BOULDER COUNTY

CRIME, LOVE, AND CANNABIS,
WEST OF THE 100TH MERIDIAN

MARC KRULEWITCH

ALSO BY MARC KRULEWITCH

Maxwell Street Blues

Windy City Blues

Gold Coast Blues

Doubt in the 2nd Degree

Something to Call Your Own

For Leslie, whose love and support
made every word possible

1

MARTIN CAMPBELL TURNED off Claim-Jumper Trail onto Quartz Way, parked his blue Jeep, and bushwhacked down the low slope of national forest bordering Buddy Fisher's property. Martin was no stranger to the property, but it had been a couple of months since his last visit and recent developments dictated he be more careful.

Martin paused at the row of ponderosa pines bordering Buddy's meadow, swallowed against the butterflies in his stomach, and then stepped into the native shrubs and grasses Buddy had so diligently cultivated. Chokecherry, wild plum, and hawthorn stood in abundance. In drier sections, buffalo grass brushed the mountain breezes, while tufts of fluffy switchgrass and wheatgrass filled out wetter parts. As a kid, he had accompanied his Uncle Jake to buy weed from Buddy, even though Jake could buy it legally, since he had a medical marijuana card for chemotherapy nausea. Buddy's weed was special, Jake used to say, as did most people active in the weed culture in Boulder County.

When he was about halfway across the meadow, Martin saw Buddy spreading leaves over screens attached to a drying rack on a sunny area of driveway between the house and the storage shed. His ponytail fell straight down his spine, reaching mid-back. Across the side of the shed you could still make out the "Fisher's Soap" logo in 1930's geometric typeface.

A wooden vestibule connected the house to a rectangular quarter-acre garden defined by bamboo stalks covered with vines and broadleaf shrubs. The tops of the stalks were sharpened into daggers, some of which had small searchlights attached. It didn't take a genius to know what the bamboo concealed or the significance of Peppermint Creek flowing twenty yards away. Behind the garden, a treeless slope led up to Quartz Way, the result of clear-cutting decades earlier. Inside that bamboo enclosure Martin first learned about the importance of collecting dead leaves and raking up litter. Buddy said a messy garden filled plants with sadness, made their fruit less sweet.

Martin thought he should give Buddy a heads-up so as not to startle him. He searched for a rock to accidentally kick but the meadow was too thick with foliage. Buddy would know the only rocks skipping over his driveway would've been thrown. How would it look walking onto a man's property throwing rocks? In the end, it didn't matter because Buddy had already picked up on his visitor.

"What's the matter, Marty?" Buddy said, still bent over the drying screens. "You got your driver's license now. Did you forget where my driveway was?"

Martin anticipated Buddy turning around, staring at him the remainder of the journey. But Buddy continued laying leaves over screens, even ignoring Martin's shadow when it crossed his line of vision.

"I'm sorry, Mr. Fisher," Martin said. "I didn't want to draw attention. So I parked up on Quartz Way and cut through the forest."

Buddy placed his hands over his lower back, straightened up slowly, and turned around.

"C'mon, Marty, you're old enough to call me Buddy like everyone else. Now what do you mean draw attention? Attention from whom? Why're you acting so nervous?"

"You know. The rangers. And those other guys who used to come around to try to check up on you. Mom said they used to write down all the license plate numbers of any cars parked in the driveway."

Buddy stared at Martin a moment. "I didn't know she talked about that stuff."

Martin shrugged.

"Those stories were about what *my* father had to put up with when I was a kid. You don't have to worry about that crap anymore, Marty. Weed's legal now—more or less."

Martin almost laughed. He wanted to say, "As if you ever cared about what was legal," but he felt foolish enough for having cut across the property for no reason. "I got some news for you—"

"You think you can get away to help with the harvest this year without your old man finding out?"

It puzzled him that Buddy should bother asking. Helping with the harvest had been an annual routine since Martin was a little kid. "Of course. Mom never cared as long as my grades were good. Anyway, I wanted you to know that the Kansas guys are coming tomorrow to meet with the commissioners."

"What Kansas guys?"

"I thought Mom would've—"

"Just tell me."

"Cody Crawford's a good friend of mine. His mom works at the commissioner's office. She tells him what's going on over there and Cody leaks the info."

"*Leaks* the info? What info? Who does he leak it to?"

"Development applications, open space acquisition proposals. Stuff the slow-growth people would want to get a jump on. Cody likes to stir things up. Anyway, he told me the Boulder County sheriff showed up at his mom's office several weeks ago and was talking to Commissioner Brandt about a bunch of Kansas officials wanting to have a meeting."

"What's this got to do with me?"

"Well, at first Cody's mom didn't think much of it. Then, yesterday, Commissioner Brandt told her to put together a bunch of packets about marijuana laws and have them ready for a meeting tomorrow afternoon."

Buddy folded his arms, stared into the asphalt. "I guess I should be flattered you think this has anything to do with me. I mean, lots of people predicted neighboring states wouldn't sit still after Colorado flung open the gates of hell and released the cannabis hound."

Martin suppressed another laugh. "Cody's mom said it *has* to be about you. Why else would they come to Boulder County instead of Denver?"

"And that's why you're here."

"Something's up, don't you think? Like maybe they're planning a raid?"

Buddy gave Martin a long look. "Marty, you're a super kid. And you'll always have my property as a second home, a place to hang out with me and learn whatever I can teach you. But times have changed. Maybe you should start thinking more seriously about your own future, a future where I'm more in the background—"

"I want to do what you do, and you're the best at it. If you get in trouble—"

"Trust me. I'm not someone whose footsteps you should aspire to follow. Just keep getting good grades and look forward to college. *Enjoy* being young. That's all you gotta do right now." He turned to continue working on the screens then glanced back to add, "That's an order."

Martin walked around Buddy to face him. "What's so bad about your way of doing things? You get along fine, don't you?"

"There is no *my way* of doing things anymore. Everything's changed. Old outlaws like me need not apply."

"That doesn't make sense. If it's legal, you're in the clear, right? Just keep doing what you've always done."

Buddy straightened up, wiped his hands on his thighs. "Cultivating cannabis requires licensing. Do you know what *licensing* means?"

Martin didn't respond.

"Licensing means managers and supervisors and all kinds of cogs in the machine, all huddled in their cubicles, bitching about wholesale prices and retail excise taxes and state sales taxes and 'safe' THC levels." Buddy started counting on his fingers. "They control the number of plants allowed, the number of simultaneously flowering buds allowed, and any other rule the bureaucracy gets paid to think of. All these worker bees can't see the machine operating outside their carpeted partition walls. They're just little gears trying to squeak loud enough to be heard and get promoted to a larger gear. And it all comes down to one belief—unchecked grow operations are a menace. Is that who you want to be? A menace?"

"Then why not follow their rules? At least you're still doing what you want."

Buddy took a deep breath. "Because they wouldn't have me. Anyway, it doesn't matter—"

"You're not worried about this whole Kansas thing?"

"They're not gonna raid me, Marty. It's not like I'm cookin' meth. And as far as I know, there's still something called the Fourth Amendment."

"But the dope-cops will know you're growing more than six lousy plants." Martin was well-versed in the laws of personal use. "Everyone from here to New Jersey knows how potent your weed is. And you can bet everyone's heard the rumors about your secret stash. Fifty-five, sixty percent potency, people say."

Buddy laughed, bent down to pick out several blades of grass piled neatly at his feet, and started chewing them. "The percentage gets higher every time I hear about it," Buddy said. "Well, it is what it is. I appreciate you coming by, Marty. You want a ride back to Quartz Way so you don't have to climb that hill?"

Martin declined Buddy's offer, said he didn't mind the exercise. The truth was he couldn't stomach any more discouragement.

Buddy watched him make his way across the meadow. It hardly seemed possible this was the same boy who had so charmed Buddy with his insatiable curiosity during visits with his Uncle Jake. Buddy saw the exuberant little worker he remembered, crouched on a mound of dirt, tugging a fat stem with all his might. Martin's mother had liked the idea of her son working alongside adults, flushing, cutting, and curing. After Jake died, the boy's stepfather put an end to the "dope apprenticeship"—or so he thought.

Buddy cupped his hands around his mouth. "You're welcome here anytime you want, Marty."

Martin turned, waved, then disappeared into the wooded slope. Buddy continued staring. He knew everything had changed. He knew the very near future would be fraught with choices—none of them good. Buddy walked into the kitchen, picked up the phone. "Hey there, Cousin Alex, it's Buddy. I got some news."

2

THERE WAS AN ongoing debate in Boulder County over who first coined the phrase *Fisher's Forest*, but the name stuck and eventually begat *Fisher's Forest Way*, the unofficial name of the road merging into the compacted gravel of Buddy's driveway. Libby Campbell stopped her hybrid SUV in front of the drying screens. *Buddy should get plenty of crystals out of that leafy strain*, she thought then stepped out and walked into the kitchen. Through the living room threshold she spied the ancient leather armchair looking just as tattered and comfy as when Buddy's father, Abe Fisher, sat absorbed in one of his books. Friends and family cherished Abe's "salons," the large brick fireplace ensuring a warm setting for music, wine, and weed on a cold winter's night. Libby was well acquainted with those cold winter nights, had thought of them often before ending her and Buddy's two-decade estrangement a month earlier. Until then, they had communicated only when the logistics of Martin's so-called apprenticeship required discussion.

Through the open vestibule door she saw light flickering up the stairwell to the root cellar Buddy had long since renamed *Ye Olde Macabre Reading Chamber*, as stated by a wooden plaque hanging above the doorway. Libby had never liked the creepy room. By the time she descended the stairs and saw Buddy's candlelit face hunched over his antique walnut writing desk, scanning through a book on some arcane botanical subject, she was ready to get out. Her approach didn't stir him, but she knew better than to believe he was too occupied not to have heard her footfalls coming down the stairs and across the concrete floor.

"Excuse me? Mr. Poe?" she said in a voice just above the silence. She placed her hand lightly on his shoulder, and without a word, Buddy closed the book.

*

Buddy's chin rested on top of Libby's head, hair stuck to his lips. He'd fallen in love with her for the second time during the separation, when her hair began turning prematurely white. It pained him to watch her change like that and not be a party to the process. She had since returned to the brunette color he first fell in love with.

"I loved when you had white hair," Buddy said. "Sexy as hell."

"I looked *old* as hell."

"That's what Donny probably said." He regretted his words for spoiling the moment. Libby didn't respond. A black-capped chickadee sang, *chick-a-dee-dee-dee.* Buddy could've apologized for mentioning Donny but instead he said, "Remember all those years ago when we were lying just like we are now, in your bedroom? I said I wanted to tell you something, but I was scared it would freak you out."

A tear rolled off the bridge of Libby's nose onto Buddy's bicep. "Don't," she said.

"I told you that I would never, ever, love someone as much as I loved you."

More tears fell. "You're trying to make me cry, aren't you?"

"I could never keep my mouth shut."

"We were sixteen."

"We were sixteen. But I knew then what I still know now."

"Please don't."

Buddy pulled the sheet up, dabbed Libby's tears. "Did you know you have a spy for a son?"

Libby sat up, looked down at Buddy. "What are you talking about?"

"Marty stopped by this morning. Told me some folks from Kansas are in town to talk about their cannabis problem."

She blinked a few times. "Marty told you this?"

Buddy nodded.

Libby lay back down. "Marty's always been more interested in local news than I have, always telling me things he heard or read from somewhere or another. But I don't remember him saying anything about people from Kansas coming into town."

This time Buddy sat up. "Cody Crawford—"

"Liz's son. Oh shit. Is this about that marijuana meeting at the commissioner's office?"

"Aha! So you knew."

"I just thought it was another meeting about legalization issues. Why does Marty think this has anything to do with you?"

Buddy dropped back down to his pillow. "Maybe it doesn't."

"It's not like you're selling pot in Kansas, right?"

"C'mon, Lib, you know I'm not a *dealer*—not directly, I mean. Maybe very, very indirectly. And I've never set foot in Kansas."

Libby turned onto her side and began stroking Buddy's cheek with the tips of her fingers. "I can't help but think of your father, how he let big pharma ruin his life."

"Dad was tricked into hooking people on cigarettes. My situation is totally different."

"Maybe it's different, but if this meeting has to do with your very very indirect *selling* of illegal pot—never mind growing it—they'll find a reason to ruin you."

"Lots of people illegally grow and sell pot."

"But lots of people aren't Buddy Fisher from Boulder County."

"So let 'em ruin me. I was born ruined; therefore, I have nothing to lose."

"Really? You have nothing to lose? How about your freedom? Ever been to prison? And what about me? You think your jailers will give us a couple of days each week to lie in bed together? And what about all your co-op friends? How do you think they'll react when you, their guiding light all these years, is frog-marched away in handcuffs? And—"

"Okay, point taken. Now, please, tell me the truth. Has Donny ever chimed in about how they'll ruin me if I don't change my evil ways?"

Libby sighed. "Something to do with growing cannabis violating the easement agreement."

Buddy's grandfather, Papa George, had gifted Boulder

County his land in exchange for a conservation easement. Included in the agreement was a property tax exemption for five of the thirty acres, where Papa George built a low, broad-framed cottage with a steeply pitched gabled tin roof and wrap-around porch. Apart from updated plumbing, heating, and exterior cedar shingles, Papa George's cottage was the same house Buddy grew up in.

Libby continued, "Or maybe they'll say you got too many plants, or they'll make up some other damn reason. There are lots of forces working against you now, Buddy. You gotta play by their rules or else."

"I know what's going on, Lib. I'll be okay."

"Will you?"

"Yes. I'm not in this alone, you know. I've got friends."

Libby frowned. "Oh God, you mean like the Mackys and Beaubiens and McKennas?"

"What? They're good old boys. Not as sophisticated as us who live at lower elevations, but their hearts are in the right place—usually."

Libby choked on a laugh. "Emphasis on *usually* with Beaubien, a descendant of cannibals!"

Uncontrollably giggling, Buddy managed to say, "It was never proven, and Alfie's a great kid."

It took another minute for the levity to give way. Libby said, "If they find all those kilos, they'll skewer you."

"They won't find anything."

"Maybe it's time you told Marty—"

"I'm way ahead of you. I've taught him all I can teach. Now he needs to take his passion and run with it. A kid as smart as Marty is perfectly positioned for combining legalization with a college education. But I can't forbid him from coming here, Lib. I love that kid—"

"I know you do. But I want him to have a future here, have the same choices we had. He's going to need a real income if he wants to stay in Boulder County. Donny's not going to support him forever."

Droves of moneyed transplants had been moving to Boulder County, hell-bent on restoring the old houses with their steep roofs, sloping towers, gabled windows, and lacy decorative wood trimming. Buddy had watched the transformation unfolding for years, the charm of reclaimed cast iron gates and colorful exterior paint schemes replaced by pretension and arrogance. Nothing that old should look that new.

"Why not support him forever?" Buddy said. "That's probably how most of the young people manage to live here. You think a store specializing in 100% certified organic cotton socks or a shop that sells only coffee grown in the shade of a poor Central American farmer's tree brings in the kind of cash you need to live here?"

"I'm just saying Donny isn't keen on the idea of supporting Marty—"

"Don't tell me. Unless Marty becomes a lawyer like Donny."

"He's just being practical."

Buddy hated that word. "I still miss your brother."

"God, Marty was so hurt by Jake's death—"

"I told him that damn chemo would kill him before the cancer ever did."

"Donny wishes Marty could just get past it already."

Buddy sat up. "Are you serious? Marty was only ten years

old when Jake died! And now, at the ripe old age of sixteen, he's supposed to have gotten over it? That son-of-a—"

Libby sat up and swung her legs off the bed.

"C'mon, don't be angry—"

"It's not that. I should get going."

Buddy leaned over, wrapped his arms around her waist. "Let's get the hell away from here. You, me, and Marty."

Libby ran her fingers through his hair. "And where would we go?"

"After I sell the keys, we could live anywhere. Even Boulder County."

"That's not really running away, is it?"

"Hey! I'm going to get a smart phone. Tell me I'm not irresistible."

"I'll believe it when I see it. Oh, Donny's going to pay you a visit soon. Probably tomorrow."

Buddy looked up from Libby's hip. "Oh Christ. Why?"

"I'm not sure. He sounded serious. 'I need to talk to Buddy about something.'"

Buddy rolled onto his back, tucked his hands behind his head. "To think there was a time I would've died for that guy. Right now, I could kill him."

3

THAT NIGHT, FIFTEEN men from small towns dotting
the foothills congregated at Buddy's house. A few sat
in the kitchen, others on couches and chairs scattered
around the fireplace. Several hung out on the driveway leaning against pickup trucks. Known collectively as the Western
Boulder County Cannabis Cooperative, some of the men
shared surnames with historical luminaries now memorial-
ized on residence halls and academic buildings. An alleged
cannibal's name commemorated a university cafeteria.
Buddy provided beer and dope. Usually, someone brought
a new hybrid to test out, although pranking each other with
nasty schwag was also common.

These modern mountain men were a new breed themselves, a hybridization of authoritarian distrust with ardent
environmentalism. They were not a particularly violent
group, as mountain folks were often portrayed, but none
was shy about leveling an assault weapon between your eyes
to get a point across.

Nobody was sure when high-altitude weed cultivation
started in Boulder County, although first attempts dated

back at least to the 1920s. Billy Kittredge claimed his great granddad, Floyd "Shorty" Kittredge, brought hemp seeds to Boulder County after being run out of Bourbon County, Kentucky, by federal revenuers during Prohibition. Back then, hemp had been a principle crop on Shorty's farm. Hemp's decline in the early 20th century inspired Shorty to discover moonshine's money-making potential just in time for the Volstead Act of 1919. Pressed to explain how agricultural hemp became a psychoactive cannabis strain growing in the poor soil of the Colorado foothills, Billy Kittredge had no credible response. Instead, he usually hid behind an old saw like the one about Shorty planting a third to smoke, a third for thieves, and a third for the law. Regardless, by the end of Prohibition, weed had established deep, covert roots in Boulder County and persevered through the decades, indistinguishable from the hundreds of micro weed cultures that had sprung up since the Second World War.

Buddy's connection to this group occurred peripherally, starting as a kid who grew up between two worlds—geographically and figuratively. The Fisher homestead's lack of elevation excluded them from mountain culture, but was removed enough into the foothills to avoid "townie" affiliation. By the time Buddy reached high school, the family's oddball reputation was well known and carried equal levels of distrust from the status quo and respect from families like the Mackys, Beaubiens, and McKennas. Buddy helped those same families realize the lucrative potential of growing high-altitude weed with proper soil nutrition and an understanding of basic economics. He kept things simple, patiently explained converting pounds to grams, offered guidelines for the number of plants they could expect a row to yield per square foot of soil, and the yield per plant. "An ounce of pot," Buddy liked to say, "equals about forty joints." Through Buddy's gestures, he became an honorary brother, a de facto liaison between worlds.

*

Zebulon Macky stared into the kitchen table sipping a can of Coors, his eyes shadowed under cantilevered brows. Buddy was carving a grid into a pan of brownies he removed from the oven thirty minutes earlier, just after confirming to Zeb rumors about Kansas big shots invading their state. Ralston Macky sat drumming his fingers across the table from his older brother.

"Will you cut that shit out?" Zeb said. "At least cut your goddamn fingernails once in a while. You sound like a flicker jack-hammering chimney flashing."

Ralston pulled his hand off the table. Buddy put a brownie on a napkin, placed it in front of Zebulon. "Eat this," Buddy said. "You'll feel better."

"Someone's always got to fuck with the system," Zebulon said, shoving the entire brownie into his mouth. He chewed a bit, then said, "We're doing our thing, not bothering anyone, then some fuckers decide it ain't right. Because *they* say so."

"Hey, Rally, my friend," Buddy said. "Will you go tell those guys outside to come into the living room?"

Ralston stood then walked out the kitchen door. Zebulon said, "We're talking *war*, aren't we?"

"Try to relax, Zeb. We'll figure it out, but you gotta stay chill."

Colter McKenna and Billy Kittredge stumbled through

the door wearing stupid grins. A few others drifted in, nodded at Zebulon. Alfie Beaubien and Ralston Macky walked in together, Alfie keeping his head lowered while his upper body twitched in cough suppression.

"Here you go, Alf," Buddy said, handing him a glass of water. Alfie took the glass without looking up. Buddy watched him gulp it down. "When are you going to learn, Alf?"

Alfie said nothing, handed the empty glass back to Buddy; then he and Ralston walked into the living room.

"There they go," Zebulon said. "Dumb and Dumber."

Buddy waited for Ralston to get out of earshot then approached Zeb from behind and whacked him across the side of the head. Up to that moment, Buddy had never tested the respect boundaries of his tacit leadership role and understood the risks associated with a guy like Zebulon reverting to his more feral nature. But unsettled times called for uncharacteristic behavior, and a good leader knew the importance of keeping cool in the face of adversity.

"If this is going to be your attitude tonight," Buddy said, "then you might as well get in your truck and get the fuck out. I'll take Rally home. Yeah, we've got a serious issue going on and we'll deal with it. But not if you can't stay calm and act *rational*. Got it?"

Buddy stood in Zebulon's periphery, mentally prepared a maneuver to get a chair between them should Zebulon's body language betray violent intentions.

Zebulon slid his chair back, stood. "Okay," he said. "Let's call this bitch to order."

Buddy followed him into the living room holding the pan of brownies and handed it off to the closest guy, who took one then passed it along. The audience formed a half circle in front of the fireplace where custom dictated Buddy would stand. Zebulon dragged a wooden rocking chair about four feet stage right of Buddy and sat facing the others—a symbolic arrangement purely of Zebulon's making.

"Thank you all for coming," Buddy said, then waited for the room to quiet down. Unfortunately, Alfie Beaubien had yet to master his cough, and the jerky movements of his upper body continued providing Colter McKenna and Billy Kittredge with great amusement. Zebulon sprung out of his chair.

"You think this is goddamn funny?" Zebulon shouted. "You think we're here to make fucking jokes? How about I smash both your faces—"

"Okay, okay, they get it," Buddy said. He put his arm around the angry man, led him back to his chair.

Zebulon sat, then said, "Now shut the fuck up and let the man speak. Go ahead, Buddy."

Buddy gave Zebulon a nod of solidarity. "I'll get straight to the point. Yesterday, I took a meeting with a very reliable source who has an ear to the wall of the county commissioner's office. It seems some folks in Kansas feel mighty threatened by Colorado's cannabis legalization—"

"Kansas?" Billy Kittredge said. "Why the hell does Kansas give a shit what we do in Colorado?"

"It's complicated—"

"Are you saying the county's gonna side against us with Kansas?" Colter McKenna said, inspiring a collective groan then expletive-filled clamoring.

"Hey!" Buddy shouted. "Everyone shut up, and I'll lay it out all real simple-like. Some Kansans think legal weed equals Satan's marijuana agents breaking down doors, raping their daughters and sons. Other Kansans with corporate and political interests see dollar signs. There's more to it, but that's the bottom line."

Buddy paused and waited.

"But what does this mean to us small-timers?" Billy Kittredge said. "I mean, shit, we're just local, you know? Nobody's coming to my house from Kansas, I guarantee you that."

Buddy stared at Billy Kittredge, unsure how to respond to his naiveté. "Yeah, for now, probably not much will directly affect you and the rest, Billy, but don't ever think for a moment you're immune. Now—"

A headlight beam flashed across the window. Buddy scanned the room. "Who's not here?" he said.

The others looked around then back at Buddy. A car door shut. It sounded heavy, like a big American model. Through the window Buddy discerned the figure of a man. They listened to footsteps scraping, anticipated knuckles rapping against wood. Instead, the door opened. Then a sixty-ish man walked through the kitchen, appeared on the living room threshold. He wore a gray tweed sport coat, skinny knitted tie, and black slacks. "Is this the Buddy Fisher residence?" He sniffed the air, chuckled. "Something tells me I'm in the right place."

"And who the fuck are you?" Zebulon said, leaning forward, ready to pounce.

"Good evening, gentlemen," the man said. "My name is Stanley Carson from Wichita, Kansas."

"Who you with, Mary Kay or Avon?" Colter McKenna said, which got a pretty good snicker out of the group and a gap-toothed grin from Carson.

"Good one," Carson said, "but they stopped door-to-door cosmetics-selling years ago."

"Tell me, Mr. Stanley Carson," Zebulon said. "Do people in Wichita just walk into a man's house anytime they fucking feel like it?"

"Nah. Folks don't do that in big cities like Wichita," Carson said.

"But you thought it just fine to walk right into this house," Zebulon said.

Carson pretended to think about it. "Yeah, okay, I should've knocked, I get it. But from the driveway it was real bright inside and you all looked like a nice group of fellas and I've heard what a friendly place Boulder County was, so I thought I'd give it a try, see how a strange man in a strange county walking into a strange house is treated. But I guess that wasn't such a good idea. My sincerest apologies."

Carson stepped into the room, glanced at Buddy, then extended his hand to Zebulon. "You must be Buddy Fisher."

Zebulon didn't move. "If this was my property, Mr. Stanley Carson from Wichita, that'd be one apology you'd never have a chance to make, 'cause you'd be one dead Stanley Carson from Wichita."

"Settle down, Zeb," Buddy said.

Carson withdrew his hand.

"Hey, Mr. Carson," Billy Kittredge said. "Would you like a brownie? Or maybe you want a few hits on this new hybrid marijuana cigarette? I call it Schwag the Dog."

Another round of snickering, only louder. "Mr. Carson isn't here to eat brownies or smoke weed," Buddy said.

Carson stared at Buddy a moment then took a few steps

toward him. "And I bet you're the famous Buddy Fisher." Neither man offered his hand.

Buddy matched Carson's stare with one of his own. "Wichita, huh?" Buddy said. He stepped back, dropped to his knees, bowed, then got back to his feet. "Gentlemen, I believe we have here in our company an exalted representative from the great state of Cook Industries, land of Jayhawks and sunflowers."

Carson put his hands in his pockets, sort of leaned backward, this time with an incredulous gap-toothed expression. "Please do me the favor of explaining how you came to that conclusion," he said.

"Mr. Stanley Carson here is teasing me. But that's okay. I'll play along. Well, you referred to me as 'famous.' Only one thing a glorified gardener like me could be famous for. And judging by the way you stuck your nose in the air like a hound dog sniffing out a clue, I'd say you knew exactly what you were smelling. And since you're dressed as if for a stockholders' meeting and you're from Wichita, I'd say you worked for a corporation heavily invested in the petrochemical-pharmaceutical-agribusiness industries. You want me to—"

"Nope. No need."

"Now that we're all kissy-kissy," Zebulon said, "what the hell do you want?"

Carson said nothing, fished a piece of gum from his jacket pocket, popped it in his mouth, dropped the wrapper on the floor. Zebulon twitched.

"Stand fast, Sergeant," Buddy said. "He wants the seventy hidden kilos of magic weed and seed."

Giggling filled the ranks. Billy Kittredge said, "You've

got to be fucking kidding. I've been hearing that bullshit story for ten years."

"More than ten years," Colter McKenna said. "What would you do with it anyway? Smoke it? Eat it? Sell it?"

Several of the guys began chanting, "Smoke it, smoke it, smoke it…"

Ralston surprised everyone when he shouted, "And it's none of your goddamn business anyways!"

"Now that's what I call a right friendly welcome to your community," Carson said. "This visit was just a trial balloon, a way to take the temperature you might say. My goodness it's a short summer in Boulder County."

"Is that a fact?" Alfie Beaubien said, which was even more surprising than Ralston shouting out. "I've heard the few good things about Kansas are really in Missouri. So why don't you fuck off back to shitty Wichita and stop sticking your nose in other people's business, you stupid cunt!"

The room roared, back slaps and high-fives all around. Carson maintained his posture, his smile broader than ever.

"Simmer down, my brothers!" Buddy shouted, waited for the room to quiet, then said, "There's no surprise here. It's been a long time coming. The only question was who would be the Judas. But not to worry. Let's just thank God we still got the Fourth Amendment on our side. Isn't that right, Mr. Stanley Carson?"

Carson took a breath, let it out. "I suppose you're right, Mr. Buddy Fisher. But these days I wouldn't take anything for granted. Just a little advice, that's all. Anyway, I guess I'll just see myself out and try to warm up a bit. 'Twas nice meeting you all." Carson turned to leave then stopped and said,

"Oh, by the way, Mr. Zebulon Macky. I never been to Ward, Colorado. But I'll make sure to call first before stopping by."

Zebulon waited until Carson had walked out of the house, then jumped out of his chair. "Who the fuck was it? Who's the slimy motherfuckin' piece of shit—"

"It's none of them," Buddy said, grabbing Zebulon's elbow, leading him back to his seat. "Listen up, everyone. Now you know. It's about me and the seventy kilos."

"I don't get it," Billy Kittredge said. "Let's say they took it all. What's that gonna prove? People in Kansas will still find weed if they want it."

"Not Buddy's weed," Zebulon said, "the best goddamn weed ever grown. At least not yet."

"It's about so much more than weed," Buddy said. "But you all don't need to bother yourselves with that. Just keep your cool, don't do anything stupid, and know it's me they want."

"Yeah, and know something else," Zebulon said. "They'll come like a thief in the fucking night—the feds will. Got it? So you might as well be ready."

4

SHERIFF WYATT THOMPSON of Ellsworth County, Kansas, drove westbound on Interstate 70, silently offering blessings to passing farmers busy planting winter wheat in mid-September's morning sunshine, but also focusing on passages from Revelation. *Sorcery has no place in God's plan*, he thought then recalled Pastor Bynum's words that "the dabbler in potion-making will be excluded from heaven just as the drug user will also suffer God's wrath." Sheriff Thompson was quick to acknowledge the anger boiling up into his chest and equally quick promising not to judge the people of Boulder County for the danger they unleashed upon his young sons, Caleb and Yeshua. Then he promised not to harbor special hatred for the sorcerer himself, this Buddy Fisher, the one whom every effort must be made to stop. Thanks to DEA undercover activities along the I-70 corridor—an unvarnished "highway to hell"—Sheriff Thompson had become well acquainted with Buddy Fisher and the Boulder County culture from which he sprung. Nevertheless, it would take courage to stop a sorcerer of Buddy Fisher's magnitude. Thankfully, that kind of courage resided in the Kansas governor's mansion. Governor Brownback was fearless like Christ, Sheriff Thompson liked to say, citing the five children taken into custody because their parents were moving to Colorado to use medical marijuana as an example of his courage.

It was all part of The Plan. And salvation through Christ required following The Plan He laid out for you. "The path is always in plain sight," Pastor Bynum had said, "but the burden is on you to find it." Sheriff Thompson's path had included joining the Marines on his eighteenth birthday, a choice his grandfather, father, and two older brothers had made before him. His father liked to boast of his family's three generations of wartime duty, although some questioned whether the two older sons sitting on a troop ship during the first Gulf War should count as wartime service. Ultimately, it would be God's decision whether Sheriff Thompson's eight years of active and reserve duty would include imminent-danger pay. As it turned out, his enlistment ended shortly before the invasion of Iraq in 2003, and despite knowing he could not have foreseen the events he was told justified the conflict, Sheriff Thompson separated from the Marines with a nagging suspicion that, perhaps, God had wanted him to re-enlist.

Folks in central Kansas assumed Sheriff Thompson was named for the legendary lawman, Wyatt Earp, who may or may not have been the town marshal of Ellsworth, Kansas. The truth was much less romantic. Thompson family tradition held that the third-born son be named after the father's eldest brother. In Sheriff Thompson's case, that name happened to be Wyatt. Other notable residents of Ellsworth included two bishops, three gunfighters, and one prostitute.

But becoming sheriff was certainly no accident. The ease with which Sheriff Thompson sailed through POST-certification firearm training, then the deputy training program, was an obvious sign of a preordained calling, as was having supervisors gifted in the ways of the Holy Spirit. When Wyatt confided to his superiors how disgusted he had been by his fellow marines' devotion to pornography, masturbation, and video games, Captain Roberts and Lieutenant Harroway embraced the future Sheriff Thompson as one would a son or younger brother. They understood from whence his pain had come and gave tacit approval for his becoming the department's de facto morality scout. Looking back upon the previous decade, the astute observer could only wonder if Wyatt Thompson's ascension to sheriff of Ellsworth County could have ever been in question.

*

Representatives from the governor's office and the Kansas Highway Patrol rode in the car behind Sheriff Thompson, debated possible strategies that Buddy Fisher and his comrades might employ to infiltrate their state. The spirited discussion encouraged the creative process, helped the men bond before reaching a consensus that a hub-and-spoke distribution model would be the most likely method. The men also agreed that the large college town of Lawrence, Kansas, most likely represented the target hub from where the weed dissemination would begin once it arrived from Boulder County. Other sizable college towns like Lincoln, Nebraska, and Columbia, Missouri, were identified as likely near-term targets of the operation's tentacles.

No doubt, Buddy's weed had long ago permeated those

towns and others. But it was the *seeds* of the purported seventy hidden kilos—said to accompany each container in hermetically sealed plastic pouches—that kept the governor of Kansas and his confederates awake at night. Seventy kilos worth of Buddy's high-octane seeds hitting the streets of Lawrence, Kansas, would do nothing less than put someone on life support. But they were an optimistic group. After all, the dedication of the Kansas Highway Patrol, combined with the vast open spaces of western Kansas, created a damn perilous crossing for drug mules. "We'll swallow 'em up and spit 'em out," promised Major Davis of the KHP.

The men from Kansas pulled into the Motel 6 around one o'clock. "Where's Sheriff Thompson's overnight bag?" Major Davis said to Dale Dahlgren, who represented the Kansas Department of Agriculture.

"Wyatt's got a friend who lives here and he's going to stay with him and visit for a few days," Dahlgren said then turned toward Sheriff Thompson. "Isn't that right, Wyatt? You got a friend who lives here in Boulder?"

Major Davis stood in front of the open trunk looking at his leather traveling bag. After hearing Sheriff Thompson's "Yes, sir," he grabbed the bag and walked to the motel's entrance. "What about that Cook Industries guy, Carson?" Major Davis asked. "Where's he at?"

"Stanley Carson," Dale Dahlgren said. "He checked in a few days ago at some posh hotel downtown. I guess Carson's boss, David Cook, wanted him to appear independent from the state employees. He'll meet us at the county commissioner's office."

Sheriff Thompson accompanied the men into the lobby. Once they had all received room keys, they took turns shaking the sheriff's hand, said they would see him in a couple of hours. Sheriff Thompson nodded, then drove to an address in the south end of town.

*

The iron door knocker bounced hard against the strike plate. Moments later, Maria, a slight woman with long, salt-and-pepper hair, answered the door.

"Yes?"

"Yes, ma'am. I'm Wyatt Thompson, the one you spoke to on the phone—about the room?"

Maria stared at Wyatt a moment before nodding. "Yes, I remember," she said then returned to staring. This confused Wyatt.

"Uh, yes," Wyatt said. "I'm here to take some time off. You know, just to relax a bit in this pretty place."

"The ad didn't say you *had* to be a vegetarian, you know," she said, "as long as you *honor* the animal, of course."

Her breath had an antiseptic sweetness. He pretended to appreciate her comment, pretended the world didn't suddenly seem—somehow—off-kilter. Her serious, penetrating gaze magnified his confusion. Finally, she stepped aside, allowed Sheriff Thompson into the open floor plan of her tidy ranch-style house. The living room centered around a sofa, love seat, and coffee table on which a statue of an oriental man sat with an unlit candle lodged between his crossed legs. A television, chaise lounge, and end table were set up in a nearby corner.

"My life is structured around the pursuit of self-realization," Maria said. She seemed to anticipate a response.

Wyatt didn't care what Maria's life was structured

around, although, strangely enough, he was familiar with the term *self-realization*. Shortly before leaving active duty, he'd heard a marine in his unit use this term, claimed his reason for joining was to attain *self-realization*. A roadside explosion killed the marine on his fourth day in Iraq.

"Yes, self-realization," Sheriff Thompson said then remembered how that same marine once described humans as hamsters stuck on exercise wheels. "I'm trying to get off the wheel too."

Maria's eyebrows lifted. "The wheel of life is an exquisite metaphor."

He followed her into the kitchen where she said, "The kitchen," before stopping abruptly and turning around. Wyatt stepped out of her way, kicked a milk crate full of empty half-pint ginger-brandy bottles, then followed her down a hallway to a bedroom of bare white walls, a twin bed, a four-drawer dresser, and a small closet with wire hangers on a metal pole. A folding snack table served as a nightstand. The windows had no coverings, the closet had no door.

"You'll notice there are two windows," Maria said. "That creates wondrous light."

"Yes, it's very bright in here," Sheriff Thompson said. He dropped his duffel bag on the bed and sat.

Maria stepped into the hall, pointed to the bathroom just outside the bedroom, then walked away.

Sheriff Thompson thought she was on something. That would explain her weird personality. He put a picture of Jesus holding a lost lamb on the snack table, called his wife, Ariel, told her everything was fine, but didn't mention how his bedroom depressed him. He spread out a map of Boulder on the bed, the kind with cartoon versions of buildings drawn on the streets. The old courthouse was on the mall, in the middle of downtown. He thought a nap would be a good idea before the meeting, but sleep evaded him. Why not take a look around downtown instead?

*

The red-brick avenue was bordered with shop windows of scented soybean-wax candles, organic cotton chenille baby blankets, natural venison dog food, and chocolates made from small-scale African cacao farmers. At the end of the block, Sheriff Thompson saw a wooden plaque hanging from an iron post like a medieval tradesman's sign. A black-and-white cat was painted on the plaque beside Old English lettering that spelled out Punim's Mocha Madness. He didn't understand the cat, but he remembered mocha had something to do with coffee and chocolate. Even before he joined the Marines it seemed the country had been talking non-stop about coffee. He never gave the subject much attention until moving back to Ellsworth, where he discovered that a cup of coffee at the Elkhorn Diner now cost a buck and a half. Maybe it was time to see what the fuss was about.

Vintage photos of mustached cowboys bellying up to the counter suggested beer and whiskey were served long before coffee acquired the status to warrant its own oak and mahogany bar. Sheriff Thompson stood in line, struggled to read the loopy handwriting describing coffee choices.

"Can I help you?" said the girl behind the counter. She wore a green, red, and black knit cap.

"Mocha?" Wyatt said bravely.

"Coffee?"

Once again, he was confused. "Yes."

"Whipped cream?"

"No," he said. It seemed safer.

She asked for his name, wrote it on a cup, then rang up the four-dollar coffee. Wyatt paid, then sensed something was wrong.

"They'll bring your coffee to you over there," the girl said, pointing to the people standing near the end of the counter. She spoke the way they did in New York or New Jersey, or maybe some place called Long Island.

Sheriff Thompson waited for his name to be called then found a table. He brought the cup to his mouth, pulled it away, lips burning. From his pocket he took a bronze coin depicting St. Michael commanding God's army against the apostate Lucifer, began rolling the coin over his knuckles. A copy of the *Daily Camera* lay on the table. Page one, above the fold, a chubby prairie dog sat back on its haunches munching grass from clawed hands. An article described the colony's impending destruction from developers. Large bold type quoted a longtime resident. "Some complain that only in Boulder County would people be up in arms over a bunch of rodents."

Sheriff Thompson was familiar with these varmints. But through the scope of his Bull 24 rifle, he didn't remember them looking so cute, like bunnies or chipmunks. He did remember his anger when the state began poisoning the colonies, though, taking away the fun of shooting them.

"*Castor canadensis.*"

Sheriff Thompson looked up, saw a lined, weather-beaten face staring at him from an adjacent table. The overstuffed backpack gave the man a vagrant quality, although he appeared well-fed.

"Native Americans considered beavers the sacred center of the land because they created rich habitats for other mammals like fish, turtles, frogs, birds, and ducks."

"I don't know about beavers," Sheriff Thompson said.

"No?" the man said. "Well guess what? They're *rodents*, just like prairie dogs. Should we kill all the beavers because they're rodents?"

The man stared, waited for an answer. Sheriff Thompson wondered if everyone around here was as crazy as Maria. "No, sir," Sheriff Thompson said.

"And what about the golden eagles, the ferruginous hawks, and the black-footed ferrets? What do you think they eat? You kill all the prairie dogs and you can kiss the golden eagles, ferruginous hawks, and black-footed ferrets goodbye."

Sheriff Thompson nodded. "I didn't know about that."

"I'll tell you what you *should* know," the man said. "Prairie dogs. They're *native* for chrissake. They belong here. They belong here more than you or me!"

Before Sheriff Thompson could formulate a response, the man stood then walked away mumbling. Sheriff Thompson tried the mocha again. It tasted good all right, but not four-dollars good.

5

A STATUE HONORING BOULDER County's Civil War dead stood in front of the Art Deco courthouse built after the original Victorian structure caught fire in 1932. The commissioner's secretary, Liz Crawford, had been expecting Sheriff Thompson. "Straight ahead," she said.

He walked into the conference room, saw his traveling companions talking casually with three other men. A map of Colorado and Kansas hung from an easel. Sheriff Thompson looked at his watch.

"You're not late. We're early," Carson said then introduced Boulder County sheriff, Ray Castellanos, a lawyer named Donald Campbell, and County Commissioner Will Brandt, who sipped from one of those fancy metal coffee mugs with a purple lid. Sheriff Thompson didn't like sitting at the head of the table, but it was the only chair available.

"Okay, Jay, uh, Major Davis," Commissioner Brandt said, "why don't you begin?"

Major Davis stood, walked to the easel. His shaven head, black slacks, and white dress shirt resonated with Sheriff Thompson's Pentecostal sensibilities, helped provoke his feeling of kinship with a fellow law enforcement officer operating in a foreign jurisdiction. On the map, Major Davis stuck a pin in Boulder County and a pin in Lawrence, Kansas, then drew a straight line between them with a black marker.

"Gentlemen," Major Davis said, "it's no secret how the state of Kansas feels about legalized marijuana—in any form." Major Davis paused, made eye contact with the three men across the table, and then continued.

Castellanos took a breath, exhaled. "Asshole." Commissioner Brandt tried kicking him but hit a table leg.

"…It's common knowledge that this individual has been producing and *is currently* producing an illegal strain of marijuana—"

"We have no solid evidence of this claim," Castellanos interrupted.

"Let Major Davis finish, Ray," Commissioner Brandt said.

"Well, Sheriff Castellanos, maybe you don't see the evidence, but the Kansas Highway Patrol sure as hell sees it in the eyes of our kids, as they drive I-70 east, coming back from Boulder County. We're finding THC levels well above Colorado's legal limit of five nanograms per milliliter of blood."

"Maybe you should be having this discussion with the Colorado State Patrol," Castellanos said.

"Be glad to," Major Davis said. "And if they returned any of our phone calls, maybe we would."

"We'll see what we can do at our end," Commissioner Brandt said. "As you know, the CSP is under the governor's auspices."

"Let me jump in if you don't mind," Dale Dahlgren said. Dahlgren's fancy suit and the way he combed over his thinning hair brought to mind the double-dealing government bureaucrats Sheriff Thompson had been warned about. "Agriculture is very important to Kansas. All we're asking is that you rein in the problem grower. We've had our labs in Wichita test confiscated Colorado marijuana, and we routinely find THC levels over thirty percent. That's intolerable. And it's all coming from Boulder County pot shops."

"You collecting receipts from these shops?" Castellanos said.

Major Davis said, "I'm glad you brought that up, Sheriff. Because I'm not sure you realize how insidious your problem really is."

"My problem—"

"There's a whole network involved. Like the Mafia. I don't know if they all take an oath when they buy the stuff, but nobody talks. We sit these kids down and they give us a name of some dope shop but they never have a receipt. Isn't that strange?"

Castellanos said, "So these kids from Kansas—and I got a feeling they're not all kids—throw their receipts away and that's Boulder County's problem?"

"You're goddamn right it is—"

"Let me give it a try, Major Davis," Carson said.

"Hang on," Castellanos said. "Who are you again?"

"Stanley Carson, communications director for Cook Industries."

"Cook Industries? Energy?"

"And all related products," Commissioner Brandt said.

Carson coughed. "Speaking of agriculture," he said,

"let's talk about the threat posed by the seeds your Buddy Fisher is trying to spread."

"Does he hail from a family of fishermen?" Dale Dahlgren said, grinning, trying to lighten things up. "Maybe he's like an exotic species threatening to destroy our native plants, like the zebra mussel choking El Dorado and Cheney Lakes."

"The original name was *Fischbein*," Donald said. "German immigrants."

Something about the name made Sheriff Thompson cringe. He took a hard look at Castellanos, wondered how the sheriff's family had found themselves north of the border.

"You know about Humboldt County in California, right?" Carson said. "The potheads own the county. It's the backbone of their economy, and most of it's illegal. We don't want western Kansas to become one big Humboldt County."

Castellanos laughed. "You're going to compare the people of western Kansas to the people of Humboldt County?"

"The laws of economics make no distinction of background," Carson said. "I had the good fortune of meeting Mr. Buddy Fisher and some of his constituents. They're a young, serious-minded bunch. And that scares me. If people start planting those seeds and start realizing the kind of cash they could make—tax-free cash I might add—the farmer won't be able to resist. They'll first start planting small plots of marijuana in the middle of their fields and then that plot will grow, exponentially we fear, as the money pours in. The more pot they grow, the less corn, wheat, and soybeans they'll grow."

"And the laws will become unenforceable, completely worthless," Major Davis said. "We'd have to hire thousands of troopers to figure out who's growing it and who isn't. Or the goddamn federal government will send in *agents* with all their high-tech toys and black helicopters, and you'll have those damn drones hovering over your land or peeking in your windows—God help us. That's why it's important that we pool our resources so we can avoid that kind of disaster and nip this whole thing in the bud!"

The three men from Boulder County laughed at Major Davis's unintentional pun.

"Forgive us," Donald said. "We're not laughing at you—and I think I speak for the three of us when I say that we understand and appreciate the predicament you describe."

Major Davis held his gaze on Castellanos then looked back at Donald and said, "Tell me who you are again?"

"Donald Campbell. I'm a water rights attorney."

"You work for the county?"

Commissioner Brandt straightened up, knocked over his coffee mug with an elbow. "Donald is more like a consultant," Brandt said as he blotted a few drops of liquid with a napkin.

"Is water rights relevant to this issue?" Dale Dahlgren said.

"We can make it an issue if it'll help solve the problem," Donald said. "Assuming Buddy is illegally diverting water from a creek that runs through his property."

Castellanos stood, glared down at Donald. "You can prove this?"

Sheriff Thompson stared at Castellanos's holstered pistol. It looked like the new Glock 45 with the high magazine capacity, but he couldn't be sure.

"Relax, Ray, it's just an idea," Commissioner Brandt said. Castellanos sat back down.

Dale Dahlgren winced. "How much water could he possibly be using? Good god, does this Buddy Fisher have *acres* of pot out there?"

"We're not sure how much he's growing," Donald said. "But every drop of water in the state is already owned before it hits the ground. Being from Kansas, you know what I'm talking about."

Major Davis again looked directly at Castellanos. "So tell us about some of your ideas to bust this Buddy fellow."

Castellanos leaned forward, supporting his body on his elbows. "Whatever we do, Major, will be within the boundaries of the law and with the approval of the district attorney. And whatever we decide, Major, will first have the unanimous support of the county commissioners—"

"We haven't heard from Sheriff Thompson yet," Commissioner Brandt said. Sheriff Thompson straightened up, appeared shocked to hear his name.

"Like your Mr. Campbell," Carson said, "Sheriff Thompson's here as a kind of consultant. A liaison, if you like, between Topeka and Wichita, to help the other sheriffs of western Kansas get a grip on what's happening and how they could approach the problem."

"I noticed that Sheriff Thompson has a mouth of his own," Castellanos said.

Sheriff Thompson shifted in his seat. The chair moved back a bit. "Well," he said, "if this Buddy Fisher continues to defy the law, then with the good Lord's help, I'm sure we can stop his destructive ways—"

Major Davis cut in, "We thought maybe you wouldn't mind if Wyatt stuck around your nice little city for a while. Maybe he could work with you, Sheriff Castellanos, or some of your deputies, in an official capacity, like on a special assignment. He may come up with some good ideas on how to help solve your—I mean *our* problem."

Castellanos was still leaning on his elbows but had let his chin drop against his chest. Without looking up he said, "It's a free country, Major. If Sheriff Thompson wants to hang around and see the sights of Boulder County, it's his right as an American citizen to do so. But Sheriff Thompson needs to understand that he has no jurisdiction to act in a manner that even *remotely* suggests he has any law enforcement authority. So as long as that is understood, I hope Sheriff Thompson has a most enjoyable stay in Boulder County."

Major Davis stood. "Well, I think it's understood where we all stand on this matter," he said. "And I don't know about you all, but I could sure use a good steak."

The Kansas men laughed, except for Sheriff Thompson.

"I know the perfect place," Commissioner Brandt said.

On the way out, Commissioner Brandt gave Castellanos a savage look. Donald tipped his chair back, fingers laced behind his head. They could hear Commissioner Brandt's voice rise and fall outside the room, depending on whether he was throwing in reassuring words. The outside door banged shut. Donald righted his chair. Commissioner Brandt walked in, flung the door closed.

"Goddamn you, Ray! Remember when we agreed to just go along for now? Not sound *resistant*?"

"I was supposed to say, 'Sure, let your cracker sheriff run around the county looking for the devil's weed'?"

Commissioner Brandt sat. "Yes! That's exactly what you were supposed to say. It doesn't mean you let it happen, but we gotta placate these fuckers, you know? At least give the *appearance* of cooperation? Didn't we agree on that?"

Castellanos walked to the window overlooking the lawn in front of the courthouse.

Donald said, "You understand what that Cook Industries guy is all about, right?"

"What's this water lawyer doing here?" Castellanos said.

"Ray, you're really being a prick," Commissioner Brandt said. "Donny's known Buddy as long as you have."

Castellanos turned around. "Sorry, Donny. What can you tell us about Stanley-fucking-Carson?"

"When the Cook brothers hear about legal marijuana, they don't give a damn about kids getting high; they're worried about marijuana's cousin, *hemp*."

"I know what hemp is," Castellanos said, looked at Commissioner Brandt. "And just to be clear, I didn't become friends with Buddy until high school, and I have no clue about the alleged seventy kilos of demon dope-seed or have the faintest fucking idea where he would hide it."

"His grandfather built a bomb shelter in the early sixties," Donny said. "I never saw it, but Buddy's dad used to talk about it. I'm positive you get to it from the cellar, and I'm just as positive it's underneath the dope garden."

"If the pot's really there," Commissioner Brandt said, "what's his plan? I mean what the hell does he want to do with it all? Make money? Is that what it's all about?"

"He's not out for one big score and then retiring," Castellanos said. "He's always known if he'd tried distributing on a large scale, he would've been busted a long time ago. He's harmless."

"Well, Kansas doesn't think he's harmless," Commissioner

Brandt said. "And none of us are getting any younger. That land's worth millions. Five acres surrounded by protected parks and open space? He could sell that shack to some billionaire who'll scrape it and build their vacation palace, and he'd have all the money he ever dreamed of."

"Of all people, *Commissioner*," Donald said, "you should know Buddy's property is a conservation easement. Only direct descendants can live there. Buddy's an only child with no children. If he dies or moves out, the land reverts back to county parks and open space. And the agreement requires the county to rehabilitate the land back to its natural state before incorporating it into the open space system."

"Sounds like you're saying he *does* need the money?" Brandt said.

Castellanos and Brandt looked at Donald. "Well yeah, of course he needs money. It's not like he's got a pension plan waiting for him. But he'd have to keep the cash under the mattress, launder it through selling vegetables or whatever else he does for money. That bomb shelter might be one big bank vault for all I know."

"What were you saying about hemp?" Commissioner Brandt said.

"Cook Industries is not just about oil and gas. They're a petrochemical-agricultural-biotechnology company. Every acre of soybeans, corn, or wheat lost to hemp is an acre that's *not* going to use Cook Industries' fertilizers and pesticides, because you don't need any of that to grow hemp."

"They're scared of hemp but not marijuana?" Commissioner Brandt said.

"Yeah, because you don't get high from hemp. The less afraid the public becomes about hemp, the more they'll learn about it. Hemp oil for bio-fuels, plastics, paints, detergents—all Cook Industries' *petroleum* products. Then there's clothes from hemp fiber. That means less *cotton*, which, again, means less Cook Industries' fertilizers and pesticides. You get it?"

"I get it," Commissioner Brandt said.

"I hope so," Donald said. "They're used to getting what they want. They'll destroy us if they have to. This is war, gentlemen. They gave a lot of money trying to defeat the medical weed referendum and lost. They gave even more money trying to kill the recreational weed referendum and lost. As far as the Cook brothers are concerned, if Kansas falls, then it's only a matter of time before the whole Midwest falls."

"What do you mean 'destroy' us?" Commissioner Brandt said.

"From the top down, slowly eroding living standards with budget-destroying lawsuits. Make the citizens suffer because their elected officials don't know how the game is played…"

"Are you listening, Ray?" Commissioner Brandt said. "We gotta get Buddy to play along. Give 'em what they want."

Castellanos walked to Commissioner Brandt, looked down at him. "Maybe I should remind you of something, Will. You're not my boss."

Commissioner Brandt sat up. "Maybe I should remind you of something. The county commissioners control your funding."

Castellanos retreated to the window. Brandt said, "Oh c'mon, Ray, we've known each other too long to go down this road. The lieutenant governor is waiting for my call. Can I tell him you're going to play ball or not?"

6

DONALD DIDN'T BOTHER downshifting as he took the curves on Fisher's Forest Way. He bought the Roadster because it was fun to drive and he'd be damned if a few pine trees along the road would coerce him into stressing out his clutch. Earlier in the day he'd vowed to punch in the face the next person who commented on the Roadster's impracticality. On snowy days he would drive the Porsche Cayenne. What was so hard to understand?

Late September snow was not unheard of in Boulder County, but as Donald raced through Fisher's Forest, the only moisture on his mind belonged to the ancient prospecting town of Paradox, a mix of artists and fly fishermen trying to stop Donald's ski-resort client, Cimarron Resorts, from sucking water out of Bunny Creek. Snowmaking contributed to the destruction of an already fragile ecosystem, they moaned, and taking that water would be a death sentence for the eggs of native fish. Trout-kissers drove Donald crazy. It wasn't always that way.

Like Buddy, Donald was a son of Colorado. Unlike Buddy, he owed his lifestyle to America's westward expansion, beyond a geographical line running through North America where the ownership of every raindrop or snowflake was determined before it touched the ground. That is, the *right* to use all moisture had been decided west of this theoretical boundary called the 100th meridian, where water flowed through arid fields of short grasses via ditches dug by drunken gold prospectors who a hundred or more years earlier had instituted a juvenile methodology decreeing the first to use a given water source had the right to use it over those arriving later. The two friends used to laugh that such a callow plan was still the basis of "water law," and a court system existed solely to interpret the desires of liquored-up miners.

Donald's romance with what he called "a uniquely western concern dating back to the range wars of the Old West" began in law school, after he accepted an internship with a water rights law firm. By graduation, Buddy was accusing Donald of "water arrogance," the way he bristled at a new arrival's indifference to how water had transformed their adopted landscape. Especially galling to Donald was how the engineering miracle of diverting water across the Continental Divide elicited only polite nods from those spoiled immigrants accustomed to more than twenty inches of precipitation a year.

*

Buddy had just put his salad on the kitchen table when the whine of Donald's beloved 2.5-liter turbocharged appliance intruded. He sat hunched over his bowl of spinach, two kinds of lettuce, three colors of peppers, speared the innocent vegetables as if they'd done him personal harm. A minute later he looked up, knew the idiot hadn't bothered turning on his lights despite entering the foothills' late September shadow the moment he exited Highway 36. He stood, walked to the screen door, barely able to discern the Roadster twisting and turning in exaggerated movements, like a kid playing speed racer. When Donald turned into the driveway, the rear wheels spun before the car shot forward. Buddy expected the drying screens to catapult through the kitchen windows, but the Roadster stopped just short.

"Buddy!" Donald shouted as he got out of the car, held up his hands. "Don't shoot, I come in peace."

"Spinning ruts into my driveway, asshole?"

Donald dropped his hands, glanced back. "That? Oh c'mon, I remember when you put that stone down. This is the most compacted piece of driveway east of Los Angeles."

Buddy walked back to the kitchen table. Donald stuck his head inside the door. "May I?"

"When have you ever asked to enter my kitchen?"

"Sheesh! Just being polite." Donald walked in, sat at the table. "Satellite dish on the roof but a cordless phone in the kitchen. Buddy, the walking contradiction. Whose truck is that with the Illinois plates?"

"Alex is in town a couple of days."

Donald smiled. "How the heck is Cousin Alex? Holy cow, when was the last time I saw him? You guys just hanging out, catching up on old times?"

Donald's phony enthusiasm grated Buddy. "Five thousand acres isn't enough? Cimarron needs more land to spray snow over?"

"Do you know how much revenue Cimarron brings in for the state?"

"You don't think there are *costs* associated with putting Disneyland on the side of a mountain?"

"I'm not here to argue about Cimarron." Donald looked toward the vestibule. "A padlock on the dope-tunnel door?"

"What about it?"

"I don't know. How long you been padlocking that door? Someone try to steal your pot plants?"

"What pot plants?"

Donald chuckled. "Really?"

"Why're you here, Donny?"

"I'm just here to give you a heads-up on what's going on."

"Oh yeah? You're tuned in to what's going on, huh?"

"I was called to a meeting, Buddy. Castellanos, Commissioner Brandt, and some yokels they dragged in from Kansas. One of them's a sheriff."

"Why were you invited?"

"They know you're diverting water out of Peppermint Creek."

Buddy waited for the gag line, faked a laugh. "You're shittin' me, right? Suddenly that's an issue? Three hundred and twenty-six thousand gallons in a single acre-foot of water. What I take out of that creek wouldn't qualify as a rounding error. And you know damn well it's my water, so what the hell are you talking about?"

"You lease your water to Paradox to keep the trout in Bunny Creek happy. When that water dumps into Peppermint Creek and flows through your property, it's already been used and is no longer yours to divert."

"You're full of shit."

"Am I? Remember *beneficial use*, old friend? The water has to be put to beneficial use. Growing illegal weed ain't beneficial use. And that's all the excuse they need to bust your ass. They'll get farmers and ranchers to file complaints claiming water rights violations."

"Very hard to believe."

"Believe it. They've done it before. It took, what, fifty years to legalize rain barrels? And that's just water running off your roof—not coming out a creek."

Buddy laughed, this time for real. "Kansas is worried about Peppermint Creek water? Does Kansas know Peppermint Creek feeds the Platte River and that the Platte River runs through *Nebraska* not Kansas?"

Now Buddy roared, his joy too infectious for Donald to hold it together. Suddenly, it was like the old days, two friends passing a joint, sipping beer, making fun of rich brats from California and Texas driving around in Daddy's Mercedes, griping about I-70 traffic to the ski resorts. Or when the library refused to display an American flag, concerned someone might be offended, but had no qualms presenting an "art" exhibit of penises hanging from a clothesline.

Donald gained control first. "The point is, they're going to find a reason to come busting in here and rip everything apart."

"Just to see if I have more than three plants flowering at the same time."

"You know damn well what they want."

The carefree past vanished. Donald was still an asshole, after all. "I do? What might that be?"

"I was *here*, remember? Your dad treated me like a son, remember? Don't talk to me like you two were never up to something."

"We weren't."

Donald stood, looked away for a second, leaned over the table. "You don't think I know why you got that door padlocked? You don't think I know about that bomb shelter your grandfather built? You think I don't remember you bragging about how *you* would do things? Like connecting the garden to the bomb shelter?"

Buddy carried his bowl to the sink. "How's Libby?"

Donald sat back down, waited for Buddy to do the same before saying, "Fine. Give her a call—if you want."

Buddy sensed an ambiguous tone, caught the enhanced moment Donald eyeballed him. "How's Marty doing?" Buddy said.

"Fine, I guess. He should stay on track, though. He's been getting good grades. But now he's—I don't know. All of a sudden he's not sure what he wants to do. Anyway, I'm not here to talk about me—"

"I'm well aware that every sheriff west of Wichita is on a crusade to keep the devil-weed out of their county—in Jesus's name, of course."

"You can make jokes, but I'm telling you they mean business. You want to go to prison? And there's a whole shit-storm of lawsuits waiting to be tested on who's responsible for keeping their weed within state boundaries. If Kansas can prove weed with illegally high THC levels is infiltrating their children's bloodstreams, they could argue Boulder County is liable for whatever happens once they cross back into Kansas. They got the commissioners scared shitless. That's why they're cooperating. Lawsuits can drain a budget pretty fast."

Buddy knew bull crap when he smelled it. "And all that water I'm stealing from Nebraska will be somebody's excuse to violate my Fourth Amendment rights."

"They're coming, Buddy. You can spout off all you want about the Fourth Amendment, but there's nothing you can do to stop them from coming in here and digging your whole damn place up."

"So what shall I do, old friend?"

"Just cooperate. That's all you gotta do. I'll tell them you'll turn the weed over as long as they won't prosecute. Start with a sample they can test. When they know you're not fucking with them, we'll arrange to collect it all. Then maybe you can start following the rules and go legit."

"Okay, Donny, you've done your job. Consider me warned."

"Don't give me that crap. What do you think of my plan?"

"Unlikely."

"You're a goddamn fool, you know that? At least tell me you'll think about it." Donald rubbed his forehead. "Ask Libby. Of course, you'll have to explain what's going on to her." Silence, then Donald said, "Assuming she doesn't know already."

Buddy faked a yawn. "It's getting late."

"Oh Jesus Christ, don't—"

"Goodbye, Donny."

"What is it with you Fishers? Taking the moral high ground didn't do shit for Abe Fisher, did it? And you know as well as I do the Fourth Amendment is meaningless. Do you want to go the same route as your old man and let a big corporation ruin your life? Is that what you want?"

Buddy stood. He was not a violent man, but he did have a limit, especially with someone sitting in his kitchen. "Am I going to have to *show* you the door?"

Donny cursed under his breath, stormed out.

Buddy thought maybe it was time to shut up about the Bill of Rights already. The Fourth Amendment and Abe Fisher, after all, had both been dead too long for any ironic point to be made. Buddy knew this as sure as he knew Donald's reason for coming over had more to do with getting additional water for Cimarron than warning an old friend.

7

Sheriff Thompson walked into Maria's house holding a bag of groceries. Maria was lying on the chaise lounge in her yellow robe, sipping from a paper cup, watching a courtroom drama on television. A half-empty ginger-brandy bottle stood on the end table. From the kitchen he heard Maria shout, "Hah!" several times as he put groceries away. On the way back to his bedroom, Maria stopped him.

"Oh, Wyatt, sit down," she said, slurring his name. He obeyed.

"What are you watching?" Wyatt said more out of a sense of duty than curiosity. She mumbled something to do with "justice for all."

He stared at the screen, thought about the Boulder County men at the meeting. Commissioner Brandt seemed like a decent enough American. The other two he wasn't so sure about. That lawyer had a devious way about him with that crazy talk about *owning water before it hit the ground.* Did he own the clouds and the sunshine and the rainbows too? That sheriff was a troublemaker, no doubt about it.

"Hah!" Maria said again, startling Sheriff Thompson. "There's no justice for all…"

Maria said she didn't remember the last time she had filed a tax return and that she paid someone three hundred dollars to be part of a lawsuit against the IRS for stealing her money all that time she didn't know any better. She expected a large check within the year.

"You should know," Maria said, "that government is inherently evil. Because it's run by men." She then broadened her attack to include *all* men as evil, especially the ones who had forced her to type so fast she developed carpal tunnel syndrome. The next time Maria lifted the cup to her mouth, Sheriff Thompson said, "Goodnight," then fast-walked to his bedroom.

He awoke the next morning puzzled by the cold. Late summer mornings in Kansas never felt this cold. He dressed, walked down the gravel road. The air was dry, fragrant. Pine trees and massive rock formations bathed in sunlight brought to him a glorious sense of peace. The chill he felt was a message from the Lord, he decided, reassurance that traveling to Boulder County was indeed part of His plan. The road stopped at an aspen grove where Sheriff Thompson leaned back on an ancient split rail fence, closed his eyes, then listened to the bubbling, flute-like notes of the meadowlark's song. It was the same song he heard Kansas meadowlarks sing from fence posts at the edge of his property. Hunger pangs interrupted his contemplation. He walked back to Maria's house to see a dingy green Plymouth Duster in the driveway. Maria stumbled through the front door with one arm around a vacuum canister, a snarl of hoses draped over the other arm.

"Let me help you," Sheriff Thompson said, reaching for the canister.

Maria flinched. "Put it in the backseat," she said.

Sheriff Thompson did as told while Maria opened the trunk, dropped the hoses on yellowed newspapers, sausage McMuffin wrappers, and empty bottles, before slamming the trunk closed. "Okay," she said then climbed into the car.

He watched the Duster sputter away, consciously not dwelling on her lack of gratitude, but wondered if Maria had the comfort of church in her life. He pictured her bent over a vacuum, backbones outlined through her T-shirt. Then he saw her scrubbing toilets and it seemed her biceps would give out and all the muscles in her bony arms would pop through her skin, unravel like a spool of string. Surely, she couldn't go on like this without the spirit of the Lord giving her strength. He returned to his bedroom to find his bed made.

8

BUDDY RECOGNIZED THE engine's hum as an automatic transmission driven by someone not accustomed to the winding curves along Fisher's Forest Way. He pushed cut-up stems off the kitchen table into a bucket, walked outside, sat on the single step in front of the screen door. Minutes later, a Ford Fiesta turned onto the driveway, rolled to a stop about fifteen yards in front of the drying screens. The driver and backseat passenger stepped out, both looking business casual in dark slacks, white button-down shirts, and shiny heads. Their facial expressions, however, were strictly business. The front seat passenger finished folding a map before stepping out. He looked like an accountant. All three stood beside their respective doors, staring at Buddy. Buddy stared back, curious who would blink first, but ended up surrendering a smile to avoid laughing. He walked over to the strangers, hand extended.

"Kansas?" Buddy said.

"I hope you don't mind us dropping in uninvited," the accountant said as he took Buddy's hand.

"Not at all," Buddy said. "Always glad when folks come for a visit. It gets lonely out here."

The man introduced himself as Dale Dahlgren, representing the Kansas Department of Agriculture. Then he introduced Major Davis of the Kansas Highway Patrol and Sheriff Wyatt Thompson of Ellsworth County, Kansas.

"It's a pleasure to meet all of you," Buddy said, noted the sheriff was not wearing a sidearm, then pointed to a wooden picnic table in the shade. "Take a seat, gentlemen. I'll get some iced tea."

Dahlgren and Major Davis exchanged looks. Sheriff Thompson watched Buddy walk into the house. "C'mon," Dahlgren said, walking toward the picnic table. The others followed. Buddy returned a few minutes later with a pitcher and four glasses.

"I get the idea you were expecting us," Major Davis said as Buddy poured the tea.

Buddy laughed. "Well, yeah, I guess I was. I mean, I wouldn't call Boulder County a small town, but for those of us who've lived here all our lives, we kind of operate with a single mind."

Dahlgren and Major Davis sipped. "Whaddya think?" Buddy said.

"Not bad," Dahlgren said. "Tangy."

"Yep. Lemon ginger," Buddy said. "Not thirsty, Sheriff Thompson?"

"Mr. Fisher—" Major Davis said.

"No, no, no. Please call me Buddy."

"Okay, Buddy, I'll get right to the point of our visit. It's well known that you grow a particularly potent strain of marijuana. And now that Colorado tolerates the recreational use of this drug, we in Kansas have serious concerns—"

"Concerns with *any* marijuana, I would say. Medical or otherwise."

"Uh, well, so be it. Anyway, now that pot has been officially *endorsed* by Colorado, we fear our kids will see this statement as permission to go ahead and experiment with drug use. In fact, according to our statistics, it's already started. Kids driving over the border, buying your marijuana, then driving back, is what I mean."

"Gosh, I can't help but be flattered that you think I created something special, but I'm not a licensed grower. Therefore, I don't sell marijuana to licensed retailers. So you must be mistaken."

"The amount of THC in their bloodstreams is far higher than any pot shop is allowed to sell under Colorado law. Word gets around, Mr. Fish—I mean, Buddy—that this marijuana could only come from you."

"I'm sorry, Major Davis, but I just told you—"

"We're not the stupid bumpkins you think we are. Maybe you, personally, are not selling to legal shops, but somehow your marijuana is finding its way there."

"What does *somehow* have to do with me?"

"If you grew it, it has to do with you."

"We won't even mention what it's costing the state of Kansas to test these kids," Dahlgren said. "And that affects all taxpaying citizens."

"Well, I suggest you stop testing and save the taxpayers a lot of money."

Sheriff Thompson straightened up. Major Davis said, "We were hoping that you would take us seriously—uh,

Buddy. It would be in your best interests to understand that we are taking you *very* seriously. And we're especially serious about those seventy kilos hidden on your property that you plan to distribute into Kansas and beyond—seeds and all."

A pause. Dale Dahlgren and Major Davis took more sips.

"The taste kind of grows on you after a while, doesn't it?" Buddy said.

Nobody responded then Dahlgren said, "Look, Buddy, I know us barging in on you like this—"

"Sorry, fellas, but I gotta ask. Why do you believe some fairytale about seventy kilos with magic seeds?"

Major Davis took one more quick sip then licked his lips. "Sheriff Thompson and I initiated a task force to examine the impact of Colorado's pot law on Kansas law enforcement. In the process of conducting interviews of the youngsters we pulled over—and sometimes arrested—of the ones we got to talk, they all seemed to have the same things in common, and one of those things was the name, Buddy Fisher. It seems you're famous to these kids."

"Golly, I sure don't feel famous. Are these Kansas young-sters you've been pulling over?"

The question caught Major Davis off guard. "Uh, some are Kansas teens taking road trips to buy pot. Some are those hippie types from all over—but that's not the point. Especially alarming is that, to a person—both boys and girls—they all demonstrated an alarming disregard for consequences, not to mention a lack of respect for law enforcement. It was a cockiness I'd never seen in my thirty years on the force. 'Your time is coming to an end.' Or 'Closing the barn door a little late, aren't ya?' Or something about Pandora's box already being open. That kind of crap. I pressed some of them on this attitude, and they'd just push back about some Boulder County dope farmer ready to 'change the game' with his pot. And that's when your name would come up."

"You realize that's all hearsay," Buddy said. "None of those kids have ever been on my property." Buddy looked at Sheriff Thompson. "You know what hearsay is, Wyatt?"

"You're absolutely right," Major Davis said. "And the people of Kansas have the highest respect for private property rights. Our mission here is not about intimidation or anything like that. We just want to have a chat, see if we can't find some common ground."

Buddy pretended to think about it. "It'll be hard to find common ground when you just walk in here and blame me for all your problems."

"Colorado is sick," Sheriff Thompson said. "You're a symptom of the sickness."

Dahlgren said, "I don't think Sheriff Thompson meant that to sound as rude as it—"

"No worries. I'm thankful the sheriff didn't refer to me as the *disease* itself! Say, Major, what reason did your troopers cite for pulling over all these youngsters?"

Major Davis sipped again. "I couldn't tell you offhand, only that they had reasonable belief that the car should be pulled over."

Buddy nodded. Dahlgren was about to say something, but Buddy beat him to it. "Well, Sheriff Thompson, are you pulling over a lot of marijuana-crazed teens in your part of Kansas?"

Dahlgren laughed. "*Marijuana-crazed* might be overdoing it a—"

"There's nothing I wouldn't do to protect the children of Ellsworth County from you people," Sheriff Thompson said.

"Sheriff—" Dahlgren said before Buddy cut him off.

"You familiar with the Fourth Amendment, Sheriff Thompson?"

"The Fourth Amendment is some men's words written on paper. Our children belong to God. They come into this world pure and are expected to return to God just as pure."

"Does the Boulder County Sheriff know you all planned on visiting me?"

Dale Dahlgren and Major Davis squirmed a bit. Major Davis said, "We met with Sheriff Castellanos yesterday. He knows we're here."

"Look, gentlemen," Buddy said. "I'm just a small, independent, *businessman*, really. A horticulturist-slash-farmer, living off the land like the pioneers who settled this great country—hey, I have an idea." Buddy stood up. "How about I give you all a tour of the land? Maybe it'll give you a different perspective."

Major Davis and Dale Dahlgren stood.

"C'mon, Wyatt," Major Davis said. His voice had acquired a touch of playfulness. "Let's stretch our legs a little bit and see what old Buddy here has been up to."

Sheriff Thompson took his time getting up. Buddy guided them into the meadow, pointed out grasses called bluestem, Indian rice, eyelash, and fescue. Sheriff Thompson heard the sinister-sounding names, recognized the tricky way the sorcerer spoke, the way he went on and on about *nature* painting the landscapes with purples, yellows, blues, and reds from plants called sage, columbine, penstemon, and coneflower— as if this was all nature's doing and not the Holy Spirit's work.

"What are those over there?" Dahlgren asked, pointing to an area of pink, yellow, and blue.

"Well, Mr. Dahlgren," Buddy said. "You just picked out some fine examples of fireweed, sulfur flower, and flax."

Sheriff Thompson bristled at Dahlgren for daring to fraternize with the sorcerer. As they neared the bamboo enclosure, Sheriff Thompson took one look at the spiny labyrinth of vines and instantly recognized the demarcation of an insidious garden of evil.

"You probably guessed that inside these bamboo walls is where I grow my vegetables," Buddy said.

"What exactly do you grow there?" Major Davis said.

"Oh, just the hardier veggies. Broccoli, cabbage, onions, lettuce, peas, radishes, spinach, turnips—and some herbs."

"You forget about the marijuana?" Dahlgren said.

"Marijuana is an herb," Buddy said.

"Is that forest all your land too?" Major Davis asked.

"That's national forest, all the way up to a little road at the top of the slope called Quartz Way. But first you'd better find Claim Jumper Trail if you ever hope to find Quartz Way."

Sheriff Thompson noticed the back of the garden extending to the slope. "You get curious folks trying to climb your fence?" Major Davis said.

"Oh, you mean the lights," Buddy said. "Well, I really don't want to see somebody impale themselves on top of the bamboo. So if someone's going to scale that fence, they're going to have to do it under a very bright light. Just a little discouragement tactic."

Sheriff Thompson thought one could stand on Quartz Way and see down into the garden. He also noticed how this one slope was not forested like the other areas, but a tangle of rusty shrubbery speckled with bits of green and yellow. It didn't seem natural. A perfect place to hollow out a cave or mask a tunnel entrance.

Dahlgren yawned behind his hand. "Well," he said, "maybe it's time we quit pestering Buddy and let him be."

"Oh, geez, guys, you're not pestering me. I understand your concerns and all. It's only normal. At least I got a chance to show you that I'm not the devil-worshiping hell-hound you thought I was."

Dahlgren and Major Davis laughed then turned to see Sheriff Thompson already walking toward the car. Buddy accompanied his guests across the meadow, but had to shorten his strides on account of the other two becoming a little heavy in the legs. They walked in silence until Dahlgren said, "Don't pay Sheriff Thompson too much mind, Buddy. I think I can speak for Major Davis when I say that we both see in you a reasonable man. Sure, we may not agree philosophically on some things, but if you'll work with us, I've no doubt we can come to terms with the situation."

"No doubt," Buddy said.

Dahlgren continued, "You being a businessman—like you said—I'm sure we'll figure something out as long as we keep the lines of communication open. Do I speak out of turn, Major Davis?"

"No, Dale, you spoke pretty good for one of the governor's aggy-crats."

The three men laughed.

9

L ATE SEPTEMBER'S SUN held Buddy spellbound, oblivious to the "clank" of the spray nozzle bouncing off a steel drum. His father used to stand on that same spot on Quartz Way, contemplating crop orientation according to the sun's angle. Buddy thought of their mid-August "reaping festivals," before the development of more cold-tolerant strains pushed the cutting and trimming into September. Two horn blasts from Castellanos's truck creeping up the driveway brought him back to the present. Buddy waited for Castellanos to get out then whistled and waved before securing the drum on a portable hydraulic lift and loading it onto the bed of his truck. Two hikers approached as he wiped oily goo from his hands. They wondered out loud what he'd been spraying on the slope.

"Roundup," Buddy said without looking up then heard, "Asshole," as they walked past.

*

The two men shook hands, cautiously semi-embraced the way men did. Castellanos added a playful punch to Buddy's shoulder.

"What's with the Illinois plates?"

"Remember Alex?"

"Yeah, I do! How the hell is Cousin Alex?"

"He's good."

"Get him out here. I wanna say hi."

"Oh, he's out communing with nature on one of his five-hour walks."

Castellanos nodded. "I remember. Not much of a talker. An *interesting* guy—I guess."

Buddy laughed. "We were an *interesting* family. So what's the latest?"

"Well, supposedly you been supplying the western US with high-altitude seeds you got from a Nepalese shaman and you're teaching everyone to soak the leaves in the juice of some Asian asparagus root. A couple of puffs and you're instantly a heroin addict. That kind of stuff."

"Sounds about right. Head over. I shall be there forthwith."

Castellanos walked past the picnic table, rounded the corner, and fell back in one of two Adirondack chairs, dropping his feet on a tree stump. Buddy returned holding two bottles and a cigar box. Castellanos extended an arm, with open palm, into which Buddy deftly placed the bottle. Buddy sat, put the cigar box on the ground, watched Castellanos guzzle his beer, drop the empty, then let loose a ferocious belch. "Ready?"

Buddy shook his head in disgust. "Only a sick bastard drinks like that."

The two sat quietly as Buddy sipped. Twenty minutes later he put his half-empty bottle on the ground next to the cigar box. "Ready," he said then whacked Castellanos's arm with the back of his hand. "Wake up, Sheriff. Dog at large!"

Castellanos opened his eyes. Buddy handed him a joint. "Kind of thin."

"You want a fatty of this weed, you better call out of service for the rest of the day—and tomorrow too."

Castellanos's face lit up. He put the joint in his mouth and leaned into Buddy's lighter. Buddy took a drag, blew out a lungful. "You let those hayseed sons-of-bitches come to my house? Unescorted? Are you still the sheriff of Boulder County by any chance?"

"Take it easy. Yeah, I knew they were in town, but they didn't say anything about paying you a visit. I found out just a couple of hours ago when they came by—out of respect." Castellanos laughed. "Out of respect for the Boulder County Sheriff's Department."

"And?"

"They wanted to tell me they had *already* visited you." He laughed harder.

Buddy watched. "Okay. I think I get it."

"When outside law enforcement visits, it's customary to tell the host what they're up to and expect an escort. But they didn't do that until *after* they said hello to you."

"I guess they felt guilty over dissing you."

"I said, 'You just showed up at Buddy Fisher's house!? Just did what you damn well pleased!? This is 'merica, damn it!'" Now they both laughed. "You should've seen them falling over themselves apologizing. Except for that turd, Sheriff Thompson. He just stood there watching then walked out."

Buddy took another drag. "This is 'merica, and Sheriff Reyes Castellanos is one hell of a good 'merican who can trace his roots to the Sangre de Cristo Land Grant."

"Damn right! I'm more 'merican than any of those Kansas boys could ever dream of being."

"Then what?"

"I calmed them down, said they were forgiven, then they started talking about this Buddy Fisher and what a nice guy he was and how optimistic they were about figuring things out. Oh, and then they wanted to make sure I knew they didn't have anything against the people of Boulder County and deep down we were all the same blah, blah, blah. I don't know what you did, but those two boys were a hell of a lot different than when I first met them yesterday. Sheriff Thompson, that's another story. We gotta keep an eye on that fucker. But how'd you win those other two over?"

Buddy sat up, tried to keep a straight face. "Oh, just killed 'em with kindness. Major Davis and Dahlgren really liked my iced tea—by the way. Sheriff Thompson barely touched his."

Buddy waited for his friend's brain to crunch the data.

"You didn't!"

"I swear to God Almighty there wasn't enough dope in that iced tea to get a mouse buzzed."

Castellanos pulled up his knees, hugged them to his chest, his lungs filling before spasms of laughter gushed out. Both men lay helpless for a while until Castellanos managed to say, "What did you give them?"

"A hybrid for crabby folks. I call it Terrapin Lemonade."

More laughing, then Sheriff Castellanos sighed loudly and said, "Uh, Buddy?"

"Say it."

"I don't gotta tell you that if this thing goes federal—we're all fucked. You more than anyone else."

"No, Ray. You don't gotta tell me."

Castellanos dropped his roach into the empty bottle. "Remind me. Way back when, what did they nail you for?"

"Over twelve ounces of weed. Another time, over three ounces of hash oil."

Castellanos groaned. "Class 6 felonies. You're fucked."

"Yes, Ray, it's been long established that I'm fucked. They'll never give me a commercial license. *I know that.*"

"So whaddya gonna do?"

"About what?"

"Don't bullshit me. You know what I'm talking about."

"What do you want to hear? That's why you came over, right? So I'll say what you want to hear?"

Castellanos turned to Buddy. "You think I like this? You think I'd give a damn about a tidal wave of shit I saw headed toward Donny? Did you see the look in that Sheriff Thompson's eyes? He's one scary motherfucker—on a mission from God. You got no chance against a crusading Kansas redneck like him. He'll cut your throat and praise Jesus at the same time. And if that wasn't bad enough, there's a Cook Industries prick—"

"We met."

"Oh? Well that should've put a burr in your underpants. *Cook Industries*, Buddy. I don't understand all that corporate-blueprint shit, but it sounds a lot like what your dad used to talk about. I used to think he was nuts, but Abe saw it coming way back when."

Buddy smiled at his friend. "He *did* see it coming, didn't he?"

"Why're you acting like this?"

"What do you want me to do, Ray?"

"Give 'em what they want and move on to something else. Hey! Why not go back to soap-making? That's where you came from, right? Make Papa George proud."

"Now you're talking out your ass. What they want is all I've ever known."

"So what? The Wild West is over, Buddy. The frontier is closing. Grow your organic veggies or whatever, but stay away from weed."

It sounded so easy, logical. And it did make sense if one ignored Buddy's age, the massive amounts of labor, and small, if non-existent profit margins.

"You have no idea what you're talking about."

"Maybe I don't. But I do know you weren't always like this—so damn negative. And it's not like I don't know why. What's it been? At least twenty years?"

Buddy thought that meme had finally run dry. He was wrong. "Let me rephrase. You have no *fucking* idea what you're talking about."

"Arrrrrgh! You're so goddamn self-absorbed you don't even realize the position you're putting me in. I worked hard to get to where I am. But you don't care. Screw me. Screw all the people who care about you. Let 'em all watch as you martyr yourself fighting the unbeatable enemy until it crushes you, because you're a man of *principle*, who would never sell out to some evil corporate—" Castellanos stopped then said, "I haven't slept in two days—"

Buddy swung his legs over the side of the chair. "Ray, it's fine. I get it. Just do your job. Be a sheriff. I don't blame you. I won't ever blame you."

Castellanos wiped his eyes. "It's your goddamn weed

turning me into Sheriff Pussy. You did this on purpose, you shit."

Neither spoke awhile. "By the way," Castellanos said, "did you have one of your co-op dope meetings the other night?"

"Yep. That's where I met Stanley Carson from Cook Industries."

"Ah. How did Zeb react?"

Buddy waved him off. "Your little pal, Alfie, was the star. Told Stanley to fuck off, called him a cunt."

Laughter roared back. "No shit?"

"None at all."

"Best news I've heard in a long time. Although—I better talk to him, make sure he understands what diplomacy means."

"So how do you think it'll go down if I don't behave?"

"I was gonna get to that. Speaking of cunts, has Donny been here lately?"

"Last night."

Castellanos lay back again, put his feet back on the stump. "They're holding off on strong-arming you with law enforcement to see if you'll just play ball and make it an easy transition, so to speak. Today's visit was about testing the waters. Next, they'll want to get friendly with those nice boys we grew up with from Nederland and Ward and Jamestown. You remember them, don't you? Those boys you trained in growing high-altitude dope? Kansas will graciously ask them to convince Buddy Fisher to turn over the seventy kilos."

"I'd pay good money just to watch Zeb Macky's reaction."

"Yeah, I know. But after Zeb tells Kansas to go fuck themselves, they'll start with the lawsuits."

"Lawsuits, huh? You don't think they'd get more radical

than lawsuits? I mean lawsuits can take a while. And there're still one or two hippie lawyers left to go pro bono for guys like me and Zeb."

"It's bigger than that. They sue the governor—"

"They'll sue the sheriff of Boulder County!"

"Hell yes they will. They'll sue everyone and their fucking uncle for all kinds of reasons, and they'll keep doing it—even if it's all frivolous bullshit—just to bleed everyone dry. Eventually, they're gonna look at me, the sheriff, and say it's time to start cracking down on all the illegal growing, blah, blah, blah. And guess whose name will be at the top of the list? *Yours* goddamn it. Buddy-fucking-Fisher."

Buddy remembered Castellanos was up for re-election. "How about this," Buddy said. "Some quasi-government, contractor, men-in-black types will pay Zeb a visit and see if he might not reconsider getting all the foothills weed clans to come down on me. That way, they stand to keep their little operations if they just get me to play along. And when good old Zeb says, 'No thank you,' the men-in-black will start talking about unacknowledged, federal-marshal types digging up, burning, and poisoning their land to the point they'd have trouble raising a crop of knapweed."

Castellanos's jaw tightened. "I don't know if you're kidding with that conspiracy crap or what. But it's kind of pissing me off."

"Pissed off after smoking my weed? I must be losing my touch. Why'd you ask if Donny had been here?"

"Because he knows all about this plan. I guess the prick didn't think it was important enough to mention."

"You have any idea how many families up in those towns depend on dope revenue just to make ends meet? Without it, they'd never make it through the winter. And they'd rather starve than ask for help."

"Hell yes, I know. And I know at the end of the day nobody gives a damn about a bunch of paranoid, off-the-grid, libertarian nutjobs."

"They might give a damn when an AR-15 is shoved into their mouths. Those boys are heavily armed."

"And it'll be *my* mouth or one of my deputies' mouths, and they'll give us no choice but to use extreme measures—get it?"

"They're not stupid, Ray. Waco, Ruby Ridge—that Philadelphia compound going up in flames? It's all stamped on their brains. They'll only go so far."

"You're wrong. They worship you. And loyalty is sacred to those guys. Snitches get stitches, you know."

Loyalty. Buddy once knew what the word meant. The sheriff of Boulder County copped a weed and beer buzz out of loyalty. But once the kids and mortgage came along, loyalties had a habit of changing.

10

AT TWO-THIRTY THE next morning Buddy sat comfortably in a swivel chair, arms folded against the cellar's chill. It would come back slowly: getting out of bed, putting on a robe, lighting a candle, descending the stairs where three laptops displayed different angles of the slope behind the garden. Lost was any recollection of lighting wall sconces above the desk or turning on the space heater blowing over his ankles. Usually, it wasn't until breakfast that a faint memory of beeping would resurface: a coyote, no doubt, breaking the laser shining across Quartz Way—although one time a mountain lion with her three cubs strolled across the computer screens. But this was different. Never had Buddy just found himself sitting in the cellar, semi-conscious, Papa George's voice exuding from the walls in his clumsy immigrant syntax, *From a story you know who you are and how you're coming here...*

Buddy knew the story, superficially at least, having learned it the way a child learned prayer, that is, dogmatically, the way parents instilled reverence for something invisible yet all powerful. Castellanos had been right about his father.

Abe saw it coming way back when. But Papa George must've seen it too, whatever *it* was, and only from the source, Buddy reasoned, could *it* be truly known. Straddling the seen and unseen worlds in the candlelit darkness, Buddy inserted himself into the story, began imagining a realistic account, not as a chronicler of anecdotes, but as one needing to *become* the story in order to know the story—and to know himself.

Because Buddy Fisher owed his existence to soap—a product of chemistry—it made sense that he first saw Papa George's grandfather, Emil, who worked as an apothecary's assistant, so the story went, serving the Royal House of Hanover. Emil had obtained the position after ingratiating himself with the royal chemist, Herr Stahl, a man said to have carried the spark of Enlightenment in his soul.

This was the latter part of the 19th century, when an apothecary's assistant could expect—at best—cautious civility from their employer, albeit with a bridled disdain in their speech. The exception was Herr Stahl, the oldest of the royal chemists, whose disorderly head of hair and pleasant smile gave him a rather lovable Bohemian persona. It was through the generosity of this man that Emil gained access to the library and was even permitted to take home chemistry and pharmacy books once updated versions had been acquired. From Herr Stahl's kindness, Emil began assembling a library that eventually grew to encompass subjects ranging from Darwin's biological theories to Zola's literary naturalism. Herr Stahl's generosity also enabled Emil to move his wife and four children from the *Kellerstrasse* ghetto into two large rooms behind a "front house" apartment in the Old Town district—the epitome of opulence compared to their dark claustrophobic attic.

Emil loved all his children but derived his greatest joy from Jakob—Papa George's father—his first born and only son. By age four, Emil had taught the boy how to read. By age ten, Jakob comprehended his father's books with a preternatural understanding that could only have been a message from God Almighty Himself. And as Noah built his ark, so did Emil construct two small bookcases he positioned at right angles in a corner, barely large enough for two chairs and a table with an oil lamp—their little study tantamount to the queen's Marienburg Castle library.

The latter 19th century was also a time when apothecaries began transitioning to the bulk manufacturing of plant-based extracts for medicines and dyes. From this development, the farsighted Emil recognized the practicality of nurturing in his son a passion for chemistry, an ambition Jakob happily obliged his beloved father. But Emil knew passion without state-accredited education was useless in their world; Jakob's future needed, if not required, the influence of a man such as Herr Stahl. With his wife's help, an encounter was planned and executed, Rachel bringing Jakob into the apothecary at precisely the time Emil knew his employer would undertake a cursory lab inspection. In this "chance" meeting, Jakob graciously thanked the royal chemist for his generosity with books, then expressed his fascination over the isolation of chemical compounds from plants, particularly *papaver somniferum*, from which the chemist Friedrich Sertürner had extracted a soporific alkaloid Jakob thought held great promise for medicinal use. So impressed was Herr Stahl with the boy's intelligence, his breadth of knowledge, his general self-possession, that he ensured Jakob's placement in *gymnasium* the following year.

As time passed, Emil kept Herr Stahl apprised of his son's superior class ranking, but never elicited more than a muted "Well done." Inevitably, thoughts of university dared show signs of life in both father and son. Emil had purposely avoided the subject in the face of deficient funds and a quota system, but did his best to sound supportive. After Jakob turned sixteen, Emil took a chance, gathered his courage to tell Herr Stahl—with unmistakable self-abasement—of Jakob's naive desire to attend university. The royal chemist smiled weakly, nodded. His expression would haunt Emil through the coming months, especially when Jakob sat in their library poring over Latin, Greek, algebra, logarithms, and trigonometry, in preparation for university entrance exams.

As Jakob's eighteenth birthday neared, Emil had all but given up hope. Then, as if by a miracle, Herr Stahl summoned Emil to his office, where he stood trembling before the royal chemist's enormous rosewood desk.

"Jakob should be done with his studies soon, no?"

"Yes, Herr Stahl."

"And what of his future? An apothecary's assistant like his father?"

Emil knew only too well that Jakob's life could be much worse than what an apothecary's assistant offered, but squandering his son's intellect on dispensing prescriptions, compounding tinctures, and dressing injuries seemed wasteful, if not cruel. Before Emil could respond, Herr Stahl said, "Perhaps something different? I'm prepared to provide financial backing for an apprenticeship with Herr Neubek, a prominent soap maker. I would be happy to make this a reality should the boy show an interest."

Emil saw benevolence in the royal chemist's eyes, but as the seconds ticked away, he also saw impatience. As painful as it was to accept less than what he thought Jakob deserved, Emil couldn't deny the unique opportunity Herr Stahl presented.

"You are kind beyond words, Herr Stahl. Your generosity knows no bounds. God shall certainly reward you for your charitable soul. I will speak with Jakob tonight and tell him the wonderful news."

"I know you had higher hopes, Emil. But we must recognize the best option available, regardless of one's aspirations."

"Yes, Herr Stahl. You are of course right. And I'll make sure Jakob understands the value of your generosity. God bless you."

Walking home that night, Emil wondered if this was God's punishment for sustaining faith in the human guise of a royal chemist—a false prophet, perhaps?—therefore renouncing trust in the creator. Then he thought of how pride destroyed the Moabites. Had he, too, replaced the holy with worldly ambition?

Emil discerned in Jakob's face that his son understood the source of his father's furrowed brow, why his father picked at the stuffed goose neck and salt herring. Had they not shared the same dream for eight years? After dinner, Emil put his arm around Jakob, walked him to their little library.

"I have good news for you," Emil said, his words the embodiment of irony. "Herr Stahl has arranged an apprenticeship for you with a prominent soap maker."

Emil's chin quivered; tears dropped from his eyes. Jakob fought the lump in his throat long enough for a positive glimmer to surface. Despite its dowdy nature, soap-making did require chemistry skills and a chance to elevate the family's financial and social status. Jakob walked behind Emil's chair, wrapped his arms around his father's shoulders.

"That's fantastic news, Papa. I shall become the best soap maker in the world. I will make you proud of me."

*

That Herr Neubek would consider entrusting his heritage to Jakob, an "ethnic German," testified to the strength of his conviction that the family's living legacy endured—the income of which the sons-in-law found no objection to accepting. Master soap maker Herr Neubek hailed from a tradition of recipes certified by edicts dating back two hundred years. By the late 19th century, his family had established itself on the more prosperous end of the upper middle class, a notch or two below, perhaps, the "lesser nobility" of the landowning families. Ensuring his ancestral expertise passed to future generations was for Herr Neubek a sacred duty. Providence, however, had not seen fit to provide him a male heir. To make matters worse, Herr Neubek's prosperity had enabled his three daughters to marry *above* their social class, a mixed blessing, as it turned out, since the newly acquired sons-in-law shunned identification with the trades. Yet Jakob's introduction would not have been possible without Herr Stahl and Herr Neubek's common social circles. And then there was Herr Stahl's force of personality—"don't be a silly ass and meet the boy!"

The interview took place in the soap maker's study, a stately room of elk antler chandeliers and tapestries of falconry drama. With the aplomb of one accustomed to speaking in Prussian hunting lodges, Jakob demonstrated his knowledge of fats and alkalis. Then he expounded on soap-making history from ancient Babylon, Rome, and China, to medieval Europe when the French centers of Marseilles, Toulon, Provence, and Hyères established dominance. Observing the encounter from a plush Queen Anne armchair, Herr Stahl found great amusement with Herr Neubek's determination to appear uninspired by the boy's assimilated appearance and pure, unaccented German.

The meeting proceeded nicely until Jakob mentioned the recent development of potash and soda for alkali extraction. Herr Neubek's posture stiffened. Herr Stahl cringed, only then realizing his underestimation of Jakob's innocence. Considering the cultural divide, a peddler's son appearing to know more than his future master was particularly acute. Perhaps it was from this same innocence that Jakob then praised the soap tax's repeal and correctly identified the room's paintings as the Duke of Brunswick-Lüneburg, the first member of the House of Hanover; George V, the last Hanoverian king, and a superb oil-on-canvas depiction of the moated castle Wasserschloss Hülsede.

*

By the time Buddy heard the quote "Two hundred years of soap-making must be respected," it had been reduced to a comic euphemism for obeying one's parents. His great-great-grandfather, Emil, however, saw nothing funny when he allegedly used the phrase before Jakob's apprenticeship began, and then made his son promise to speak only when questioned and reveal nothing of himself beyond deference and conformity. "Tame your inquisitive mind. Outside our home, we are just lambs among wolves."

Jakob behaved as his father advised, quickly gleaned from Herr Neubek's disapproving looks and haughty comportment that the slightest allusion to deviating from animal fats, lye, and water would be interpreted as insolence. At the end of his first week, Jakob gave his father an unsolicited description of Herr Neubek's factory—antiquated, crude, bereft of imagination, looking every day of its two-hundred-year existence. A horrified Emil closed his eyes, braced against childhood stories of terror, dispossession, and annihilation. He wondered if it had been a mistake to spare his children such visions. Maybe it would have been better impressing upon young minds how quickly circumstances could change. Emil begged Jakob's assurance of never talking in such a manner outside their home.

Jakob apologized, pledged his silence, but then sent Emil to his knees, sobbing, when he compared the next five years of his life to a prison sentence. A guilt-stricken Jakob apologized through his own tears, unaware the source of his father's grief came not from Jakob's sentiment, but from *knowing* his son's frustration, as he knew himself.

"Just tell me what you want to hear, Papa. I give you my word I'll do whatever you ask."

Emil wiped his eyes, laid his hands on Jakob's shoulders. "For God's sake, embrace their world for these five years. Make it something to call your own—if only to help us *believe* in a future. This is what I ask."

Jakob would do as asked, but grew to despise the memory of his father sobbing, particularly the fear and humiliation it represented. The library became Jakob's refuge, a place to write down thoughts, ideas, conclusions, and questions that had crossed his mind during the day. Never again did he speak disparagingly of Herr Neubek. Only once during the five-year apprenticeship did he test fate, rhetorically pondering—couched in childlike curiosity—the feasibility of vegetable oils. Herr Neubek scowled at such folly, lectured Jakob on the seriousness of tradition, demanded his thoughts remain fixed upon measurement and consistency.

Jakob's Master Soap Maker certificate from the guild's trade school came with the expectation that Herr Neubek would bring Jakob into his employ, although details had not been discussed. Jakob's feelings on the matter also had not been discussed. Staying put was the safest course, but Jakob's ambition to succeed on his own told him otherwise. Emil agonized over his son's confidence. "We don't have the luxury of turning our backs on opportunity."

"I did as you asked, Papa. This certificate gives me rights. We can do better than what Herr Neubek dictates. He is no longer my master. I'm no longer his slave."

Emil recoiled. "Can't you see we are only guests in Hanover and that appearing ungrateful could be the end of us?"

"I have a plan to make something new, something better that costs much less to produce. Mama told me you two saved every pfennig since I started gymnasium. From that money we can buy capital, start our own business."

It was true that additional income from his mother's and sisters' seamstress work had enabled Emil and Rachel to squirrel away a tidy sum—for when their good luck might run out. Not a single book had been added to the library.

"Herr Stahl is an old man," Emil said. "What do I say to him? That my son took your gift of a living and gambled it away? Should Herr Stahl die, my position becomes tenuous. The family needs security."

"Herr Neubek is also old, Papa. What guarantee would I have after he dies? We have only ourselves on which to depend."

"You're right, Jakob. There are no guarantees. We can only do what we think is best. But we must always be prepared for our world to change—the way society views us, I mean. I've failed to teach you this and I'm sorry." Emil saw Jakob's confusion, placed a hand on each side of his face. "Wait for Herr Neubek to present his terms. Then we'll talk again."

*

As Buddy learned more about his soap-making forefathers, so did he theorize how the fear of change mutated their DNA to become an intergenerational curse. The capricious nature of change that his great-great-grandfather, Emil, so feared would be brutally demonstrated during the forthcoming influenza pandemic that killed Herr Neubek. Herr Stahl, too, was laid low but managed to recover, albeit in a much weakened state. Herr Neubek's will had designated the business pass in equal shares to the three sons-in-law, but his failure to provide instructions regarding an apprentice's terms of employment put Jakob's future in the hands of the three aristocrats. While the family waited for news, Jakob continued overseeing the pouring and mixing of Herr Neubek's soaps, ensuring consistency was maintained. He noticed the hollow look of anxiety in the workers' faces, pitied them for their lack of education, fantasized of one day employing them all.

The new circumstances shattered Emil. Herr Stahl took notice, summoned Emil to his office. "Good god, man,"

Herr Stahl said, his voice depleted by illness. "You look as if any moment Cossacks will smash down your doors."

Emil was struck with how the enormous desk enhanced Herr Stahl's withered appearance. "I'm sorry, Herr Stahl."

Herr Stahl wiped his nose. "Such a pity Herr Neubek did not have the foresight to leave instructions—the damn fool."

"Yes, Herr Stahl. The uncertainty is upsetting."

"How is the boy?"

"Jakob does not fear uncertainty. He wants to start his own business. It is my fault that he should feel this way."

Herr Stahl began coughing violently, taking several minutes to compose himself. "I know the families with whom Jakob's future will be decided. They come from houses of high nobility. Soap-making is but a trifle to them—as is Jakob. Never will they have your family's best interests in mind. Your son has brilliant instincts, Emil. But a boy needs his father to stand with him, help him find what he seeks. 'So those who rely on faith are blessed along with Abraham, the man of faith.'"

Emil was not familiar with the quote, but appreciated it nonetheless. That evening father and son sat in the library. "Herr Stahl agrees with you," Emil said, the words sticking in his throat. "One with your talents should be allowed to find the opportunity he seeks. And I will help you."

This time, father and son shared joyous tears.

Unfettered to pursue his vision, Jakob leased a derelict potash ashery on the outskirts of Hanover, having anticipated such vacancies early in his apprenticeship after learning mineral salts were fast replacing wood ash for potash extraction. Within a year, he was traveling throughout the province, handing out sample-sized flasks of an olive-oil-based liquid soap. The soap's popularity spread quickly, proving especially popular with proprietors seeking inexpensive detergents for public facilities.

Beeping computers transitioned Buddy back to the 21st century, but not before a brief stop in a 20th-century garden, where a little boy assisted his delighted grandfather with pruning dead branches, eliminating weeds, and managing mulch. "Always plant a flower or herb beside the vegetable," Papa George told Buddy. "We should all grow with something lovely to look at."

Buddy watched the car move slowly across three laptop screens before pulling over beside the retaining wall. Sheriff Thompson stepped out wearing night vision goggles and a pistol holstered high on his hip. *He's a passionate man all right*, Buddy thought.

11

AFTER CONSIDERING THE rashness of the sheriff's actions Buddy decided *rabid* might be a better adjective. Had the sheriff maintained his composure and thought things through a little bit, he would've seen fit to wait a week in order to conduct covert ops under an eleven percent crescent moon instead of an eighty-two percent waxing moon.

From the trunk Sheriff Thompson took a pickaxe and shovel then slung them over his shoulder. Along the road between one end of the clear-cut parcel to the other, he paced with his eyes fixated downhill. Moonshine sparkled off the oily foliage. Several times he stopped, zeroed in as a hunter looked for camouflaged prey. Finally, he tossed the shovel aside, raised the pick over his head, then plunged it into the top of the slope. Buddy winced at the torque he imagined testing the sheriff's lower back. Sheriff Thompson repeated the action, establishing a rhythm of lifting, plunging, and sidestepping along the lip of Quartz Way all the way to where the slope became forested again, then stopped to shed his windbreaker and wipe his brow.

Buddy sat up, assumed the sheriff had sensed his

corporeal vulnerability from assaulting the land this way, but then saw the sheriff step onto the slope and position himself perpendicular to the road, legs astride, preparing to dispense punishment worthy of Samson slaying a thousand Philistines. Samson, however, most likely stood on dry, level ground, and not askew on a thirty-degree angle susceptible to a sudden change of posture. Nevertheless, Sheriff Thompson raised the pickaxe and delivered a blow with all the force one would expect from a Kansas sheriff overcome with the spirit of the Lord. The slope responded in kind, rocking the sheriff's body with an earthly agony, buckling his knees, sending him downhill.

The weight of future consequences crushed any joyful impulse inspired by the drama playing out across Buddy's laptops. It would still be a few more hours before Sheriff Thompson felt the full brunt of his misfortune. A few more hours before a poison ivy rash of red, swollen, itchy skin would appear on his arms, hands, and face. And besides the associated problems of pulled, twisted, and torn back muscles, Sheriff Thompson would also have to confront tiny needle-like hairs once attached to stinging nettle stems, which now pierced his skin and clothing.

*

Commissioner Brandt met with Castellanos later that morning, about an hour before Major Davis, Stanley Carson, and Dale Dahlgren were scheduled for an emergency meeting. The commissioner's secretary, Liz Crawford, noticed Castellanos's whimsical mood as he breezed into the office holding a laptop. Before shutting the conference room door, he winked at her. She lingered near the door, unable to decipher every word, but knew from Commissioner Brandt's tone he wasn't happy.

"What the hell's so funny?" Commissioner Brandt said.

"I already know," Castellanos said.

"Who told you?"

"You didn't see the video? Don't you check your email as soon as you get to work? It's in the county's employment guidelines, you know."

Commissioner Brandt sat down. He looked sick. Using his indoor voice he said, "What video?"

Liz Crawford hadn't checked her Outlook account either. She double-clicked on the envelope icon, saw a list of messages, including one from "CastellanosR" with the subject line "Criminal trespass, C.R.S. § 18-4-503 example" and an AVI attachment. The video opened to the sheriff from central Kansas unearthing a row of dirt along the top edge of a slope. Then the video cut to the sheriff slamming the pickaxe into the ground and the structural failure that followed. Liz Crawford watched the video several times, a hand covering her mouth.

Commissioner Brandt didn't react. He'd already received a detailed description of Sheriff Thompson's injuries.

"Buddy's taken up biological warfare?" Commissioner Brandt said.

"That stupid cracker was trespassing," Castellanos said. "He got what he deserved. I could have him arrested based on that video alone. This guy's a *sheriff* for fuck's sake."

"And now the sheriff's in bed, covered with blisters, throat closed, face blown up like a pumpkin, eyes swollen practically shut."

"Whoa," Castellanos said, legitimately surprised. "He

must've been allergic. I've had it before, but never reacted like that. It's still his own damn fault, Will. He had no business being on Buddy's property, and if his Kansas comrades think they have some legal recourse over this, I've got bad news for them."

Commissioner Brandt stared at Castellanos with the same unemotional expression with which he watched the video. "What else happened yesterday? At Buddy's place?"

Castellanos screwed up his face so as not to laugh. "Whaddya mean?"

"Did Buddy spike the lemonade with weed juice or whatever you call it?"

"What? Lemonade? No, no, no—hell no! It was iced tea." Acting as his own straight man sent Castellanos into hysterics. "It was *harmless*."

"Harmless? You've no idea how badly Buddy just screwed things up. As far as those Kansas boys are concerned, they offer an olive branch and Buddy gives 'em a vial of poison. He just declared war for chrissake."

Commissioner Brandt rested his forehead in his hand.

"You don't think you're overreacting, Will?"

"It's going federal. We're screwed. How do you feel about going back to being a patrolman on the graveyard shift?"

"Oh fuck you."

"Think so? You still don't get these people, do you?"

"The video clearly shows—"

"Do me a favor and get out. I'll deal with these guys myself. All you'll do is piss 'em off even more. Just get the fuck out."

*

Buddy grabbed a handful of stem chunks, funneled them into an electric coffee grinder, then held the switch down for several seconds before dumping the grounds into a glass jar. He repeated the process until the jar was half-full, then added an alcohol-water mixture and shook the jar. Martin's blue Jeep rolled into view through the kitchen window as Buddy was straining the mixture through coffee filters. Buddy walked to the screen door, watched Martin step out of the Jeep, said, "Uh-oh. Another visit so soon? I must've really stepped in it this time."

"I don't mean to be a pest," Martin said.

"I might start calling you Cassandra. Anyway, I said you were welcome anytime and I meant it." Buddy held the door open. "*Entrez*, Agent Marty. Grab a chair."

Martin sat, looked at the paraphernalia on the table. "You're making bubble hash."

"You're damn right I am. And as the famous Bubbleman said in *High Times* magazine, 'If it don't bubble, it ain't worth the trouble.'"

"I bet you make the purest trichome resin possible."

Buddy smiled, shook his head. "And I bet not one in ten thousand people know what a trichome is, yet you walk into my kitchen knowing exactly what you're talking about. You'd make a great pharmacognosist, you know that?"

"A what?"

"Pharmacognosist. They look for medicinal properties in plant chemicals."

"Like marijuana."

"Yeah, yeah, like marijuana, but that's not what I had in mind."

"Why not? There's a whole market opening up to it. Lots of money being made."

Buddy wanted to avoid the other day's polemics. "And money means big pharma's going to move in, cheapen the product, and put everybody out of business—anyway, what's going on? You got more shitty news for me?"

"Sheriff Castellanos sent Cody's mom and Commissioner Brandt a video of that Kansas sheriff digging up your property and taking a nasty spill. She said he's stuck in bed now, skin all blistered and nasty. Brandt had an emergency meeting this morning with those Kansas guys. They're declaring war on you."

"Hang on. Cody's mom actually *heard* the Kansas guys say they're declaring war on me?"

Martin thought about it. "I'll double-check. Maybe not literally."

Buddy sat across the table from Martin. "Fuck it. Doesn't matter. No school today?"

"I took a lot of summer school so my schedule's pretty light this year. What if you just went along with the government's game and—"

"Marty, for the last time, it's over for me. If you want to pursue this line of work one day then do it. Study the botanical sciences and take it from there."

"But I want your help. Teach me everything you know and we'll go into business together."

Buddy leaned back, saw Libby's face in Marty's forehead, brow ridge, and eyes.

"For now, watch me finish making the purest trichome resin you ever saw."

"You know they got CO_2 bubble hash washing machines

now. And 220 micron screen bags that hold, like, three pounds of weed."

"Well, there you go. That's the future. That's *your* future. You don't need me, Marty. Figure out the best course of study for what you want to do, then learn, learn, learn. Shit, you're way ahead of me already. In the meantime, let me tell you about the importance of soil nutrition…"

Buddy continued straining the jar's contents through coffee filters while talking about worm castings, blood meal, and guano. The vestibule door opened then closed.

"Alex!" Buddy yelled. "Get in here."

A man about Buddy's age with a head of wavy black hair walked out.

"You remember little Marty who used to help us with the harvest way back when? He still helps me when he can get time away from school."

Alex smiled, walked to Martin, extended his hand. "All grown up, huh?"

"Alex and your Uncle Jake were good friends. Jake was always trying to convince Alex to move out here. Isn't that right, Alex?"

Alex looked down, eyes blinking. "Yeah, Jake was a real good guy."

"How things look?" Buddy said.

Alex gave the thumbs-up sign. "Things look all right."

"Awesome. I'll join you in a little bit."

Alex grinned at Martin then walked back into the vestibule. The change in Martin's demeanor had been palpable as soon as Alex appeared. For now, Buddy said nothing, allowed Martin to sit quietly with his thoughts. After Buddy finished filtering the remaining stem grounds he said, "Seeing Alex again after all this time must've brought back a lot of memories, huh?"

"How come Mom never hung out with us and Uncle Jake?"

The question hadn't surprised Buddy, but he had expected it years ago. When it wasn't asked, he assumed Libby or Jake had given Martin a sufficient explanation. Maybe not.

"Well, your mom and I were very close as kids. But people change as they grow up. Times change, too. She went away to school and I stayed local, living and working with my dad, going to CU part-time." Buddy stopped, swallowed hard.

"Did you know my real dad?"

"No. I don't know much about your mom's life in Los Angeles—when you were born."

Buddy knew his answer sounded as unsatisfying to Marty as it did to his own ears. "You didn't *ask* her?"

"You gotta remember, Marty, you and I became pals all those years ago thanks to your Uncle Jake. Your mom and I have only been back in touch for a few months. For now, I think it's best to let her decide what I should or shouldn't know. What do you know about your dad?"

"Not much. All she says is that he was a coward who ran out on us. She gets upset when I ask, so I stopped asking."

"Well, it's his loss. He's missing out on watching you become the man you're becoming." Martin frowned. Buddy said, "You getting along with your step-dad?"

"Uncle Jake hated him. Called him The Asshole."

Buddy muzzled a laugh. He and Jake had spent many weed-infused afternoons disparaging Donny. "You didn't answer my question."

"Mom said you and Donny were thick as thieves."

"Oh yeah, we used to be good pals. Made lots of plans. But like I said, things change over time. People change."

"What plans did you make?"

Buddy took a breath. "First it was an organic-farm-cooperative thing. We were going to supply the whole front range with the freshest, greatest, in-season produce they'd ever seen. Somewhere there's a picture of us with an arm around each other's shoulders standing behind a basket overflowing with all kinds of fruits and veggies. Of course, that's before we knew anything about economies of scale, soil classifications, drainage, yield data, water rights, what the word *organic* actually meant, labor costs, transportation costs—you name it, we knew nothing about it."

"Except for weed."

"Except for weed. But until recently, that was always an outlaw's crop. And by the time medical pot became legal, idealism had been in Donny's rearview mirror for quite a while."

"In other words, he's an asshole."

"Maybe. But he's nice to your mom and he's giving you a good home."

"I remember as a little kid telling Uncle Jake I wished you or him were my father."

Buddy smiled. "He told me."

"And he probably told you his airy-fairy response about being a spiritual daddy or some crap."

"Yep."

"I said the same thing to mom once. She said that since you and Uncle Jake didn't want kids that you two could never understand the bond between parent and child."

"Did she now? And how did Jake respond?"

"Uncle Jake said it's *because* you guys knew you weren't cut out to be parents that you understood the bond better than most parents did, or something like that."

Buddy's grin reached ear to ear. "That's totally something he would've said. That uncle of yours was one of the smartest men I ever knew. Holy shit, I miss him. You could probably tell that Alex also misses him. And I know you do too."

12

CASTELLANOS PARKED HIS truck at the base of Flagstaff Mountain next to Alfie's green pickup, then began the gradual ascent on Horsetooth Trail under the shade of ponderosa and lodgepole pines. The cool air smelled refreshingly sweet, bringing back youthful memories. His panting reminded him of his age. Twenty minutes later, the path opened to a cluster of dramatic granite outcroppings. Castellanos scrambled down a pile of boulders to sit beside Alfie, their legs dangling above an evergreen slope interspersed with fields of rock fragments.

"Hi, Uncle Reyes."

Castellanos struggled to catch his breath. "Whaddya say, Alf? How've you been?"

Alfie shrugged. "What did you want to talk about?"

Castellanos mopped his forehead with his sleeve. "Just wanted to see how you're doing. Got so used to running into you at the Trident Cafe or Guild Books that I kind of took for granted we'd be in touch. But it seems like you haven't been around as much—or we keep missing each other. Everything's okay?"

Alfie stared down the slope, bounced his bootheels against the rock. "Yep," he said. "I'm fine."

Castellanos wasn't convinced. "Good to hear. Gettin' enough work? In a few months Uncle Sam'll be expecting his pound of flesh as usual."

"Not a problem."

Alfie's father, Fernando Beaubien, began growing cannabis when Buddy's father noticed the flat, southern exposure of Fernando's property and suggested he give it a try. Fernando took Abe Fisher's advice, but he ensured Alfie became a competent carpenter and mason. After his parents died in a car crash, Castellanos and Buddy assisted eighteen-year-old Alfie's transition into the adult world. Buddy taught him to exploit the growing cannabis market. With the help of weed revenue, Alfie never failed to cover his living expenses.

"In high school, me, Buddy, and your dad used to sit here and get stoned out of our gourds. It's a miracle we didn't end up at the bottom of this cliff."

"Dad told me."

Like Castellanos, Fernando Beaubien traced his family to the first Spanish settlers of the San Luis Valley. As teenagers, they called themselves *Hispanic blue bloods*, a term lost on their Anglo-derived peers. Beaubien said their feeling of ethnic-otherness inspired admiration for the Fisher family's nonconformist standing.

"Funny thing about your dad—he didn't care about getting high unless Buddy and I put him up to it. Never once do I remember him suggesting we light up. I know he never had his own stash. It wouldn't of cost nothing, not with having Buddy as a friend. Even when he started growing his own crop it was all for swapping goods and services, none for personal use. But he enjoyed the hell out of it when we hung out together, that I can tell you. Your dad had some serious will power."

Alfie stopped bouncing his bootheels, turned to Castellanos. "Mom wasn't into smoking weed. I think Dad didn't want to worry her since the laws were different back then."

"Yep. Your mom was some special lady. But I don't have to tell you that."

Alfie smiled for the first time. "The cannibal's granddaughter."

Alfie's cabin sat on ten secluded acres originally purchased by his great-great-grandfather, who may or may not have killed and eaten his companions after the party became snowbound crossing the mountains.

"So you and Rally keeping in touch with Buddy?"

"We saw him a few days ago."

Alfie didn't elaborate; Castellanos quit fishing. Sharing ancestry with an alleged cannibal had presented special challenges to Alfie's childhood. While some kids might have adopted this distinction with a kind of backhanded pride, Alfie struggled against merciless teasing. Through the trials of adolescence, Ralston stayed at Alfie's side, gladly shared the burden of classmates calling them "cannibal cousins."

"You all had a co-op meeting the other night, right?"

"Yep."

"I heard there was an unexpected visitor."

Alfie smiled again. "What'd you hear?"

"You holding back on me, Alf? C'mon, man, that ain't fair."

It felt more like old times now, shy Alfie showing signs of life through silliness. "This guy shows up from Wichita," Alfie said. "Mr. Carson. Cocky as hell, like his shit don't smell."

"What did Mr. Wichita want?"

"I'm not even sure. Buddy and Carson went back and forth about things I don't know anything about. Something about a stash of weed Buddy was hiding? All I know is that the guy was such an ass-clown, I was hoping Zeb would beat the crap out of him."

"I heard you offered him some advice."

"I called him a cunt and told him to fuck off—if that's what you mean."

They laughed together, exchanged high-fives, then sat quietly in the *esprit de corps*. "Listen, Alf, I'm glad to see you're really coming out of your shell, not afraid to speak your mind and all. But with this whole Kansas thing, be careful—"

"What do you mean *Kansas thing*? What thing?"

"Well, I don't one hundred percent understand it all, but it has to do with cannabis being legal now in Colorado. And I'm talking about hemp as well as marijuana—you know more about that shit than I do. Mr. Wichita and his friends see legal weed as a threat to their business interests. And then there are the religious nuts who think marijuana is the devil's weed. Anyway, they're here because of Buddy. They're trying to stop Buddy from doing what he's been doing his whole life."

"What're you scared of?"

Alfie's tone caught him off guard. "I'm concerned. That's all. These people, they're a bunch of creepy fuckers. It's all about money and power and they'll use the resources they have to ruin people if they want. And we're not just talking about billionaire brothers from Wichita. You've also got the governor of Kansas involved. That guy says God told him the solution to Kansas's financial problems would be divinely revealed if everyone prayed and fasted!"

This last statement got a big smile from Alfie.

"Oh and that's not all. There's a sheriff from the middle of nowhere who says the *good Lord* will help him defeat the evil Buddy Fisher."

"Shut the fuck up!"

"I wish I was kidding, Alf. But that's why I'm saying to just stay in the background while all this bullshit plays out. I know you think a lot of Buddy; we all do. But he's got to fight his own battles. Don't go throwing yourself on any hand grenades for him—or anyone else."

"What could they really do to me?"

"Probably nothing, but you never know. I'm just asking you not to be reckless, keep it chill, you know? Why invite attention from these lunatics? Calling that guy a *cunt*, you know—you don't gotta do that. Although, to be perfectly honest, I wish I could've been there."

"Buddy's one of your oldest friends. You just gonna blow him off?"

"No. Hell no. I'll help him, but he's gonna have to help himself too. There's the way Buddy thinks the world should be, and there's reality—money. Who do you think's gonna win that fight?"

Alfie nodded several times, watched a prairie falcon cruise past before landing on a cliff across the gully. "I get what you're saying," Alfie said. "Don't worry. I'll stay in the background. As long as they don't get in my face."

"They're not going to get in your face. It's Buddy they're after. Thing is, if Buddy just went along with them, he could weather this storm and come out pretty good."

Alfie turned to face Castellanos. He had his biggest smile yet. "And we'd all live happily ever after."

Alfie's mischievous expression made Castellanos a touch uneasy.

"So the story goes, my friend."

13

CARSON SAT ON the edge of Sheriff Thompson's bed, told him the dry crustiness forming on his skin was a good sign. Sheriff Thompson was propped up, leaning back on several pillows. His eyes were alert although still a bit oblong. He heard the positive news but offered no discernible reaction.

The previous three days had been spent in a Benadryl-induced reverie on repaying afflictions to those who had afflicted. Confronting evil with love, as he had been taught, had become the most challenging of God's tests. During periods of extreme distress, Sheriff Thompson called upon the Book of Revelation for guidance, and took comfort in knowing that the stinging, weeping blisters paled compared to the vengeance awaiting those who did not accept and obey God.

As it turned out, God's test also included Maria's insistence that he drink the foul-tasting tea she brought him throughout those three days. When he balked at its flavor, she responded with short, biting lectures on the disrespectful implications associated with rejecting nature's medicine, even hinted that residing in her home, perhaps, required compliance. Sheriff Thompson's church forbid turning one's back on acts of kindness, so he took small sips in her presence then dumped the rest into the bathroom sink when he could.

Carson's first visit had occurred on the morning of Sheriff Thompson's misfortune. Maria flung open the door without a word then retreated into the living where she gadded about in a state of high agitation among scattered pieces of cleaning equipment.

"Pardon me, is this where Mr. Wyatt Thompson is staying?"

"Of course!" Maria said as if just asked the stupidest question she'd ever heard. "He's paid up through the month, but I don't have time to supervise his healing. I have work to do."

Carson looked back at the driveway, saw Maria's Duster with the trunk open. "You want help loading—?"

"Yes! But hurry up, c'mon."

The two worked quickly to get Maria on her way. Before driving off, she said a pot of herbal tea was ready on the stove and that she had written her phone number on the dry erase board. "But don't you dare call me between noon and two when I might be eating my lunch."

Carson reassured Maria. *Strange woman*, he thought, then wondered if he'd find Sheriff Thompson unconscious in a pool of blood. Instead, he found him slumbering fitfully in bed, crimson and puffy. Carson walked back to the living room, sat on the love seat where memories of a penicillin allergy sparked his own rumination. These Colorado boys didn't scare him, but he knew he could be the one on his back all inflamed and bloated. Sheriff Thompson was supposed to confer with him about any ideas he had, not go all soldier of fortune on him. Carson hoped the sheriff wouldn't have second thoughts about the mission. He didn't think so considering the sheriff's motivation stemmed from something other than his own $100K bonus. He flashed back a few days to the meeting at Buddy's house, when someone joked about what he would do with seventy kilos of weed. Carson was no dummy; he had researched the matter, understood its potential value to Cook Industries. He wasn't ignorant of enterprising teenagers getting $200 an ounce and that the same ounce often resold for $250. Carson figured the street value alone of Buddy's seventy kilos would be at least $500K, which was chewing gum money compared to the long-term potential that companies like Cook Industries could realize from it. Even in the dark recesses of Monsanto, some number-crunching sons-of-bitches knew it was only a matter of time before the coffers of every state in the union would fill with legal-weed tax revenue. And it was only a matter of time before Roundup Ready cannabis seeds flooded the market, followed by joint ventures and licensing agreements. Imagine Buddy's seeds becoming the intellectual property of Cook Industries, a patented commodity generating streams of royalty payments from farmers. Genetic modification would ensure non-renewable seedless plants raised production costs, thus encouraging more efficiently grown monocultures—which meant more Cook Industries pesticide and fertilizer revenue. Carson sighed. *All that future income for a lousy hundred grand?*

*

"Wyatt," Carson said, "did you hear me? You're getting better."

"Uh-huh."

"You up to hearing the latest?"

"Uh-huh."

"We've had a couple of meetings with Commissioner Brandt since—uh, what happened. He insists we can still come to terms with Buddy Fisher, practically begged us not to proceed with any *punitive* actions." Carson snickered. "That is one pathetic man they got there representing Boulder County…"

Sheriff Thompson watched Carson's lips, heard words, identified the tone of fellowship, but perceived a hint of unrighteousness as well. Was this voice motivated by the holy spirit or something corruptible?

"…And don't worry about the money, Wyatt. You take all the time you need to heal and accomplish the mission. And tell your wife not to worry; she'll get that fiber-glass swimming pool she always wanted."

"What that lawyer was saying," Wyatt said, "you think we should go ahead and do it?"

Carson smiled. "As a matter of fact, we talked about that just yesterday. Jay and Dale thought maybe we should give it another try with Buddy before playing hardball. But I don't see the point in waiting. Buddy spiking that drink with some kind of marijuana juice showed his blatant disrespect for our kind."

Sheriff Thompson assumed *our kind* meant Christian. "What then?"

"The lawyer you mentioned, Donald Campbell, is acting as a liaison between me and some boys who live up in the hills. I already got a glimpse of some of them. They're kind of an underground marijuana ring. They won't talk about it, though. It's like a secret society. They all know who each other are, and the only folks allowed to join have to be recommended by someone already in the group."

"Sound like squirrelly potheads."

Carson laughed. "Yeah, I think you're probably right about that. Regardless, we can't show them any fear. We have to tell them how it's going to be whether they like it or not."

"I don't fear these people."

"Of course not. I'm not implying you do, Wyatt. No, sir. I just meant that you got *truth* on your side and they can't scare us, and that all those boys have to do is help us out a little bit and it'll be like we never knew they existed—"

"Stop pissin' yourself and tell me what's next."

"I think another day or two for you to relax and—"

"Just say what's next already."

"A meeting this afternoon, up the canyon a ways. I got directions to a pull-out."

Sheriff Thompson's eyes closed. Carson thought he had drifted off. "You'll pick me up," Sheriff Thompson said, eyes still closed. "I'll be waiting in front of the house."

*

Sheriff Thompson's heart skipped a beat when Carson turned onto Lefthand Canyon Drive. Expecting one day to sit at the right hand of the Lord, meeting Buddy's disciples on a road named as such must've been a sign. *Blessed are the peacemakers*, he reminded himself, still trying to reconcile the anger that had dominated his thoughts the previous three days.

The pull-out appeared about one hundred yards west

of mile-marker twelve. The well-worn trailhead was easy to spot. Sheriff Thompson stepped out of the car, adjusted his belt holster. He noticed sunshine streaming through pine and fir trees, but not in a good way. There was something sinister about the path.

"In fifty or sixty yards there'll be a clearing," Carson said then took the lead walking down the trail.

Following an unarmed man had logistical advantages to the mission's success, Sheriff Thompson thought, and promised—should events dictate—that Carson's sacrifice would be immortalized as a selfless act for God's glory. The men walked in silence until they detected light banter just before the trail curled around a large juniper bush. Rounding the turn, they saw a small clearing where Zebulon Macky sat on a boulder. Ralston Macky, Colter McKenna, and Billy Kittredge loitered nearby.

Carson stopped, backed up into the bush's shadow. "Let me see if I can get through to them," he whispered. "If things go sour, jump in as you see fit."

Sheriff Thompson grunted.

"Gentlemen," Carson said, stepping into the open, "so nice to see you again."

Zebulon stood, hands on hips, his men closing ranks around him. Sheriff Thompson followed Carson into the clearing. Carson offered his hand to Zebulon, who hesitated before shaking it.

"This here is Sheriff Wyatt Thompson," Carson said.

"This here is my crew," Zebulon said, gesturing to the others.

"Sheriff of what?" Colter McKenna said.

"Ellsworth County, Kansas," Carson said.

"Hey, Sheriff," Zebulon said. "Don't they got poison ivy in Kansas?"

Laughter. "You're not in Kansas anymore, Dorothy," Billy Kittredge said, prompting more laughs.

Carson embraced the levity. "Well, it would be nice if everything in Colorado stayed in Colorado, but that's a pretty porous border we share. In fact, I bet if you blindfolded someone and dropped them anywhere between Limon and Lawrence, then took off the blindfold, they wouldn't know which state they stood in."

"Maybe Kansas should build a wall to keep all the Colorado poison ivy out," Billy Kittredge said.

Carson retained his smile. Sheriff Thompson stared at Zebulon. *You shall not take vengeance, nor bear any grudge…*

"Excuse me, Sheriff," Zebulon said. "You shouldn't be carrying that gun in Boulder County open space."

"State law says it's okay," Carson said.

"Bullshit," Ralston said.

"No, I don't think so," Carson said. "The Colorado Supreme Court never resolved home rule versus state law. So I say state law wins the day. Anyway, you boys want to talk business or just make fun of us Kansans?"

"You're right," Zebulon said. "Settle down, boys, and let's hear what Mr. Stanley Carson from Wichita has to say."

"All right then," Carson said. "I think you all were present the other night so I'll get right to the point. Buddy's got seventy kilos of marijuana and seeds stashed somewhere and I want it."

Someone nickered like a horse.

"And how the fuck you know this is even true?" Zebulon said.

Sheriff Thompson shifted his feet. Carson glanced at him then back at Zebulon. "Sir, I'm not here to argue or debate the matter. I'm working on the assumption it is true—period. Now you can all work with us or you can fight us. Thing is, though, if you want to fight, you're not going to win."

Zebulon's crew responded with various sounds of revelry.

"Shut the fuck up!" Zebulon shouted then locked eyes with Carson. "That sounds like a threat."

Like he did at Buddy's house, Carson unwrapped a piece of gum, popped it into his mouth, dropped the wrapper on the ground. "No, sir," he said, "I make no threats, only statements of fact."

"Statements of fact, huh?" Zebulon said. "So you and your girlfriend here are going to make me and my men tell you where Buddy's hiding all that weed? I see a couple of problems with your statement of fact. You want to hear about 'em?"

"I'd be delighted."

"What about you, Deputy Doggy? You want to hear about what I think of your girlfriend's statement of fact?"

Sheriff Thompson was too distracted by the unnatural shimmering of Zebulon's face to think of an appropriate Bible verse. *A demon's aura*, he thought, then fixated on facial features, how Zebulon's nose, cheekbones, and chin appeared sharp-edged, and how each word tumbling out of his mouth stung his wounds.

"Feeling kind of shy, huh? That's okay. Here's the thing—"

"Before you start," Carson said, "let me try to clarify a bit. First and foremost, we want you to think of this as a *transaction*, something worth your while. You get me? You help us achieve our mission, you also reap the rewards."

"How much?" Zebulon said.

"Oh, something we both find agreeable. What're you thinking?"

"How about a million bucks? And a million for each of my men?"

Carson's smile dulled around the edges. "You're determined to make this transaction a difficult one, aren't you?" Carson looked down, kicked a rock. "Twenty grand. Five for each of you."

Zebulon glanced at his crew. "I tried telling you this at Buddy's house the other night. Was a time, especially in my granddad's and great-granddad's day, when a man like you come up into the foothills, uninvited, with an attitude, dropping gum wrappers and trash like you own the place, you'd find yourself shot full of holes. That's just the way things were back then."

Sheriff Thompson scratched the back of his neck. Carson said, "Thank goodness things have changed. Now, you were going to tell us about your problems with my statements of fact, weren't you?"

"Hey, Zeb," Ralston said. "I'm not sure, but it looked like that sheriff made the slightest move toward his gun a second ago."

"Oh, c'mon," Carson said. "What do you take us for, Mafia? Your pal's overreacting."

"Yeah?" Ralston said. "Then why's his holster unsnapped?"

Carson laughed. "It was already unsnapped when we walked up, son. That's just standard law enforcement procedure when walking into a possibly unpredictable situation."

Zebulon gave his brother a thumbs-up then turned back to Carson. "First problem: Buddy's one of us. We don't turn on our own. Second problem: Even if I wanted to be a backstabbing Judas, none of us have any fucking idea where Buddy's hiding that weed. Nobody's ever seen it, only heard about it. So you're shit out of luck—although there's one thing you could do for me before you leave. Might even help improve my attitude toward y'all."

Carson didn't need to ask what he had in mind because Zebulon's crew was already in hysterics seeing their boss stepping forward, unzipping his fly. The provocation proved irresistible for Sheriff Thompson, who, in a single stride, met Zebulon's neck with his left hand as his right hand unholstered the Beretta M9 and his knee drove into the choking man's thigh. On Zebulon's way down, the sheriff's gun muzzle found the back of Zebulon's throat, having first smashed through his front teeth, a fact that wasn't obvious until blood smeared over Zebulon's lips and down the corners of his mouth.

"'Then shall he say also unto them on the left hand,'" Sheriff Thompson shouted, "'depart from me, ye cursed, into everlasting fire, prepared for the devil and his angels!…'"

Carson watched, fairly confident Sheriff Thompson wouldn't pull the trigger—three others were watching in wide-eyed horror, after all. But he also knew from his own Kansas upbringing how the power of scripture persuaded rational brains to act otherwise, which prompted him to walk behind the kneeling, gurgling man.

"Wyatt," Carson said. Sheriff Thompson looked up, showed the sweaty, wild-eyed fervor Carson remembered from various preachers of his childhood. "I think we've made our point. Maybe it's time you and me walk away out of this place of darkness—back into the light of the Lord."

Sheriff Thompson looked down at the demon in hand, glanced toward the others, then removed the muzzle from the demon's mouth and released his neck. Zebulon fell to his side, spitting blood and teeth. Carson put a hand on Sheriff Thompson's shoulder. He holstered his weapon and followed Carson back down the path from whence they came.

14

BUDDY SAT CROSS-LEGGED on the bed watching Libby take off her sweater and shoes then put her watch on the nightstand. Her eyes looked tired but Buddy knew it was more worry than weary. He doubted Zeb getting his teeth knocked out would cause that look in her, assuming she knew about it. Buddy was about to ask what was on her mind, but she pushed him onto his back, stretched out over him, wrapped her arms around his neck. They could talk later. For the moment he would match her embrace and float through time, a kid again with nothing to fear.

*

Voices spoke softly, busy with tools, scraping, digging, cutting. Libby opened her eyes, lifted her head off the pillow.

"Kids in the garden," Buddy mumbled.

He meant teenagers gathering beets, broccoli, carrots, onions, peas. Flower children, they were usually called, but were more reminiscent of Depression-era migrants than the "Summer of Love." The kids camped outside his property in national forest, worked diligently bringing in crops, keeping a portion for themselves before moving toward warmer climes. Buddy made sure they had more than just vegetables to eat, provided clean water, a composting toilet, blankets, and if need be, the use of his home.

"I wonder how their parents feel about their children wandering the country, living off the land?" Libby said. "I wonder if they know—or even care."

Buddy propped himself up on an elbow. "Rally told me what happened to Zeb Macky—if that's what's bothering you."

Libby shook her head. "Anything that happens to that Neanderthal wouldn't bother me. You didn't hear about Roy Mitchell?"

Buddy sat up. "What about Roy Mitchell?"

"Donny said a bunch of guys showed up in the middle of the night and destroyed his whole crop."

"What? What're they messing with Roy Mitchell for? He grows *industrial* hemp for fuck's sake."

"This is what Donny told me."

"His whole crop? That's thousands of plants."

"Terrorized his family."

"Does Ray know?"

"I assumed someone called 9-1-1."

Buddy picked up his phone.

*

"We're looking into it," Castellanos said.

"What've you found out?"

"I said we're looking into it, Buddy. Now just chill. When we know something, I'll get back to you."

Buddy hung up, stared into the distance. "This is the

thanks I give to the sweetest, gentlest man who ever lived. I should get over there and see how Roy's doing."

"Was Roy here the other night with the rest of the guys?"

"No. He's got nothing to do with us. Industrial hemp isn't for smoking." Buddy opened the nightstand drawer, rummaged around for his wallet and keys. "Those pieces of shit always go for the weakest, most vulnerable. I should've seen this coming."

"And what could you have done about it? This is what scares me, Buddy. If they'd do that to Roy Mitchell, what do you think they'd do to you?"

"What can they do? I don't have a family to worry about. You mean they'd kill me? Well there's nothing I can do about that so let 'em kill me."

"What do you mean *nothing* you can do? Just give them what they want!"

"They want my *soul*, Libby. They can't have it."

"They want your pot."

"It's bigger than that—the symbolism, the subtext—I don't expect you to understand." Buddy regretted his condescending tone. Luckily, Libby didn't take it personally.

"Understand what? Dumb pride?"

"I don't want to be a slave, literally or figuratively."

"I want you to be alive, literally."

Buddy slipped his shirt over his head, sat back down on the bed, lay across Libby's legs. "I wasn't serious about not caring if they killed me. Don't let my cynicism worry you."

"It's too late. You can't *un*-say it, and I can't *un*-hear it."

Buddy took her hand. "You've got Marty to think about. And Donny needs you."

Libby pulled her hand away, blinked away a tear. "What

about me? I don't want him or need him. All Donny needs or cares about is money."

They stared at each other knowing a lot more needed to be said. He wanted nothing more than to undress again, climb back under the covers, but the news about Roy Mitchell was in the way.

Buddy said, "Maybe we should talk more about the future—*our* future."

"Suddenly we have a future?"

Buddy smiled. "I say, 'yes to a future.'"

"Okay. What's it look like?"

"I'm not sure yet. Let's talk about it."

"Deal. Now go see how Roy's doing."

*

Roy Mitchell's first memory of Buddy's grandfather, Papa George, went back to the early 1950s, as Roy rode a tractor across his wheat field and noticed a man holding a young boy's hand walking past his property. Both the man and the boy smiled and waved; both wore rolled denim pants and flannel shirts with herringbone patterns. Roy smiled, waved back. Over time, the two men would see each other in town, exchange perfunctory nods. It took about a year before they finally put two and two together, which prompted a good laugh. From then on, hiking past Roy Mitchell's land often included a stop to chat across his fence. At first, Roy didn't know what to make of Papa George's manner, the genuine interest the older man showed in a stranger's life, as if personally invested. Boulder County folks just weren't accustomed to such behavior. Eventually, *whimsical* was the word Roy settled upon to describe the man with the funny accent and unusual zest for life.

Roy Mitchell never understood the difference between the marijuana people smoked and the hemp nobody smoked, nor did he care. He knew only that since Papa George convinced him to transition nineteen of his twenty acres of hay and wheat into hemp—leaving one acre for hardy vegetables—his net income had steadily risen, his daughter had graduated college, and life had been generally good. Who could've seen hemp's potential for high-quality horse and chicken bedding, or that hemp paper and hemp clothing would also become profitable markets? Papa George saw it.

By the time Buddy's truck came to a stop, the quiet, soft-spoken, eighty-five-year-old Roy Mitchell stood waiting on his gravel driveway, wearing the same shaggy-fringed straw farmer's hat Buddy had always known him to wear. Roy greeted Buddy with a handshake and a weak smile, unable to hide the shell-shock.

Buddy put a hand on Roy's shoulder. "I'm sorry," he said.

Roy nodded, said, "C'mon," then turned and walked to a picnic table about ten feet away.

"How did it happen?"

"I'm not exactly sure. Helicopters, it must've been, about two, three in the morning. That sound of blades chopping the air. I couldn't really see 'em 'cause the moon was already down. But they were swoopin' in low, I'm sure of it, several abreast I think. They'd swoop in over the fields, then come back from a different direction and do it again. At some point, a strange noise started, a weird staticky racket, like when you can't get a radio station tuned in right. This went on for a good hour at least."

Roy gazed a thousand yards into the distance. Buddy said, "So, did they spray something?"

Roy stood, motioned for Buddy to follow. They walked to a slight rise in the property behind his house that gave a commanding view of Roy's flat, south-facing land. Tsunami devastation came to Buddy's mind as he looked over fields of broken, mangled, charred stalks—like a hurricane had followed a fire storm.

"I came out at first light—" Roy said then took a few seconds to fight back emotion. "It's all dead."

Just a week or two before harvest, Buddy thought. "We can plow it under, replant," Buddy said. "I'll help—"

Roy motioned for Buddy to follow him again. This time they walked to an outbuilding. The scene inside resembled the fields except with twisted, mutilated machinery.

"I don't believe it," Buddy whispered. "Some guys came in here with—explosives?"

"Well, if they did, I sure didn't hear them go off. Those copters were loud, but I think I would've heard bombs going off."

"You call the sheriff?"

"A couple of deputies were here earlier, wrote a lot of notes, took a lot of pictures. They seemed kind of out of their league, if you know what I mean." Buddy nodded. Roy said, "Let's get the hell out of here."

They walked back to the picnic table where Roy's daughter, Carrie, sat holding his great-grandson. She handed the boy to Roy then gave Buddy a big hug.

"Good to see you, Carrie," Buddy said. "I wish it was under better circumstances."

"How're you holding up?" Carrie said. "I heard you've had some visitors of your own."

"This is all my fault," Buddy said.

"Don't," Carrie said. "I've been trying to get him to sell this place for at least a decade. Now he's got no excuse. Similar property closer to Lyons just fetched $4 million."

"This land's worth at least ten," Buddy said. "What do you think, Roy?"

Roy handed the child back to Carrie. "She wants me to move into one of those fancy retirement homes popping up all over the place."

Buddy said, "Well, if you sell this place, you'll be able to afford one hell of a nice retirement. You'll have your own apartment, all your meals taken care of, activities planned. Nothing to do but relax and enjoy yourself. And you'll have folks your own age for company instead of grubby kids migrating through like a bunch of hobos. And you'd be just a quick drive from Carrie and all your grandchildren and great-grandchildren. Why not? You deserve it."

Roy didn't say anything. No need. Buddy knew what this land meant to him. It was the only place Roy had ever lived except when he was in the army.

"Papa George and your daddy predicted all this, you know," Roy said. His face softened. "Abe and me would sit on that porch right there while you were swingin' on the tire we used to have." Roy pointed to a rope still hanging from an ancient cottonwood tree.

Carrie laughed. "I used to spin you around, remember?"

"Of course!"

"Abe would repeat all that stuff I remember Papa George used to say about the real value of hemp and marijuana and all that. Big business would see all the money and then Uncle Sam would have to change his tune. I'd listen but not really take notice. I guess you gotta get bit in the ass; then you wake up."

"Papa George thought the world of you. So did my dad."

"That's nice of you to say, but I don't think I deserve a whole lot—"

"But why?" Carrie said. "Why're they picking on my dad?"

"Because they know what you know," Buddy said. "Roy can just walk away a rich man and be done with it all. Can't be any fight in a man his age sitting on all that money. In the meantime, word gets out to the others how bad it can be if they don't just go along and play nice."

"But what do they *want*?"

"Control," Roy said. "That's what your daddy always said—which I don't have to tell you."

Buddy nodded. "Yep. But in this case we've got competing interests. Did Dad ever tell you about this special project—"

"He tried. He wanted me to know about something he was doing with mixing and matching something or other. Way over my understanding. I think that's why he stopped talking about it with me. Ever since, it's been only rumors and I didn't care to pay attention to it."

"You boys mind telling me what the heck you're talking about?"

"Oh, it doesn't matter," Buddy said. "For God's sake, Roy, listen to your daughter. I bet you'll like living a couple of thousand feet lower in elevation. Easier on your lungs."

"Are you listening, Dad?"

Roy had returned to his thousand-yard stare, but Buddy knew he hadn't gone anywhere. "Well, I should get back," Buddy said. "Let me know if I can help you out—in any way. You're both like family to me. I hope you know that."

"We know," Carrie said.

Buddy stood up from the picnic table. "Hey, Buddy," Roy said. "If there's one thing I learned from the army, it's that nothing worse could happen than what I saw in Korea. So I still got plenty of fight left in me. Remember that."

"You're damn right I'll remember," Buddy said, then walked to his truck.

15

BUDDY HADN'T NOTICED the lump in his throat until he turned onto Fisher's Forest Way. The tightness reminded him of when he was a kid and his tonsils had swelled up like golf balls. After turning into his driveway, the golf balls migrated lower, lodged behind his sternum. Leaning on his elbows over the desk in the cellar, he lit a joint, took several deep drags, then waited in vain for his emotions to dull. There was no escaping an old man's blue eyes and kind leathery face. Tears brimmed forth. *What's the point?* Buddy thought, unsure if he was even asking the right question. He closed his eyes. *What's the fucking point?* he thought again, this time with a visceral rage that knocked him back in his chair and reduced him to a sobbing mess. When the catharsis abated, Roy Mitchell was gone. Buddy lifted his head, saw a newborn Papa George in the arms of Buddy's great-grandfather, Jakob, then heard Papa George say, *How did I get here?*

*

Who knew how anyone got anywhere? Georg—Papa George—Fischbein got here after the Fischbein Soap

Company's twenty-year narrative had already brought the family into upper-middle-class respectability. Jakob and his wife, Ruth, had shared a large house with Georg's five siblings and his grandparents, Emil and Rachel. Having three adoring sisters and two older brothers guaranteed Georg received the special status often given a family's youngest member—they often referred to Georg as the family pet. Emmanuel, the eldest, would grow up to manage the soap company's strategic and mechanical aspects while the next in line, Sigmund, kept the books. Jakob took great pride in his sons' embrace of the family business, but as Georg's precocious intellect became more and more evident, Jakob dreamed that a university education would give his youngest son a life beyond soap.

The Great War put dreams on hold. Emmanuel and Sigmund were initially spared the horror thanks to the essential nature of the family business. But by 1916, the same year Georg started gymnasium, the olive oil on which the business depended fell victim to the British blockade. Facing the conscription of his two oldest sons and financial ruin, Jakob found in his father's chemistry manuals the inspiration to create a crude synthetic detergent using alcohol and coal tar distillations. Despite the soap's inferior quality, the company remained solvent. War's privations also forced cutbacks to Georg's gymnasium, hitting the science curriculum especially hard. Classrooms became barracks. Boys were required to help with grueling farm work. Through it all, the headmaster did his best to maintain an intellectual environment, extolled the virtues of toiling in the fatherland's soil from which the potato's nutrients would nourish their soldiers to victory. Not until the 1918 armistice did the gymnasium begin reinstating its original emphasis on laboratory science. To Jakob's delight—and what could've been viewed as divinely decreed—Georg took to chemistry just as the proverbial apple fell close to the tree.

Just as Roy Mitchell's calamity made the thought of acquiescence ever more reproachful to Buddy, so did his great-grandfather, Jakob, see as shameful a return to soap-making in the aftermath of so much suffering. And while a childless Buddy Fisher had only his own future to consider, Jakob Fischbein felt his son's destiny should have meaning beyond soap. He imagined himself Georg's age, a young man spared the ravages of war and whose only demand on his thoughts involved deciding in which direction to take his life. He wondered how the agony of war had influenced medicinal pain relief since his late father's days as an apothecary's assistant. He sat down with Georg, promised his support in whatever he chose to pursue, but reminded him that only through the fortunate timing of his birth did he have the luxury of choice.

"Before university," Jakob said, "why not stand awhile in your grandfather's shadow? Perhaps a passion for medicine will arise."

*

Georg would first learn of the cannabis plant's 16th-century medicinal uses from an apothecary chemist said to have been trained by the famed Dominican monks of Santa Maria Novella. He enjoyed the two-year apprenticeship, but rather than studying medicine as his father privately hoped, he chose the more commercially viable field of chemical dyes. Cannabis would remain a footnote in his consciousness until several years later, at the University of Berlin, when Georg met Markus Lanzmann, an introverted PhD student living in the same rooming house. Given their shared secular backgrounds of unapologetic assimilation, it made perfect sense a close friendship should quickly develop. It turned out Lanzmann's research involved textile science, specifically cellulose isolation and refining technologies. He spoke with particular reverence of fiber extracted from a cannabis variety called hemp. When Georg expressed curiosity in the dyeing and finishing of hemp-derived fabrics, the shy Lanzmann came alive, describing chemistry's critical role in broadening the scope of hemp-fiber use. Somewhere in Lanzmann's discourse—Georg couldn't recall—Lanzmann steered the emphasis of his passion to the interconnectedness of color, nature, and humanity.

"I am a color occultist," Lanzmann said, then quoted a lengthy, unattributed passage about soaring through the heavens with spirit wings. Georg struggled with Lanzmann's correlation, but that hardly mattered.

"I'm afraid I can only comment on my familiarity with some curative applications of cannabis," Georg said. "For you, however, it's the *fiber* which inspires such—emotion?"

Georg waited, confused over why his classmate appeared to be on the verge of weeping. "Germany was once alive with cannabis," Lanzmann said. "Our fleets sailed on hemp's strength and resistance to moisture. Towing ropes, uniforms, flags, nets, everything our ships needed came from hemp. Over time, cheaper commodities like jute and sisal were introduced." Lanzmann's face darkened; he looked away. "And then came the wood pulping."

"Wood pulping upsets you?"

"All my life I've dreamed of linden groves swaying in the breeze, so beautiful in their gestures, branches full of joyous green life. I often awoke with tears in my eyes."

"And what brought you to study textiles?"

Lanzmann gave his new friend a discerning look of approval, as if Georg's question had paid him the highest of compliments.

"The truth arrived while I was studying Goethe as a young man at gymnasium," Lanzmann said. "It came gradually at first, then like a bolt of lightning. Goethe's views on color and light, his emphasis on the *experiential* instead of theoretical. It all combined with my dreams, and I saw that cutting down trees for wood pulp was an affront to nature."

"And that's where hemp comes in."

"Precisely! Nature has a way of providing man with the proper tools for civilization—if man is awake enough to see the gifts. Consider that forests take at least twenty years to grow, yet hemp matures in *four months* and produces *four times* as much fine pulp. Could you imagine a world in which no more trees have to be cut down?"

"No," Georg said, undeterred by his own failure to grasp the essence of what Lanzmann suggested. "I couldn't imagine such a world."

So it was that a friendship evolved amid the backdrop of Weimar Berlin. As communists fought street battles with Nazis, and an avant-garde Bohemianism filled cabarets, art studios, and nightclubs, Georg Fischbein and Markus Lanzmann sat in cafes discussing subjects related to whether a universal conscious intelligence was responsible for chemical reactions and plant fiber physiology and which touched upon their hopes and dreams. The two friends parted in 1928, after Georg earned his PhD and was hired by I.G. Farben, a Frankfurt chemical conglomerate formed three years earlier after the merging of several German manufacturers of industrial dyes. Despite the following year's global economic collapse, Georg's expertise with dyes kept his position reasonably secure. National socialism's arrival in 1933 helped solidify the industry's future. Why the youngest, most privileged of the Fischbeins should've grasped the perilous nature of the political climate, one might again see as divinely inspired. In the late autumn of 1935, Georg made a special trip home. He had a plan.

"The Great Western Sugar Company is in Colorado, America," Georg said to his father. "We know how clay soaps can be used to clean sugar beet juice. This is valuable knowledge. We can start there until we can establish ourselves again."

"You come all the way from Frankfurt to talk craziness?" Jakob said. "You sound like my father before he died. Suddenly he starts going on and on about horrible things that could happen at any moment. Georg, think about what you're saying. Not only do you want to throw away your career but you want the family to abandon everything we've worked so long and hard to create. And why? Because of changing politics?"

"Not just politics, Papa. A changing *culture*."

"We are not a religious family, so let the culture change. Or do you prefer to blame God? Is God telling you that we must leave? We are part of this culture, Georg. Your grandfather worked for the royal chemists of Hanover. Hard work is what gains respect."

Georg returned to Frankfurt, tried to see the world through his father's eyes, calmed down enough to consider, perhaps, he had overreacted. Government-sanctioned boycotts and daily Nazi marches soon dashed such thoughts.

On his next visit home, Georg again spoke of America, the Land of Opportunity.

"Opportunity?" Jakob said. "Look around you. Look at the buildings, the equipment. Sales are steady. I know nothing of boycotts. Here is the opportunity. Right now, at this moment, we are prospering from opportunity. So we should leave it all for America and start over?"

Georg watched his father walk away. Emmanuel took him aside. "Papa is past seventy for God's sake. Do you know what a gift it is to still have him in our lives? You owe your education and career to what Papa has built, yet you badger him about leaving it all?"

"None of you can see what's happening?"

"We see only what's happening to you."

"I've applied for a visa."

Emmanuel looked shocked, as if until that moment he hadn't taken his youngest sibling seriously. "And what makes you think America would even want you?"

"I'm healthy, relatively young, educated, and single. I think I have a good chance."

Emmanuel didn't respond; Georg watched him, too, walk away. Shortly after he returned to Frankfurt, the "racially inferior" of the lower-skilled workforce began losing their jobs. University students sponsored book burnings across the country. Georg traveled home for what would be the last time.

"Books were your life as a child, Papa. You and Papa Emil cherished books. What do you think of people who would burn what you hold sacred?"

For a moment, Georg thought he had gotten through to his father. "What do you know of these books they burned?" Jakob said. "Do you see *my* books burning? When they come and burn *my* books, then I'll take that as a sign from God it's time to leave."

When Georg's visa was approved, he wrote home begging for his father's blessing. A reply came from Emmanuel. "You've broken Papa's heart" was all it said.

Georg arrived in Fort Collins, Colorado, and Americanized his name to George Fisher. He never saw his family again.

*

Where George Fisher saw opportunity, the Great Western Sugar Company saw only a German immigrant with little command of the English language. The harsh reality of being an unemployed immigrant set in. Although unaccustomed to manual labor, George was willing to work anywhere, including the coal mines of Boulder County.

The work was exhausting but didn't prevent George from spending off-hours making soap in the boarding house basement. His Bohemian landlady, Alena, took an immediate liking to her German-speaking tenant; she was the first to try his olive-oil soap and eagerly promoted it to her friends. Eventually, George began peddling his product door to door, stashing every extra penny inside a steamer trunk. Without financial backing, George expected a decade of laboring underground before soap could improve his life. But life, as it turned out, decided otherwise. Within two years, George had courted and married twenty-year-old Clara, the only child of Ludwig Eller, a prosperous German widower who had come to Boulder County in 1912 to start a gold mining supply company. A shrewd man, George's father-in-law had been well positioned to exploit the US Treasury's demand for gold, enabling him to help George and Clara capitalize on depressed land prices. Defying the Great Depression, they became owners of more property than they ever dreamed possible, built a house, and continued growing the business.

George had all but forgotten about cannabis until a chance meeting with jazz musicians in 1937 introduced him to a strain popular enough to have fostered a subculture of marijuana clubs. His first puffs of "reefer" were unremarkable, but having had little contact with American Negroes, it was the band members' kindness that touched him. Laughter came easy to these men, and as the night wore on, George found their amusement infectious. The evening passed quickly.

Reflecting on his experience the next day, George surmised that cannabis chemicals produced a subtle, relaxing effect that many people would find enjoyable. The experience also prompted recollections of his friend Markus Lanzmann's enthusiasm for hemp, which inspired thoughts of hemp oil's suitability for soap-making. But the deteriorating situation in Europe and America's slide into the Second World War pushed such thoughts aside.

The newly incorporated Fisher Soap Company would become the supplier to Army Air Force bases sprouting up around Denver, eventually becoming the supplier to the famed 10th Mountain Division stationed in Leadville. But just as the forces of change saw fit that some prospered while multitudes suffered, so could a chosen person's fortunes change. Amidst the ecstatic celebrations of Japan's surrender, a healthy Abraham Fisher came into the world the same day an undiagnosed eclampsia carried away George's beloved Clara.

16

CARSON SAT AT one end of the couch in his hotel suite. At the other end sat a man wearing a bomber jacket with shoulder patches depicting a skull between fanned out eagle wings, the words "We Own the Night" written underneath the chin.

In front of the flat screen TV, a muscular man in desert camouflage trousers and black T-shirt stood with folded arms, legs shoulder-width apart. Carson looked at his watch, frowned, grabbed the *Daily Camera* from the end table, began reading the front page. When the door opened a few minutes later, in walked a pasty-faced black-suited man with a black hat and sunglasses. He said nothing as he walked through the room then exited onto the balcony where he remained.

Carson got off the couch, stepped toward the man in front of the TV, said, "Okay, I appreciate having this, uh, *debriefing*, I guess you call it. We all know each other? Standing here is Frederick Lacerta of SLS, which, I believe, stands for Sustainable Logistic Services. Sitting here is Officer Gonzales—*Special Agent* Gonzales, I should say. The man on the balcony dressed like a Blues Brother, is, uh, secret squirrel man-in-black."

Carson laughed alone.

"Oh c'mon," Carson said to Blues Brother. "Can't we lighten up a bit? The way you're dressed, you're a goddamn cliché for chrissake."

"Last night's mission was flawless," Lacerta said.

"That's my understanding too, Mr. Lacerta. You and Special Agent Gonzales are both to be congratulated. And you *will* be congratulated—rewarded, I mean. Don't you worry. We all need motivation. Otherwise, what's the point? Now what about the other guys? Back to Fort Worth in time for breakfast? Or is it El Paso?"

Gonzales said, "Our birds get 'em in. They do the job. We get 'em out."

"Don't I know it!" Carson said. "You boys do a damn good job. A great job. I'd just like to know who *them* all is that I'm dealing with. That's all."

"You don't need to know who *them* is," Lacerta said. "I deal directly with the assets."

"Good, good," Carson said. "It's just that I have to answer to other people who ask me these kinds of questions, see. Real control freaks they are. I'm sure you know the type. As far as they're concerned, no matter how much you plan and plan—when it comes to the mission, you never know—"

"I'm the *first* one off the *first* bird arriving," Lacerta said. "And I'm the *last* one on the *last* bird leaving." I see everything. I make sure the mission is accomplished to the standards we promised."

"SLS is very good at what they do," Gonzales said.

"Oh, and don't I know it!" Carson said. "Everyone knows

it. Masters of the exothermic-reduction-oxidation universe. What do you all call that powdery stuff that burns through steel like a red-hot knife through butter? Nano-something or other?"

Lacerta held Carson's gaze. "Anyway," Carson said. "You ever have an asset go *rogue*-like? Maybe his conscience starts gettin' to him?"

"Our assets don't make trouble for our clients," Lacerta said.

Carson smiled, glanced at Blues Brother. "Well, they're only human, after all."

"We know well ahead of time if someone is thinking about making trouble," Lacerta said. "Then it's handled."

"But—"

"They sign an oath, yes?" Blues Brother said, stepping into the room. His voice sounded automated, with a slight Germanic inflection. Blues Brother took a .45-caliber bullet from his jacket pocket and held it up to Carson's eyes. "Before they sign the oath, they are told that speaking of such things will result in this having their name on it, yes? If we hear only *rumor* they want to make trouble, this will have their name on it, yes?"

Carson retreated a step, glanced at Lacerta and Gonzales. Blues Brother returned to the balcony. "Okay then," Carson said.

"The sheriff," Lacerta said. "How's he doing?"

The question caught Carson off guard. "Wyatt? Don't worry about Wyatt. He's my man."

"Can you control the asset?" Gonzales said.

Carson gave Gonzales a queer look. "What do you mean?"

"You mentioned reward," Gonzales said. "The target's welfare is important for our rewards to be realized."

Carson laughed. "You don't got to worry about that, boys. Wyatt's a bit *fundamental* in his thinking, but he's not crazy. He was a *marine*, remember. He respects the chain of command."

"He respects a higher power," Lacerta said. "If you're not that higher power, we may have a problem."

"Who the hell—who've you all been talking to?"

"If he gets to be a problem," Gonzales said, "your asset can be handled. That's all we're saying."

Carson paced around a bit. "Well, at least I hope you all will check in with me first before deciding to *handle* one of my assets."

"That's what we're doing," Lacerta said. "That's why we have debriefings. We're checking in with you. But we're also here to plan for contingencies, so let's have a look at that map."

Carson glanced at Blues Brother. He remained motionless, buttoned up in black. From the breast pocket of his jacket, Carson took out a map of Boulder County, spread it over the glass coffee table in front of the couch.

17

COMMISSIONER BRANDT WAS leaning back in his office chair, staring at a 19th-century engraving of two men opening a wooden headgate as water surged into an irrigation chute. Brandt closed his eyes, imagined snow-covered peaks under a deep blue sky and sparkling, crystal-clear mountain runoff flowing through the Hollywood technicolor landscape of his youth.

Somebody knocked on the door. Donald stuck his head in. "Okay?"

Brandt straightened up, waved him in. Donald took a chair in front of Brandt's desk.

"Well?" Donald said.

"Well what?"

"You talk to the water commissioner?"

"Just have Cimarron buy the goddamn water from Buddy."

"He'll be more motivated to sell if the water commissioner starts asking questions."

"You think the state wants to waste their money on proving an illegal water diversion by some backyard farmer?"

"You haven't been paying attention, have you?"

"Fuck you."

"No, fuck you. Buddy owns six shares of Big Thompson water. That's *federal* water. No state-water-court bullshit. If he's growing pot with the feds' water, they'll shut his ass down tomorrow."

"And you think the feds will sell you and Cimarron Buddy's water."

"I'm saying if Buddy *thinks* selling the water will keep fed noses out of his business so he can keep his home—then I think he might see the value in selling. Say what you want about my motives, Will, but I don't want to see Buddy go to prison. Maybe Castellanos will help me get through to him, but Castellanos has always hated me—"

"In the meantime you'll just say to your old friend, 'sell or else.'"

"Save it, Will. I know all about your inflated bids and consulting fees for imaginary work. One way or another, Buddy's stubbornness will bring him down. We all know it. Those shares are worth at least 150K."

"You think Buddy knows that?" Donald didn't answer. Brandt said, "He'll sell for a fraction of that and still think he's getting a good deal. And the lower the price, the more money Cimarron kicks back to you—I mean us."

Donald stood, stepped away. "If not you, it'll just be someone else. But you can get the water commissioner's ear. All he'd have to do is make a phone call. You can cut him in or just tell him to do his job and enforce water rights law. Jesus, Will, just give him a nudge. What's the big deal?"

Brandt leaned his chair back again, stared at the engraving. He imagined those two men lifting the gate, steadfastly going about their business with no complaints, certain their hard work would be rewarded.

"Will," Donald said. "Getting the water is just the beginning. Cimarron will still need an environmental consultant. That's worth a couple of years of income. And like I said, if it's not you, it'll just be some other engineering company."

"Does Kansas know what you're up to?"

"Why the hell would they? All they care about is finding those seventy kilos. They got nothing to do with this side-project of mine."

"Yeah, well, Sheriff Thompson worries me. He's got a screw loose."

"You worry too much."

"You hear what happened to Roy Mitchell?"

"Yeah, I hear he's about to become a multi-millionaire."

"Did you know they traumatized his daughter, grand-children, great-grandchildren?"

Donald thought about it. "No, and I'm sorry. I'm sure they didn't know kids would be around."

"So you knew—"

"I didn't know anything. Carson gives me hints, but swears nobody gets hurt, not really."

"Great-grandchildren—"

"With all that money those kids will get everything they ever wanted to forget about some boogeymen showing up in the middle of the night."

Brandt stared at Donald. "Tell me the truth. Are you a human being? Seriously. Are you flesh and blood?"

Donald put his hands flat on Brandt's desk, leaned forward. "I see reality and I go with it. My fighting days are over, and I'm not apologizing for it."

"Carson is as slimy a piece of shit as you'll ever find. You like being associated with slimy shit?"

"*Everybody's* a slimy piece of shit deep down. That's just the way the world works."

Brandt stood up. "Don't talk to me like you're some world-weary veteran who had to pull himself up by his bootstraps. You don't know shit about hard work."

"You want to play grown-up, Will? Fine, then start acting like an adult."

Brandt's right arm moved, then faltered. He imagined holding Donald by the throat as he dragged him forward over the desk.

"God Almighty, I fucking hate you," Brandt said.

"Yeah, Will, I know."

*

Workers swarmed over a three-story Victorian house framed with scaffolding. Buddy watched from a park bench across the street. Castellanos parked his truck in the adjacent block then joined Buddy on the bench.

"You were supposed to get back to me," Buddy said.

"Yeah, well, I wanted to wait until I had something to say."

"The sheriff of Boulder County has nothing to say about Roy's property?"

Castellanos sighed. "Don't start this shit. It's not like we're ignoring the whole thing."

"Did you talk to Roy?"

"Yep."

"You think a Korean War vet would know a helicopter when he heard one? Or do you think it was just some kind of freaky natural phenomenon?"

"The Forest Service wants the CDA to investigate."

"Okay, that's a start. Maybe the state's aggy experts will figure out what cauterized Roy's hemp. And that'll free up the sheriff's department to investigate how Roy's machinery got turned into scrap metal."

"Give it a rest, Buddy. I've got a forensic team out there—I'm following procedure."

"That's good to know. You could've called me to tell me this. It's not exactly state secrets."

"Will you stop acting like a whiny little bitch? You think we got nothing else to do but investigate some old man's multi-million-dollar property?"

Buddy turned to Castellanos. "Is that what's going on here? If this was my property, you'd be full of outrage vowing to leave no stone unturned until you found the truth?"

Castellanos looked up at the sky. "The FAA doesn't know anything about helicopters."

"Yeah, I assumed a flight plan hadn't been filed."

Castellanos swore. "You're saying the FAA is in on the conspiracy?"

"Where are the lawsuits you promised?"

"Call Donny. Ask him."

"Do me a favor, Ray. Let's pretend we know for a fact that helicopters did—whatever they did. Then we'd be talking about instrument-rated pilots wearing night vision goggles executing maneuvers like something out of *Apocalypse Now*."

"Yes, Buddy, I've heard of the DEA and the US Army."

"I knew you'd catch on. But what does that mean? For you? For us? What does it say we're up against?" Silence settled over the two until Buddy said, "Just say the word 'lawsuit' and you shit your pants."

Castellanos turned his head, spit. "What did I tell you four or five days ago? If this thing goes federal—"

"*It's already gone federal* and we're all fucked. Me more than anyone else. I didn't know they were going to pick on Roy, but I see how it makes sense. The lion-stalking-the-weakest-zebra kind of thing."

"I have a family depending on me."

"Aha! You're scared of losing your job."

"Oh fuck you with your *scared*. You remember the Cimarron expansion all those years ago? Fish and Wildlife said, 'No! Don't do it! Bad for lynx habitat!' Guess what?"

"Sorry, you're not scared, just practical."

"Buddy, it doesn't matter if it's lawsuits or invisible helicopters. They're going to get their way—whoever it is. You want to fight? Go ahead and fight. But I'm picking the battles I put my ass on the line for, and they better be battles the people of Boulder County care about."

"You don't think people care about what happened on Roy's land?"

"Yeah, sure they care—for a few days. Then they just go about their business thankful it happened to Roy and not them. And when they hear about all the money Roy stands to make when he sells out, then it's just one of those freak accidents of nature and it's chalked up to *all's well that ends well*. But if you keep pushing it, well, then—I don't know what's gonna happen. Can't you see the shit-storm you're putting me in the middle of? You have any idea what that feels like?"

"And you can't help but make it your own personal shit-storm. It's all about you and your goddamn feelings?"

Castellanos gave his friend a hard look. "You're a real son-of-a-bitch, you know that?"

Buddy laughed. "Hell yes, I know that. And I also know you already forgot what I said to you the other day at my place. *Just do your fucking job.* I told you I won't blame you."

"I remember, you prick. And I am doing my job; what're you talking about?"

Buddy waited, still smiling. "Was a time you would've got back to me. But times have changed. I get it."

"I don't know where you're coming from with this 'times have changed' crap. I really don't. You're the only thing that's changed. And honestly, Buddy, you're acting like such a god-damn loon that I'm close to not caring anymore. I mean, you're giving me no choice."

"Bullshit. I haven't changed. I'm still a Boulder County man through and through—and don't you forget it."

"Fine."

"No point being scared of something bad that happened, as long as it happened to someone else."

"That's the spirit."

"Papa George liked quoting Napoleon. *He who fears being conquered is sure of defeat.*"

"Yeah, well, Papa George also built a bomb shelter."

Before Buddy could respond, the conversation ended with dispatch requesting assistance on a hit-and-run a few blocks from the park. Buddy remained on the bench, watching the workers preserving the historic house. The law dictated the exterior remain in 1896. Nobody cared about the interior. Buddy wondered how his own exterior looked, wondered if his facade had become, somehow, *unlawful* in the eyes of others. Or was it just a matter of perspective? True, Papa George had built a bomb shelter. But had he been scared or was he just being practical?

18

I N THE DAYS following Roy Mitchell's tragedy, the situation in Boulder County deteriorated. Colter McKenna awoke to a gloved hand around his throat, the barrel of a gun pressed against his forehead, and a voice behind a black ski mask demanding where Buddy Fisher was hiding his seventy kilos. When Colter swore up and down he didn't know, two glancing muzzle blows tore open his cheekbone, requiring twenty-two stitches. The next night, Billy Kittredge awoke in the wee hours to his German Shepherd, Ganja, barking furiously at a bright orange glow coming through the window. Billy looked out to see a geyser of molten iron flowing over the gravel driveway. He opened the door, stared in awe at the spectacle, aware of a strange material under his bare feet. When he recognized a piece of unmelted tread as one of his brand-new mud-terrain tires, he knew the glowing, semi-liquefied hulk could only be his beloved 1982 Toyota Land Cruiser. Fortunately, this same realization jogged his memory of a half-full gas tank.

Billy dialed 9-1-1 just before the explosion rocked the house, shooting glowing metal embers around the property.

Thankfully, cooling overnight temperatures had squeezed enough moisture out of the air to prevent a wildfire, and apart from Ganja cutting his paw on broken glass, Billy managed to avoid any more serious damage. The object previously underfoot was a Kevlar pouch containing a letter. "The time has come for Buddy Fisher to give up his seventy kilos—seeds and all—or expect more unpleasantness."

*

Castellanos sat in a lounge chair on his patio sipping an IPA, the malty bitterness he usually enjoyed tarnished by the knot lodged in the pit of his stomach. It was Buddy's fault his beer tasted so lousy. If the stubborn fool wouldn't embrace change already—or at least accept it—he doubted his favorite beer would ever taste good again. Yes, Castellanos understood things weren't changing as much as *transforming*, but so what? *Adapt* for chrissake. He wished he could light up one of Buddy's joints but didn't feel like discussing events since they last spoke. It didn't feel right calling Buddy just to hit him up for more dope. He could legally buy his own, but after so many years smoking Buddy's weed on the cheap, the thought of paying retail sounded like squeaking Styrofoam.

No doubt the neighborhood had changed since Castellanos and his wife bought their house twenty-five years earlier. He hadn't minded college kids for neighbors as long as they turned down the volume, kept their properties clean, and limited parties to weekends. Having the sheriff as a neighbor made some kids nervous at first, but they relaxed upon discovering whose backyard the unmistakable marijuana odor originated from so often. Every year Castellanos anticipated another crop of daughters and sons at his front door holding a pile of parking tickets, asking if he had advice. Coincidentally, Castellanos's wife was the secretary for the city's parking services director, and after explaining the difference between city and county jurisdictions, he still volunteered to see what—if anything—he could do. When their own children were young, these encounters were often the first step in acquiring reasonably priced babysitters. Those renters choosing not to respect Sheriff Castellanos's noise and sanitation requests ran the risk of waking up one morning to find an orange boot clamped to a tire.

The last few years had seen the neighborhood entering a new phase of change as young professionals bought houses they intended to live in. Anonymous notes began appearing taped to his front door objecting to the skunky odor coming from his property. Eight-foot privacy fences became more common. The sound of bulldozers and backhoes replaced lawn mowers, leaf blowers, and miter saws. Across the street, three houses changed hands without notice before literally disappearing, having been scraped from their foundations. Then a sign appeared announcing sustainable solar and geothermal-powered green homes with gourmet kitchen islands and commercial grade induction ranges.

Suzanne walked out the backdoor, kissed her husband, sat next to him with a beer. They relaxed to sounds of diesel engines and backup-warning alarms.

"It's getting worse and worse," Suzanne said.

"Uh-huh."

"That hypocrisy I've been talking about. It's just like what your parents used to say about all bureaucracies being inherently corrupt…"

Castellanos knew what she meant but his thoughts had

turned to the fire investigator's confirmation of a thermitic accelerant doing the job on Billy Kittredge's Toyota. Kansas was sending a message, all right, but what the hell was he supposed to do about it? *Goddamn Buddy and his principles...*

"...So now we've got two former cops as supervisors, making sure the third former cop they hired to write parking tickets can just drive around all day while the other officers have to walk around in the heat and cold taking verbal abuse..."

Castellanos had warned Suzanne to expect blatant cronyism when mixing ex-cops with civilian law enforcement.

"...The city manager's office doesn't give a damn. It's just cover-your-fellow-managers'-asses—you're not listening to me, are you?"

"There's nothing new here, Suzy. It's everything I predicted."

Suzanne took a long sip. "You're really all twisted up over this Kansas thing, aren't you?"

"None of which you're supposed to know about."

"What happened at Roy's place was in the paper."

"But there's no link to Kansas and what happened at Roy's place."

"You sure think there is."

"*In the paper*, there's no link. People are talking about UFOs and having a good laugh. Trust me, it's not funny."

"Roy's gonna make out okay, so what're you worried about?"

Castellanos said nothing, sipped his beer.

"What does 'thermitic' mean?" Suzanne asked.

"It means arson."

"Billy Kittredge was probably trying to collect insurance

money or something. He's batshit crazy just like the rest of those dopers up in the hills. Always has been."

"Colter McKenna got pistol-whipped by a home intruder. His face is a mess."

"Ray, it's a different world in the foothills. Colter's an idiot; you know that. He probably got involved with harder drugs. Crack, heroin, meth. Who knows?"

Castellanos didn't respond again.

"Okay, I get it," Suzanne said. "But Buddy's a grown-up, Ray. He's going to handle things his way and there's nothing you can do about it. His family has always been that way and everyone knows it. *Nonconformist* is programmed in his DNA."

"There's more going on I haven't told you about—but don't ask because I'm not telling. Anyway, Buddy thinks I don't know what we're up against. I think he's the one who doesn't know what he's up against."

"He knows; he just doesn't care. He's never cared about anything or anybody except himself."

Castellanos turned to Suzanne. "That's bullshit. Maybe he doesn't care about the same things *you* care about, but he cares plenty about others."

"Sorry."

A backhoe engine kept stalling out, dying. "He cared about Libby. That's for sure," Suzanne said. "She was the best thing that ever happened to him."

"That, I agree with," Castellanos said. "But let's not go there. What should we do for dinner?"

Before Suzanne could answer, Castellanos's phone rang.

*

Castellanos pulled into Buddy's driveway, saw him sitting with two teenagers at the kitchen table. He stepped into the chilly air, realized he'd left without taking a jacket.

"You know Marty, don't you?" Buddy said. "And this is Cody Crawford."

Castellanos nodded at them. "You two know something about a shooting?"

"My mom works for Commissioner Brandt," Cody said. "Earlier today he said someone got shot."

The knot in Castellanos's stomach tightened. He sat down, took a breath. "Where? What happened?"

"I think it was one of those Kansas operatives," Buddy said.

"What do you mean 'operatives'?"

"None of the guys you met at Brandt's office. Probably one of the hired guns they brought in to start their little terror campaign."

Castellanos looked at Cody. "Okay, backup. What exactly did your mom say?"

"She said this Carson guy from Wichita stormed into the office demanding to see Commissioner Brandt. They go into the conference room, and Carson starts shouting about someone getting shot in the parking lot at the Motel 6."

"That's in the city limits," Castellanos said. "Your mom or Brandt didn't call the police?"

Cody looked at Buddy. Buddy said to Castellanos, "Why don't you call the area ERs and confirm someone was brought in with a gunshot wound? They're required to call the police."

Castellanos said to Cody, "What else did she say? Where was he hit?"

"She thinks in the leg. Carson said something about the victim hobbling to get in a car that came flying up and hauled him away. It sounded like someone was waiting from a hidden location, like a sniper."

Castellanos leaned back. "All right, guys," he said. "Let me and Buddy talk privately, okay?"

Buddy walked the boys out. Castellanos said, "You talk to Zeb lately?"

"It wasn't him."

"He's the only one crazy enough."

"I don't think so."

"Why the hell not?"

"Because Zeb's not smart enough to figure out who an *operative* is—" Buddy stopped, began thinking out loud. "Although, if it was Zeb, and Carson was there when it happened, *Carson* may have been the target and the other guy got in the way."

"Carson? Why would Zeb want to kill Carson?"

"Zeb's not killing anyone—on purpose. He'd just want to hurt you. And I know he's got a .22 with a scope."

"You didn't answer my question."

"On second thought, I don't think it was Zeb. It's Sheriff Thompson that Zeb would've wanted to shoot in the leg."

"You mind telling me why Zeb's thinking about shooting anyone anywhere?"

Buddy walked to the kitchen counter, hit the switch on an electric kettle, then sat back down. "The day before Roy Mitchell had his helicopter visitation, Zeb and his guys met with Carson and Sheriff Thompson up Lefthand Canyon somewhere. Apparently, things got testy and Sheriff Thompson beat down on Zeb pretty good."

"Zeb told you this?"

"Billy Kittredge told me. He was there with Rally and Colter McKenna."

Castellanos stood, walked over to the padlocked vestibule door, kicked it lightly with the toe of his shoe. "Roy Mitchell. Colter McKenna. Billy Kittredge. And now Zeb. All with a motive. Well, Buddy-boy, looks like we got a war on our hands. Happy?"

Buddy waited for Castellanos to turn around. "And why would I be happy, Ray?"

Castellanos walked back to the table, looked down at Buddy. "Why'd you even bother? Calling me, I mean."

"I thought you'd wanna know."

"So it's not about reporting a crime; it's more about *informing* me of a crime. Otherwise you would've called Boulder PD."

"You'd rather not know?"

Castellanos sat back down. "Here's the thing. PD's going to tell me that a couple of Motel 6 guests said they heard gunfire, prompting PD to send half the force to respond to a possible active shooter, but found nothing. PD'll then check all the area ERs. It's possible there's a gunshot wound or two, but what're the chances it's our guy?"

"Zero."

"And we both know it. Therefore—"

"Why did I bother calling you?"

"Bingo."

Buddy took his turn thinking about it, although he didn't need to. "I guess I just wanted confirmation that we both know what's going on."

"What I said when we were talking in the park the other

day? I didn't mean it—about not caring anymore. You can always call me, you know—or not. Right?"

"'Course I know. But I'm not gonna waste your time anymore. Next time you get a call to come over here, it'll be about something you don't know already."

Castellanos laughed. "Suzanne always said, 'Buddy is what he is and there's nothing anyone can do about it.' Anyway, just do me a favor—I'm serious. Don't do anything stupid. Is that asking too much?"

Buddy shrugged. "We'll see. Give my best to Suzanne. And take care of that family of yours."

19

BUDDY WAS UP early working a second harvest of Swiss chard, cauliflower, beets, and carrots. His ears perked up to stones popping off tires. He walked through the vestibule into the kitchen, saw a Lincoln Navigator parked down the driveway about twenty yards away. Maybe someone checking directions after a wrong turn. Carson and Sheriff Thompson stepped out, walked up the drive. Both looked around as if half-expecting an ambush. The fact that they acted nervous and parked in the driveway told Buddy this visit was not part of some coordinated "discovery" operation.

Buddy met them in front of the empty drying screens, thought Carson's gap-toothed grin almost as distasteful as Sheriff Thompson's calamine-smeared face.

"Sort of early to be visiting," Buddy said.

"We kind of assumed you'd be up early," Carson said. "You being a farmer and all."

Buddy looked at Sheriff Thompson. "Nervous, Sheriff? That's why you brought a gun?"

"It's just part of the culture where we're from," Carson

said. "Wyatt being a marine and working in law enforcement—it just comes natural to him."

Buddy nodded. "I get it. Wearing a gun's like a fashion statement in Kansas. Good ol' Wyatt's accessorizing. Poor man must've felt damn near naked not wearing a gun the other day when he came over."

"Hang on, Buddy. Let's not overreact."

"I guess I should feel fortunate two men show up at daybreak instead of the middle of the night. Although Mr. Poison Ivy here already tried that once. Do I hear helicopters in the distance?"

Carson stepped forward. "You mind bringing it down a notch?"

Buddy stood his ground. "You know, I can't help but wonder why you and your pals in Topeka haven't already executed one of your *unacknowledged* commando raids on my humble abode. I guess it's more fun to pick on defenseless old men than dangerous pot farmers like me. I mean, you think you know what I got and where it is. What're you waiting for?"

Carson retreated a step. "You overestimate my role, Buddy. My function is strictly reconnaissance. I could try to answer your question, but I'd be punching above my weight. Maybe you've got friends in high places you didn't realize you had—"

"Roy Mitchell was my friend."

"I respect that. But I really think you're overreact—"

"A stranger shows up on my property packing, what, a nine-millimeter semi-automatic handgun? How would one of your God-fearing citizens of Kansas react to such an event?"

"We're just here to talk. That's all we want to do. And considering the recent escalation of things, you can't blame us for bringing a little self-defense along."

"And who's been escalating things? I heard a guy's car blew up and another guy got pistol-whipped as he lay in bed. What else been going on?"

"You know what I'm talking about."

"Oh? So it's not a rumor? Someone did get shot?"

"You know damn well it's true."

"Why would I? Police didn't find anything except a couple of frightened motel guests. No reports from the ER."

"I think I've been damn fair to you, Buddy. But it seems you've taken on a new attitude." Carson turned to Sheriff Thompson. "Hey, Wyatt, did he get it right? The type of gun you carry. Let me have a look."

Sheriff Thompson handed over the gun. Carson disengaged the safety, pulled back the slide, aimed it to the right of Buddy's head, then shouted, "Bang!"

Buddy flinched, stumbled back a step.

Carson said, "Yep, Beretta nine-millimeter."

"Okay, okay, you win. I was just messin' with y'all. C'mon in. Let's chat."

Carson re-engaged the safety, handed the gun back to Sheriff Thompson. The two men followed Buddy into the kitchen.

"Sit down," Buddy said, pointing to the table. "Excuse me a moment."

Buddy stepped toward the vestibule door he forgot to close, stopped, then veered into the living room. A minute later he walked back into the kitchen racking a twelve-gauge shotgun. He sat down with the rifle resting across his thighs.

"This is my emotional support crutch," Buddy said. "Being from Kansas and all, I'm sure you boys don't mind me cuddling this little cutie while we talk."

Sheriff Thompson's chair screeched back. "Relax!" Carson shouted, reaching across the sheriff's lap. The two struggled for the gun, Carson yelling in Sheriff Thompson's ear until the sheriff let go. Carson slid the gun across the table to Buddy. "Okay? Can we talk now like rational human beings?"

"Sounds good to me," Buddy said.

"Look," Carson said, "I don't like what's been going on the last week or so. There's no reason for it, really. You know what I mean?"

"I absolutely agree that there's no reason for you to be here causing trouble."

"Did you hear that, Wyatt? It's *our* fault we're here."

Sheriff Thompson had no comment. Buddy said, "For a duly elected county sheriff, he sure doesn't talk much."

Sheriff Thompson cleared his throat. "A time to tear and a time to mend, a time to be silent and a time to speak."

Carson smiled. "He's a man of few words, but he chooses them wisely. By the way, how's Zeb been faring during these troubled times?"

"Why don't you ask Zeb?"

Carson laughed. "Anyway, considering what took place yesterday—and I know you know what I mean—"

"Someone got shot. I heard."

"Considering the escalation that has occurred, you may want to consider yourself lucky that Wyatt and I should nevertheless come here with the sole intention of making you a very generous offer."

"Lucky, huh?"

"Does it really matter how we got here? The point is, *we're here*. And a smart guy like you should've figured out by now that you're dealing with forces operating with, shall we say, different protocols. My hope is that you'd now understand the *commitment* of certain parties in our mission and consider the resources at their disposal."

"Yet all those resources couldn't stop someone from getting shot. Who do you think did it?"

"You know damn well who did it. Or you have a damn good idea."

Buddy crossed one leg over the other, laid the rifle across the top leg.

"Just a thigh wound, I heard," Buddy said. "Neat and clean, I bet. No major arteries hit. Simple to patch up. I don't know anyone who can shoot that well. Must've been a trained sharpshooter. Now you got the perfect excuse to escalate, which is what you corporate types love doing. Here's what I want to know. Did they tell you beforehand where to stand so you wouldn't get in the way?"

Carson swore under his breath. "You're just a goddamn Boulder leftist, aren't you? I'm offering you one hundred thousand dollars—cash—to give us what we want. No questions asked. We go home. Nobody else gets bothered with unpleasant—uh, episodes. And, well, that's all there is to it."

Scrub jays clattered in the ensuing silence, impatiently awaiting their morning peanuts. Buddy glanced at the handgun lying on the table then lifted the shotgun off his leg, laid it over his shoulder. "Five million," he said.

A couple of ravens joined the din. "You're messin' with us again," Carson said. "You can't really believe you'd get that kind of dough."

"Well, I was gonna ask for a million, but I didn't think you'd go for it. So if you're not gonna give me one million, you might as well not give me five million."

The punchline never failed to make Buddy laugh.

"Go ahead, whoop it up," Carson said. "Laugh like the selfish little dope-smoking hippie-shit you are. Just remember, it's the little folks that get hurt by your prideful arrogance. And now you've made it pretty clear you don't care if things get worse, but you go ahead and have a good laugh."

"I don't think you two have a very high opinion of me. Maybe it would be better for y'all to fuck off out of here."

Carson stood, buried his hands in his pockets, walked to the window overlooking the driveway. He seemed to be staring at the unruly saltbush pushing up against the shed. Sheriff Thompson watched him. Then Carson turned around and said, "We probably should leave. But I'm just not quite ready to give up on you. I just can't believe there's not somewhere closer to a hundred grand we can meet."

"What's a hundred grand? Or even two-fifty? Is that really going to make a big enough difference in my life to give up everything? Hey, wait a minute! I got an idea. What about five million and I kick back a million to each of you? Talk about a win-win, eh?"

Carson walked back to his chair, took a deep breath. "Marijuana will be rescheduled—eventually. It's gonna happen. Anyone with a brain knows it. But it'll still have to be grown *legally*, which your dope sure as hell isn't. In fact, you've never sprouted a single legal bud in your whole life, have you?"

Buddy rubbed his chin. "By golly, I think you're right."

"You take that hundred grand—or maybe a hundred and

fifty—and you're guaranteed to come out ahead as a winner. And then you shake the federal-government dust off your overalls once and for all. No more looking over your shoulder. What's peace of mind worth to you, Buddy?"

"That's a helluva good question. What's my peace of mind worth? Gimme a few seconds." The kitchen returned to the sounds of nature until Buddy said, "I can't help but wonder if the question should be: What are my seventy kilos worth to *you*. And from what I know of the market and future earnings and all that, I would say a fair price to bring peace to my mind would be five million dollars."

This time even the jays and ravens quieted down.

*

They drove in silence the whole of Fisher's Forest Way, which wasn't unusual considering Sheriff Thompson's reticent disposition, but Carson sensed something else going on.

"He'll see the folly of his ways," Carson said, turning onto Highway 36. "And he'll be damn glad to take a hundred grand. Hell, he'll take fifty by the time he finally wakes up."

"What if he don't?"

"He'll have lost his bargaining power, Wyatt. He'll take fifty and be glad to have it."

"What if he don't wake up?"

"Then I guess life will get pretty uncomfortable."

Silence returned until Sheriff Thompson said, "Them brothers. The Cooks? They got billions, don't they?"

"Only God Almighty Himself knows what those guys are worth."

"I bet five million ain't nothing to them."

Carson laughed. "Oh, c'mon now. Didn't you see what

that was all about? Buddy planting crazy ideas in your head. Trying to turn us against each other."

"What would you do with a million dollars?"

Carson carefully considered his response. "That's not how it works, Wyatt. What kind of message would we be sending? It would be like giving in to terrorists, you know what I mean?"

"Would make things easier, though."

"In the short run. But once the word got out about all that money? Holy Jesus, every Tom, Dick, and Harry would be wanting a handout. You gotta remember all the jobs those Cook boys are making for folks. They have to make enormous profits for the system to work right. If they start giving all their money away to leftists like Buddy Fisher, hell, our entire free-market democracy would come crashing down, and you'd have a bunch of drug addicts running the country."

Carson waited, glanced at Sheriff Thompson a few times, thought, perhaps, a breakthrough was at hand.

"Standing on the driveway," Sheriff Thompson said, "I felt the Lord staying my hand."

"I know you did, Wyatt. I could see it in you. You have a gift, son. But guys like Buddy Fisher don't understand that."

"The Lord was giving me a choice."

"And the choice you made was the right choice. How could it be otherwise if it's coming from the Lord?"

"And you said the younger brother is some kind of crystal worshiper?"

Carson had to figure out what the sheriff was talking about. "No, no. Zeb's brother's friend, Alfie, he's the crystal man. Don't worry about him, though. From what I've heard, he's pretty harmless."

"Even the devil can appear like a servant of God."

"Try to stay focused, Wyatt. Don't waste your energy on little guys like Alfie. Fastest way to kill the serpent is to cut its head off."

"The Lord was testing me with that demon Buddy, temptin' me with his money talk. I kept thinking of all the good I could do for the church with a million dollars."

"But that money would've been tainted, covered in blood. *A hundred grand*, Wyatt. Where's a guy like Buddy Fisher gonna make that kind of dough unless it's through immoral means? And here the Cooks are telling me to go ahead and offer Buddy a hundred Gs. They don't have to do it. They could crush Buddy Fisher like the cockroach he is, yet they offer him all that money—for peace and goodwill— and he just spits in their faces. That can't be allowed, I tell you. We, as a society, must make a stand. And I know that's why you're here sitting at my side, Wyatt."

Carson thought it best to shut up, let things percolate.

"I could've blowed his head off right there in the drive-way," Sheriff Thompson said as they pulled into the parking lot of Chief Black Kettle's Inn. "And then I would've thanked the Lord for saving my children. But the Lord saw fit to guide me with a different choice."

"And only a man of God like yourself knows the right choice to make, which is why Sheriff Wyatt Thompson will go far in life. It's why you're destined to be a great man."

20

TWO HOSTESSES DASHED about setting up the dining room, wondered out loud whether management had forgotten Sanctified Blood of the Lamb's semiannual mass baptism. Throngs of hungry folks in pleated khakis, polyester sport coats, pastel dresses, and Peter Pan collars watched the two teenage hostesses from behind a red velvet rope. Children pressed against their parents' thighs and hips, dreaming about bottomless cups of sparkling apple juice.

Sheriff Thompson followed Carson into the Chief Niwot room, sat at the table reserved for a party of eight. Through the entryway they watched employees rushing to prepare the main dining room for the onslaught. Even the kitchen staff was out equipping server stations with pitchers of water, napkins, condiments, and any other accoutrement required for Chief Black Kettle's famous champagne buffet brunch.

Shortly after the red rope came down, Lacerta, Gonzales, Donald, and Dale Dahlgren entered the Chief Niwot room. All sat except Donald, who stood next to his chair, looking around.

"Gentlemen," Carson said to Mr. Lacerta of Sustainable Logistics Services and Special Agent Gonzales, "this here is

Ellsworth County sheriff, Wyatt Thompson, and this here is Dale Dahlgren, Kansas Department of Agriculture."

Heads exchanged nods.

"Hey, where's the state trooper?" Carson said. "Major somebody?"

"Major Davis had to go back to Kansas for now," Dahlgren said.

"What a shame," Carson said. "Hey, Don, sit down and relax."

"I'll be right back," Donald said then walked to the entryway, stood scanning the main dining room.

"S'matter, Dale?" Carson said. "You look kind of uptight."

"A man was *shot*, Stan," Dahlgren said. "I find that troubling, as does the governor."

"You'll get no argument from me, Dale. It's troubling, all right. Let's just thank God it's not a serious wound and soldier on."

"What've you found out?" Dahlgren said. "The governor's expecting to hear from me."

Carson leaned into Dahlgren. Lacerta and Gonzales watched. "Let's eat and enjoy ourselves a little bit; then we'll discuss things."

Donald returned to the table, said, "There's supposed to be a version of that whole buffet already set up in this room, ready to go just for us."

A woman wearing a blue skirt and white blouse hurried in. She looked close to tears.

"I'm so sorry," she said. "I'll have your buffet set up immediately."

"That's okay, sweetheart," Carson said. "We can see how busy you are."

"Thank you so much for your patience," she said, backing away, almost colliding with two staff members carrying in a long table.

"Don't look so sour," Carson said to Donald. "I'll help pay for all this if it makes you feel any better."

A smile crept across Donald's face. "It's already paid for," he said, taking a seat. "Many times over."

"Really?" Carson said. "Someone owed you big-time, huh?"

"Out back, if you follow the flagstone path, you get to a garden. It's like walking into Versailles. Six pairs of trumpeter swans live on a two-acre pond four feet deep, loaded with aquatic vegetation, tiny fish, worms, frogs—everything those swans need to thrive, including fields of cropped grasses for grazing. At the edge of the water there's a redwood platform with an arbor where the bride and groom stand. From May through July, the baby swans hatch. Imagine how much money people pay to get married in this paradise with the foothills in the background and mama swan and babies floating past, sometimes a baby or two riding mama's back."

Donald waited for an answer. The others watched the staff load the buffet table with shrimp, bacon, lamb, roast beef, chicken, ham, eggs, croissants, muffins, waffles, pancakes, French toast, assorted truffles, tortes, éclairs, parfaits, and other desserts with the word "crème" in their name.

"I'd imagine it would cost quite a pretty penny to get married in that garden," Carson said.

"Put it this way," Donald said. "The owners are more than happy to provide anyone from my firm a buffet party for up to one hundred and fifty guests, anytime they want, for as long as we're both in business—as payment for procuring the water needed to create and maintain that Garden of Eden."

Carson nodded. "Okay, then. Seems the food's just about ready." He looked at the other empty seat, then at Lacerta and Gonzales. "Blues Brother not joining us today?"

"No," Lacerta said.

"Too bad," Carson said then laughed. "He's missing out on some good food. Guys like him do eat *food* like we do, don't they?"

Lacerta stood, walked to the buffet. Gonzales, Donald, and Dahlgren followed. Carson looked at Sheriff Thompson. "C'mon, I'm hungry."

The eating portion of the brunch meeting commenced in silence. The seemingly endless supply of food reminded Sheriff Thompson of the "loaves and fishes" miracle, but as some undertook their third trip to the buffet table, he wondered if the sin of gluttony was now upon them.

Carson waited until everyone was sitting up, plates pushed forward, then said, "Now that we've all had our fill. I'll get down to it. Apparently, there was a breakdown."

"You were working outside the protocol," Lacerta said.

Carson picked up a clean napkin and gave his mouth a final wipe. "Would you mind explaining?"

Lacerta glanced at Sheriff Thompson. "Someone got shot in a motel parking lot because SLS was not involved. Therefore, one hundred percent control of your assets was not achieved. SLS needs to be involved in every aspect of the mission. That's what we do—maintain control."

"The perimeter hadn't been secured," Gonzales said. "That's a very amateur SNAFU."

Carson straightened up. "Now just wait a goddamn

minute, boys. I got a call from Wichita. They told me to meet an operative at the Motel 6. I assumed you all were plugged in. Are you saying Topeka didn't know about that meeting?"

"We received no communication regarding an operative," Lacerta said. "We know our assets, we know how to correctly use them, and we know when and where they'll be deployed."

"Well then," Carson said. "Topeka and Wichita must've got their lines crossed. Either way, somebody acted out. A lone wolf kind of thing. You sure some of your boys weren't running their mouths?"

Lacerta and Gonzales glanced at each other. "Lacerta just explained that we know our operatives," Gonzales said. "Our operatives *understand* consequences. The problem's on your end, Mr. Carson. And I suggest you handle it. If not, things will have to change."

Donald leaned on an elbow, forehead in palm. The heavy silence worried him. He looked up, said, "How about we just agree to move forward? Mr. Carson will undoubtedly check into things and figure out what went wrong."

"You have no information?" Dahlgren said.

"Stan," Donald said to Carson, "have you talked with Zeb? Does he have any insight into this?"

"We know nothing about any Zeb," Lacerta said.

"Zebulon Macky," Donald said. "He's like Buddy Fisher's first lieutenant. His man in the field. Thanks to Sheriff Thompson, Zeb's come around to see the light. He understands what needs to happen. Isn't that right, Stan?"

"Thank you, Don. No, I haven't spoken to Zeb since the incident. But I doubt very much he had a hand in any of this. As Don said, Sheriff Thompson got the message across that marijuana's Wild West days are over and he might as well join the program or go down with the sinking ship. Anyway—"

"I think a reassessment may be in order," Gonzales said. "Unreliable assets put us all at risk."

"Zeb's not unreliable," Carson said.

Dahlgren stood. "Gentlemen, would you excuse Mr. Carson and myself for a moment?" Dahlgren stepped away, motioned for Carson.

"Listen, Stan, the governor's nervous. I need to know who got shot, who sent him, and what the hell he was doing there."

"You've been around long enough to know how these things work, Dale. The governor sure as hell knows."

"What's that supposed to mean?"

"It means decisions are made down the line by people who are in the business of getting things done. That's called *insulation*. The Cooks got their *assets* just like the feds do. Something's put in motion. Stuff starts happening. Things get done."

"So you have no idea what the shooting was all about?"

"A man was sent to get a feel for things, say, and report back to the Cooks. That's all. I was going to show him around a little bit, fill him in on things better said in person than over the phone or the internet. If he had additional plans, I don't know anything about it."

"And what the hell is that water lawyer doing here?"

"He's a man with an agenda. The governor's got his, the Cooks got theirs, and Don Campbell's got his. A mutually beneficial agenda, I assure you. And you can remind the governor we're all on the same side, so he can call the Cooks himself if he needs to know every goddamn detail of what they're up to. You and I both know he's too big of a pussy to do that."

Dahlgren studied Carson's face. "In a public parking lot for chrissake?"

Carson leaned into him. "Yeah, yeah, it was a fuck-up. But it won't happen again. *That* you can tell the governor. Now let's get back to the table."

The two men returned to their seats. The others sat buttoned up, avoiding eye contact.

"Good to see everybody getting along so nicely," Carson said. "Don, I know you'd rather be spending Sunday with your family, so I won't keep you. We're just gonna discuss some things you're probably not interested in knowing anyway."

Donald stood. "Thanks, Stan. Enjoy your day, everyone."

Carson waited until Donald left the room. "Dale," Carson said. "You sure you want to stay?"

"Why wouldn't I?"

"I wouldn't want to make you uncomfortable. That's all. I know the governor is waiting to hear from you. I think we can officially acknowledge that an act of unprovoked violence has been perpetrated against Wichita. And I believe Wichita has the right to defend itself. I know that's how Topeka would view things."

"The governor would not advocate violence," Dahlgren said.

"Of course he wouldn't," Carson said. "Nobody's advocating anything. It's self-defense. We all have the right to defend ourselves."

"What exactly are you saying?" Dahlgren said.

"It's kind of hard to be diplomatic when people are

shooting at you, but you can assure the governor we're still open to diplomacy."

Dahlgren stood, nodded at Lacerta and Gonzales, walked out.

"And then there were four," Carson said. "Gentlemen, I want you to think of what happened at the parking lot like getting hit over the head with a bag of lemons. Sure, it hurts. But then once you calm down and take a look around, you notice that the bag holding the lemons had busted wide open, and it wasn't lemons at all but lots of big, fat, topo maps I gave you back at my hotel room. The maps with the names and locations of all those good Boulder County folks who are gonna help us achieve our goals. I believe you did use the word *contingencies*, Mr. Lacerta?"

Lacerta nodded.

"All right then, boys," Carson said. "Stop worrying and relax. In the meantime, I'll start making lemonade."

21

ALFIE BEAUBIEN LAY on the couch paging through *Rock & Gem* magazine while his best friend, Ralston Macky, paced back and forth through colorful spectrums emanating from illuminated gems. The room used to double as a clinic for Alfie's mother, Lourdes, who saw clients seeking her healing skills as an "energy practitioner." Discussions of Lemurian crystal energy transmission or quartz orb vibrational frequency amplification had been common in the Beaubien home.

At some point, when Alfie noticed the pacing had stopped, he lowered the magazine to see Ralston staring at him. "You actually *shot* a guy?" Ralston said. "I can't believe it. What the hell's gotten into you?"

"My intention was pure," Alfie said. "I don't know why you're getting all worked up over it."

"Your intention was pure? Since when has violence ever been a part of your intention?"

Fernando and Lourdes believed their home should be an oasis of warmth and love. Sandalwood or frankincense greeted you at the door, escorted you into a world of classical

Hindu music weaving diverse tapestries of sitar, tamboura, and tabla. For Ralston, Alfie's house was a refuge from angry, bitter, alcoholic parents. He sobbed loudly at Fernando and Lourdes's funeral.

"All people have the potential for violence," Alfie said. "It's just part of being human."

"I practically grew up in this house, and there's no way your parents would've approved of you shooting someone."

Alfie sat up, slid to the end of the couch. "Things have changed. If my folks were alive and saw what was going on? I don't think they would've had a problem with shooting someone. I mean, Jesus Christ, Rally, I didn't kill the guy."

Ralston sat at the other end of the couch. "You really have no concept of the shit-storm you just started, do you?"

"After what you saw them do to Zeb? And then what they did to Colter and Billy and Roy Mitchell?"

"You should've told me you were going to do it."

"It's not like I planned it out. You told me what Zeb said. About some guy coming in from what? Texas? And I got to thinking, and I just decided it was time to take action. Send a little message. A little karmic payback I guess."

"I don't believe what I'm hearing. Your parents never talked that way."

"Oh, I don't know—maybe not explicitly. But they did talk about karmic debt, yeah? We're supposed to just let 'em beat the shit out of us? Let 'em steal our lives? Let 'em destroy who we really are and turn us into slaves?"

"Who the hell am I talking to? I don't know this person."

"People change, Rally. Not such a big goddamn deal."

"All by yourself you get the idea to shoot someone

because of something I told you. That makes me an accomplice, you prick. Did that ever occur to you?"

"An accomplice to what? There's nothing in the news. Nobody's talking about it. It's like it never happened."

"Maybe not yet."

"And why're you making everything so personal?"

"Because Zeb's out of his fucking mind now, walking around saying, 'Who the fuck did you tell?' Yesterday he was like, 'They're gonna think I did it!' Goddamn it, Alfie, you should've told me first you were thinking about shooting someone."

The two friends sat in silence. Then Alfie said, "Why the hell did Zeb tell you about this guy coming into town in the first place?"

"I don't know. He just tells me shit sometimes. It probably makes him feel like he's important, an insider. And I'm the only one he's got to talk to, I guess."

22

"I'M CALLING AN emergency meeting of the W-B triple-C," Zebulon said over the phone. Buddy heard the waver in his voice. "Expect a bunch of us." A few moments of dead air, then Zebulon added, "Is that okay?"

"Sure. Looking forward to it."

Buddy retreated to the cellar, took a long drag on a joint, then exhaled a laugh. *One hundred thousand dollars*, he thought, for his version of a "weed" that had been growing wild for thousands of years. He doubted that Bible-quoting sheriff knew Jesus wore clothes made of cannabis fiber or that early Christians would've read scripture by the light of cannabis oil lamps. No doubt Stanley Carson didn't know— or give a damn. Buddy laughed again. Maybe he should've taken the money on the condition of being paid in 1914 ten-dollar bills printed on hemp paper, the back of which portrayed farmers harvesting hemp fields.

He opened one of Papa George's antique books, stared at depictions of young girls weaving hemp into fabric on exotic landscapes covered with *cannabis sativa*. Would Papa George have taken the money?

Buddy pulled one more long drag, closed his eyes, heard Papa George talking to his eight-year-old son, Abe, in 1953.

"The health and well-being of dirt, plants, and humans is inextricably linked…"

It was the same year that Watson and Crick discovered DNA and the Soviet Union detonated its first hydrogen bomb. Although Abe Fisher was too young to understand the double helix or thermonuclear fission, his childhood had already been a healthy fusion of spiritual-botanical anthropomorphisms. In Papa George's cryptic prose, a "consciousness ballet" portrayed the fungi's symbiotic relationship with roots, and a "dance of enlightenment" depicted the Clark's nutcracker dispersing seeds of the whitebark pine.

When Papa George decided to dismantle the Fisher Soap Company, it netted a small but not insignificant amount of money earmarked for Abe's education. There had been an expectation of Papa George's father-in-law financially assisting his grandson, but so overwhelming was Ludwig Eller's grief when Clara died during childbirth that he slipped into a psychotic depression from which he never recovered. Business partners plundered what was left of his mining supply company.

The necessities of life would be provided through growing as much food as possible, backyard chickens, bartering, and, if necessary, odd jobs. By living simply and avoiding unnecessary expenditures, all would be well. But transforming into an organic-gardening evangelist during America's golden age of pesticide use did not occur without challenges. While most viewed Papa George as a harmless man undone by tragic events, others found his strange, metaphorical style of speech troubling. Preaching the evils of something called *monocultures*, and the need for something called *biodiversity*, implied unnatural changes to the accustomed order. Some even feared Papa George's unruly beard and outspoken rejection of herbicide use indicated communist sympathies.

Suggestions that Abe's childhood appeared deficient—as many in the community whispered—had no material meaning for Abe, whose memories never included hunger or a sense of lack. True, his clothes were hand-me-downs from foothills residents happy to help a widower, but any disapproval felt upon seeing the boy in baggy trousers or shirts drooping across the shoulders went unnoticed. As a visitor to the Fisher home, one encountered a pleasantly subdued disorder of books and periodicals stacked in close proximity to half-empty shelves, and a kitchen whose dull luster of enameled steel cabinets, linoleum floors, and plaster surfaces had its own baking-soda-and-vinegar warmth.

Abe's teachers thought his introspection puzzling but were charmed by his intelligence and amiability with the other children. Unfortunately, Cold War paranoia was enough for many parents to discourage socializing with the son of a nonconformist father living in the foothills. In retrospect, one could see how such an upbringing would engender a latent sense of loneliness.

As Abe entered adolescence, his awareness of how different his childhood had been from his peers' became more evident. He knew World War II accounted for a lack of cousins. He knew of Clara—his mother—dying in childbirth. He heard stories of his great-grandfather, Emil, working for the royal chemists, and his grandfather, Jakob, starting a soap company. But of his own father he knew little beyond his earning a PhD, immigrating to America, and working in the coal mines. Abe's early inquiries were met with blank stares and then a long-lost sibling's name—Hani, Gerta, Eva, Sigmund, Emmanuel—followed by glistening eyes and a trembling lip before Abe halted the ordeal with a hug and the words "Some other time."

The other times came sporadically—occasional attempts by Papa George himself—but never progressed beyond his master-soap-maker grandfather, or the luxury of having five older siblings, before emotion clogged his throat. Abe fared slightly better with Clara, his father producing a photo showing a barely recognizable Papa George, clean-shaven in a single-breasted three-piece suit of black twill, standing next to Abe's mother, in a floor-sweeping gown of sequins and appliqué beadwork.

Roy and Lorraine Mitchell were both in their early thirties during Abe's early teens, the age difference casting them more as older siblings than parents. Starting with the days when Papa George and Abe first hiked past their property, the soft-spoken couple had developed a kinship with the Fishers, an affection reinforced over the years by the suspicious undertones of community chatter that chafed at their liberal Catholic sentiments. Whenever an opportunity arose—at the VFW or Knights of Columbus—Roy was sure to describe Papa George as a devoted father and good neighbor who always had a kind word.

What the Mitchells knew of Papa George's past—what anybody knew—stemmed from hazy, fragmented rumors that had been circulating, although the coincidence of Roy's uncle having worked in the hardware business when Papa George's father-in-law built his mining supply company put Roy closer to a primary source than most. Roy's

Uncle Charles clearly remembered Ludwig Eller's excitement over Clara's union with another German immigrant, and, of course, Uncle Charles would never forget Ludwig's crushing pain upon his daughter's untimely death. Through the years, Roy and Lorraine made a point of stopping by the Fishers' house and made sure to invite them to family gatherings. To the delight of seven-year-old Carrie Mitchell, Papa George showed up at her first communion party with an elaborately carved, three-foot-tall wooden statue of St. Francis, the beloved saint cradling a fawn with birds sitting across his shoulders, while baby raccoons, chipmunks, and bunnies congregated around his feet.

It was only natural that an empathetic couple like Roy and Lorraine would sense their teenage neighbor's psychic commotion and—as unobtrusively as possible—show an interest in the boy, ask how things were at home, glean what they could from whatever thirteen-year-old Abe felt comfortable revealing. Unwittingly, the Mitchells sought some confirmation of what they suspected, that circumstances had imposed on Abe a life bereft of blood relatives. But it would take bumping into the fifteen-year-old Abe at the grocery store for a breakthrough of sorts to occur. After small talk of how he and Papa George were faring, Roy felt emboldened to say, "You know, Abe, Lorraine and I hope you think of us as family. If you should ever need something."

Unused to frank expressions of compassion, but now mature enough to appreciate the intention, Abe said, "Okay," in a tone Roy thought genuinely thankful.

"Does your dad have friends or—*relations* that visit?"

"Once in a while a friend from his mining days will stop by. But we're on our own most of the time."

Roy nodded. "I understand your family suffered terribly. And I'm sorry."

Abe considered Roy's comment. "Yeah, Dad's family died in the war."

"And losing your mother was another terrible blow."

Abe looked surprised. "You know about my mother?"

Roy hadn't expected his sudden feeling of self-consciousness. After all, what did he really know about Clara? "Well, I only heard she passed away when you were very young. That's all. I'm sure your dad has told you more than I or anyone else knows. It's nobody's business but yours, of course."

Abe shook his head. "She was a German immigrant like Dad. Her father had a mining supply company. That's all I know. Do you know what ever happened to my grandfather?"

Roy did know, which made him more self-conscious. "My Uncle Charles knew your grandfather. He said he became very sick after your mother passed away."

Abe pondered Roy's words. "What kind of sick? Mental?"

"Uh, very depressed. Uncle Charles thought your grandfather never recovered from his depression. He's buried at Columbia Cemetery, if you're interested."

Roy wished he could take back what he said about the cemetery, then regretted saying anything at all about the boy's grandfather. Who was he to talk about someone's ancestors? He would apologize to Papa George at the first opportunity.

"Have a talk with your dad," Roy said. "I'm sure he'd be glad to tell you about his family."

Abe looked down, shifted his feet. "He gets too upset when I ask him those kinds of questions, so I've stopped trying."

Roy sensed the boy's burden but was at a loss for words.

"I understand," Roy said, putting his hand on Abe's shoulder then removing it. "You take care. And I mean what I said—about thinking of Lorraine and me as family."

"Okay," Abe said.

*

Buddy awoke from his root-cellar contemplation to the sounds of Zebulon's pickup truck growling through stainless-steel side pipes and chambered muffler. He returned to the kitchen, sat waiting in the dark. "It's open!" he shouted just as Zebulon reached the door. "Hit the light, will ya?"

Zebulon found the switch, took a seat at the table. "It's gonna be crowded," Zebulon said. "Might be better to go into the living room."

"You gonna get those teeth put back in your head?"

Zebulon rubbed his eyes. "I don't know."

"Kind of weird I gotta hear about it from others."

A line of headlights began snaking down Fisher's Forest Way. Buddy counted fifteen pair, ten pulling in, the last five parking along the approach to the driveway. The room filled with the usual faces plus others Buddy hadn't seen in years, all crowded in a semi-circle around the kitchen table. Some brought wives or girlfriends. Jimmy Dufour had a sleeping child strapped in a Snugli, arms and legs hanging limp. Buddy locked eyes with Katherine Peterson holding hands with another woman.

"Great to see you, Katie," Buddy said.

Katherine smiled. "Likewise, Buddy. Love the ponytail."

They both laughed. A few others giggled. Then the room fell silent.

Buddy took a breath. "Okay, someone say something."

All eyes shifted toward Zebulon then back to Buddy. "We think you should just go ahead and give 'em what they want," Zebulon said. "The seventy kilos."

Many in the group looked at the floor, adjusted postures.

"What makes you think I've got seventy kilos of something?"

"Well, they sure as hell think you do," Colter McKenna said, the side of his face covered by a thick bandage.

"How're you feeling, Colter?"

"I feel like shit. Thanks for asking."

"If you don't have it," Billy Kittredge said, "then why not say so and let 'em search your property. Give 'em a reason to believe you."

"And you think they're gonna believe anything other than what they *want* to believe?"

"A guy knocks on my door," Jimmy Dufour said, "and he starts talking to me like we're old friends. Tells me how cute Ryder is. My wife comes over and he comments about us expecting another child. I ask who the hell he is and he laughs, wants to know if I heard about what happened to Roy Mitchell and Colter and Billy. Says that's just the beginning, that all we gotta do is get you to cooperate and we got nothing to worry about."

"Someone came to my house too," said a mousy voice from the back. The crowd opened. Ginny McCormick came forward. Buddy and Ginny had known each other since kindergarten. Their fathers had been graduate school classmates then business partners at a small-scale manufacturer of re-agents. Abe quit before a pharmaceutical giant purchased the company. Rodney became fabulously wealthy. By the time Ginny and Buddy were teenagers, Rodney had built a wood-framed stucco-and-stone mansion with a fully equipped laboratory for atomic and molecular analysis. To this day the household included the extended McCormick family. In a cruel twist of irony, a rock-climbing accident left Rodney with chronic pain that precipitated an oxycodone addiction. Buddy tutored Ginny on the latest research for replacing opiate-based pain-killers with cannabis and helped her set up a grow operation. Now in his seventies and still suffering, Rodney devoted his time to experimenting with his daughter's cannabis crop.

"I'm sorry, Ginny," Buddy said. "I didn't know. What happened?"

"This guy called the house, said he was from Dad's old company, Kiowa Chemicals, and needed to talk to Dad about his pension. I said he was out of town, and he asked if he could drop off some info—which was weird because they usually just sent stuff in the mail. Anyway, I said, 'fine,' and I swear to God as soon as I hung up there was a knock on the door. He must've been standing in the driveway when he made the call."

Katherine Peterson said, "Gin, please tell me you didn't let him in."

"Not exactly, Katie. I opened the door and there's this guy dressed in a black suit, sunglasses, and one of those round, black hats you see men wearing in photos from like a hundred years ago. His skin was milk-white. I think he had some kind of disease that makes all your hair fall out because his face and head were as bare as a cue ball. Even his eyebrows looked painted on. He was the freakiest looking person I'd ever seen."

"So what happened?" Jimmy Dufour said.

"I said, 'So you got some information you want to drop off?' And he just stands there, and I was about to repeat myself when he starts talking really weird, like someone imitating a computer. And he kept saying, 'Yes? Yes?' after everything. 'Your father working hard still, yes?' So now I'm getting really creeped out, and I tell him to just give me the info and leave. And then he starts talking about how well Dad has done for himself and what a nice life we have. This pisses me off, and I take out my phone and tell him I'm going to call the cops if he doesn't leave."

"Did he show you any kind of ID?" a voice said.

"It wouldn't have mattered," Buddy said.

"By that time, I didn't care who he was," Ginny said. "I just wanted him off the property. This is when he mentions you by name, Buddy, and starts rambling on like, 'You know Buddy Fisher, yes? He needs to cooperate. Tell your father Buddy Fisher needs to cooperate. Because life can become not-so-good for everybody, yes? This can happen. I can promise. So tell your father, and all will be happy, yes?' Then he walks away and disappears down the driveway."

The room stayed quiet until Buddy said, "Everyone here have some kind of encounter?"

"No," Zebulon said. "But they all depend on weed for money. And there's lots of others not here that know what's going on. You know damn well there're no secrets in the weed world."

"I know you're all scared," Buddy said. "That's what they *want*. But if you can keep calm and not let them intimidate you—"

"Spoken like a man who's got nothing to lose," Jimmy

Dufour said. "It's easy to talk tough when you don't have children to worry about."

"Buddy," Katherine Peterson said, "we appreciate all you and your family have done over the years for our way of life. But Jimmy's got a point. You're on your own out here. As Zeb said, we have families depending on weed income. Most of us also have mortgages or medical expenses or car payments, not to mention rising property taxes. This is our home. We want to stay here—"

"This whole thing's a lot bigger than just giving them seventy kilos, Katie. They can have my life anytime they want it, but they can't have my *soul*. Because once they take my soul, they're going to come after yours, Katie, and yours, Jimmy, and yours, Ginny. They won't be satisfied until they own all of our souls and your kids' souls and your grandchildren's souls. That's what the fear thing is all about. You keep giving away a little bit of yourself in exchange for feeling safe, until you've given it all away and they own you. You all want to be slaves?"

Sporadic chuckling. "You're starting to sound crazy paranoid," said a man with a shaved head and interlocking triangles tattooed on his right cheekbone. "You think there's some big conspiracy going on, is that it? You sure it's got nothing to do with you setting up a big score for yourself?"

Buddy locked eyes with the man. "What's that supposed to mean?"

The man said, "It means you sit back and watch everyone get put out of business and then you're the only game in town. That's how you people operate, isn't it?"

"Shut the fuck up, Chilton," Billy Kittredge said.

"Chilly!" Buddy said. "I knew you looked familiar. Love the tattoo. You found a family in prison, huh?"

Chilton stood up. Several hands grabbed him; then Alfie pushed his way to the front and stood next to Buddy. "What the hell's the matter with all of you? Listen to what Buddy's saying. It's about *consciousness*, don't you see? If you fill your brains with fear, then fear will rule your lives—"

"Don't start your crystal-energy crap!" someone yelled.

"Yeah," someone else said. "Fuck that shit. Are your consciousness and crystals gonna put food on the table? Pay my taxes?"

"This is bullshit!" Ralston shouted, shoving his way up front next to Alfie. "You come into this man's house and attack him because you want him to fight your battles for you? What a bunch of gutless assholes you are." Ralston stepped closer to his brother, looked down at him. "Zeb, why aren't you sticking up for Buddy? You get slapped around a bit and you turn into a big pussy?"

Zebulon jumped up, hooked his arm around Ralston's neck, then bent him over in a headlock. Buddy put a choke-hold on Zebulon from behind while others tried to pry his arm off Ralston's neck. "Let him go, Zeb!" Buddy shouted, increasing the pressure until Zebulon relented. Buddy shoved him in one direction, guided Ralston the opposite way.

The group shrunk back. Buddy stood catching his breath. "If I thought it would do any of us any good," Buddy said, "I'd give them the goddamn seventy kilos. But I know better, and I'm not going to do it. I can't stop them from breaking down the doors and looking for it. And I can't stop them from taking it if they find it. But I'm not giving it to them."

The room stayed quiet a few more moments before

Jimmy Dufour turned and made his way to the door, Ryder now awake and bawling. Zebulon followed, then the others, until only Alfie and Ralston remained. The three stood in the kitchen watching headlights maneuver out of the driveway, head back down Fisher's Forest Way.

"After all you've done for everyone all these years and this is how they treat you?" Ralston said.

Buddy put his hand on Ralston's shoulder. "It's all about fear—exactly as Alfie described it. Fear taking over people's lives."

Buddy sat at the table, looked up at his two young friends. "And it's my fault. Maybe I should've just given them what they wanted from day one. Who the hell am I to resist change when so many others are affected?"

"They're a bunch of cowards," Ralston said. "Instead of sticking together and fighting back, they surrender."

"It's like they've totally forgotten how much you mean to this community," Alfie said. "They're too stupid to see how much they owe you."

Buddy leaned back in his chair, smiled. "I can't tell you how happy it makes me to see what fine men you've both become. But believe me when I say that nobody owes me anything. Seriously. Nobody owes me a goddamn thing."

23

T HE FIRST HINT of blue diffused through the morning
sky as Sheriff Thompson parked on the firebreak about
fifty yards below the final switchback where Stamp Mill
Road straightened into Hardscrabble Lane. The Marines had
done their job training Sheriff Thompson in the art of land
navigation. From the Boulder quadrangle map, he easily
interpreted saddles, depressions, ridges, spurs, draws, and
cliffs, to reconnoiter his objective. The advantageous layout
of this lonely stretch of narrow road—how it ran between
a craggy cliff on one side and a thick forest on the other—
was obvious.

Sheriff Thompson scrambled up the slope having
anticipated the cold mountain air but not the challenge a
two-thousand-foot elevation gain posed to his burning lungs.
For inspiration, he thought of the marines fighting their way
up Iwo Jima's Mount Suribachi. He didn't have a flag to raise,
but his mission would be no less symbolic for God's victory.

At the brow of the hill he collapsed onto his back and lay
staring into the brightening sky until his watch pealed "The
Marines' Hymn." A pickup truck with a white topper would

soon appear. Rolling onto his stomach, he aimed binoculars about a hundred yards up the road. When the vehicle came into view, Sheriff Thompson advanced.

Alfie maintained his speed until it was obvious the fool in the road wasn't going to move. He braked hard then pumped the pedal, coming to a complete stop about ten yards in front of Sheriff Thompson. Alfie lay on the horn, threw up his hands, lowered the window. A crystal swung wildly from the rearview mirror.

"What the hell are you doing?" Alfie yelled.

"Pretty morning, huh?"

"I have to get to work, you stupid fuck. Now get out of the way."

Sheriff Thompson smiled. "Only wicked men use crooked speech like that."

Alfie let loose a string of expletives, jumped out of the pickup, walked up to Sheriff Thompson. "What the hell's wrong with you?"

"I hear you're the one that worships crystals."

Alfie stood frozen, bewildered, unable to comprehend the scene. "Who the fuck are you?"

Sheriff Thompson checked for clues like unnatural foot movement, erratic finger pointing, eye winking. He noticed all three.

"I know who I am," Sheriff Thompson said. "And I know who you are. And I ain't afraid."

Alfie stepped back, tried assimilating how this man fit into what had been a typical morning.

"Whoever the fuck you are," Alfie said, "congratulations for not being afraid. Now you're going to get out of the way." Alfie turned around, started walking back to the truck.

"You need to give up crystal-worshiping."

Alfie did an about-face, retraced his steps. "You don't know shit about me, and I don't give a flying fuck what you heard because my life is none of your goddamn business. So get out of the way, or I swear to fucking God I'll run your ass over."

Alfie was about to turn around again when Sheriff Thompson said, "You getting forgiven is my business, and it's your only chance."

Shooting someone in the leg at the Motel 6 notwithstanding, tolerance had been stressed in Alfie's upbringing, which in practice hadn't been particularly difficult given the live-and-let-live attitude of foothill denizens. But with Fernando and Lourdes now ten years gone and all that had occurred the past few weeks, turning the other cheek had lost its appeal.

"What do you mean *forgiven*?" Alfie said. "And who the hell are you to tell me what I *need*?"

"If you continue sowing discord, calamity will befall you. You will be broken and beyond healing."

Alfie's face lit up. "You're one of those Kansas pricks, aren't you? You think I'm the devil or something." Alfie began giggling. "Tell me, Mr. Kansas, what am I apologizing for?"

Sheriff Thompson wasn't falling for it. He recognized Alfie's delight as an enticement to fight as a mere mortal from outside the framework of God's word. The strength of the Lord was all Sheriff Thompson needed.

"Practicing sorcery and worshiping mystical forces is detestable."

Alfie stopped laughing, then deadpanned. "Says who?"

"Thus saith the Lord."

Alfie began giggling again, this time harder. "Well, get the Lord over here. I want to hear-eth it from His mouth."

"The Lord speaks through me."

"Really? So you're the son of God?" Alfie looked around, grabbed some rocks, dropped them at Sheriff Thompson's feet. "Okay, son of God, show me something. Make the stones into bread—I'm hungry."

There was much about Alfie that Sheriff Thompson detested, and not just because the giggling had become robust laughter. The physical characteristics he'd noticed earlier— the jerky foot movements, erratic finger pointing, sinister eye twinkling—appeared to have taken over the demon's entire being. As Sheriff Thompson searched for the appropriate Bible verse, Alfie ran back to his truck, returned with a fist-sized purple crystal he put at Sheriff Thompson's feet.

"Excuse me," Alfie said, "but I'm feeling overcome with the spirit of the Amethyst-serpent-Lord." Alfie dropped to his knees, began bowing to the gemstone. "Oh God of mystical, scaly, purple crystal forces, fill me with the power to slay the evil Kansas leviathan standing in my midst, tempting me with forgiveness…"

Sheriff Thompson took a breath, fought against nausea, abdominal cramping. Once again, he tried to imagine himself as a soldier of Christ reaching out with love, but couldn't help but succumb to a parable in Luke that included something about slaughtering enemies.

"…connect me to the lower worlds, fill me with Lucifer's purple light…"

"Stop sowing seeds of evil—" Sheriff Thompson said before his voice failed. He knew his words were useless anyway, that he was powerless to help the demon trapped inside a spell of his own making.

"Save me! Save me! Save me!…" the demon shrieked. "Forgive me! Forgive me! Forgive me!"

Maniacal laughter took possession of the body, bent the demon over in a fit of fiendish ecstasy while the sheriff of Ellsworth County struggled to find love.

He knew God was testing him, that the answer to encountering such evil had been revealed many times during his evolution to a man of God. And when the answer came, a great relief washed over him, banished the terror and revulsion.

Sheriff Thompson waited patiently, watched the spell dissipate, observed the demon's feigned composure as he climbed back to his feet just as the Holy Spirit moved Sheriff Thompson's hand into the breast pocket of his jacket.

The first gunshot hit Alfie in the chest.

He watched the demon sputter and gasp, surprised by how sweet the satisfaction tasted. *Sweeter than honey to my mouth*, he thought then became a child, unwrapping pieces of chocolate, one after the other, shoving them into his mouth until the bowl was empty.

24

UDDY SAT AGAINST a giant cottonwood tree and stared over ten square miles of short-grass prairie extending west to a line of stockade fencing bordering a condominium complex. What remained of an obscure timber-framed tower loomed above an open wound in the ground about twenty yards from the tree. Both the tree and tower had become iconic symbols of Porphyry Open Space. He saw Libby's SUV pull into the parking lot, watched her exit the car then check the door to make sure it was locked. He smiled at how she took care to stay on the designated trail until reaching an unsanctioned spur shortcutting to where he sat. Technically, they were in violation of county open space regulations.

"You're looking quite contented," Libby said then added, "in an introspective kind of way."

She sat beside him, leaned against his shoulder. A warm October breeze blew.

"Did you know there's a whole network of coal tunnels underneath us?" Buddy said.

"Nope."

Buddy pointed at the wooden structure. "There used to be a mineshaft under that winding-gear tower. It held a huge pulley that lifted up the cage."

"Aren't they supposed to seal those old mines? Looks like someone's been digging around. Or did they want it to still look like a hole to emphasize their mining heritage?"

"I don't know. Kids probably. Or maybe ghosts of miners who had toiled long and hard in those holes. Deep wounds heal slowly, I guess."

The metaphor had been unplanned. They both stared at the tower. "Okay," Libby said, "I guess that's interesting."

"Papa George used to work in this mine."

She turned to face him. "I don't think I knew that."

"Yeah. It was his first job when he got here. We used to sit in the garden when I was a little kid and talk about it."

"What did he say about those days?"

"I remember him describing miles of pitch-black tunnels with the only light coming from your helmet. Ventilation shafts intersected here and there. Wooden posts kept the roof from caving in."

Libby shuddered. "It must've been horrible working underground, especially back then."

"That's not how he described it. I don't remember fear in his voice."

"Maybe he didn't want to scare you."

"Maybe, although Dad thought Papa George liked the mines in a weird way. Up to then, his life had been about academics and laboratory research. Suddenly, he's in a strange country working alongside other immigrants—probably much less educated—using his muscles instead of his brain. I know he felt a real brotherhood with those guys. I vaguely remember him talking metaphorically about the mines. 'In darkness was a place to abandon your past'—or something like that. I was never sure what he meant, but I bet there were lots of secrets left behind down there."

"The *dark night of the soul* where everyone stashed their personal mysteries."

Buddy smiled. "Very good."

"How long did he work down there?"

"Just two or three years, I think." Buddy laughed. "He used to talk about digging out *rooms*, and my eight-year-old brain pictured comfy, carpeted dens with wood paneling, color TV, and a fridge filled with bologna sandwiches and bottles of Coke. It sounded pretty cool, like a secret underground hideout."

Libby put her arm around Buddy's shoulders. "You want to have that talk about our future? I assumed that's what we're doing here."

"Sure, but humor me and let me first talk about the past. Dad brought me here for the first time when I was fourteen."

"About the time I first asked you out, I think."

Buddy grinned, turned to Libby. "That's right. Man, he was in a weird mood that day. He told me his *soul* was dying. Can you imagine saying that to a kid? Freaked me out. Many years later, I figured out this must've been the same day Dad discovered the previous five years of his life had been spent researching ways ammonia can make nicotine more addictive. He would never talk about the time he spent working in the private sector. The mere mention of 'Kiowa Chemicals' sent him into his own private hell." Buddy looked away, wiped his eyes.

"Are you okay?"

"This place put a spell on Dad. I'm only now realizing it."

"What do you mean?"

"At home he was just trying to be Dad, going to work, messing around with all his different projects, making sure I tried hard in school and stayed out of trouble. He never talked about Papa George's life, just stories about his great-grandfather, Emil, and his grandfather, Jakob, all stories Papa George had already told me. One time he said that Papa George's days in the mines was all he really knew about his own father's life in America. Everything else he had to piece together himself."

"Did he piece it together?"

"He pieced something together. But by the time I was old enough to care, he only gave me random snippets about the past. One time I asked him why Papa George's old books had that weird odor. Dad explained the chemical reaction of mold on the cloth covers. Then he laughed—which didn't happen often—and said he once asked Papa George the same question and his response was something like, 'Should nature's magic have to always like roses smell?'"

Libby laughed. "Papa George was a magical grandfather."

"Funny you should say that because despite my grandmother, Clara, dying after giving birth to Dad, and then the horrible details coming out of the concentration camps, Dad said Papa George still extracted *magic* from his newborn son."

"Wow. And since the war was over, the soap company couldn't stay in business?"

"Dad had a theory about that. He said the cruel irony of Nazi soap allegedly made from human fat pushed Papa George into an existential crisis, and that's why he shut it down. Dad said that's when books about spiritual philosophies and nature began stacking up at the edge of the fireplace. Mysterious, dark-blue books with musty cloth covers."

"So he only worked in the mines for three years, and yet, that's just about the only part your dad knew about Papa George's life? That's pretty weird."

"Yep. There was something special about those mining years. The common bond and brotherhood, I guess. Dad said every year guys would just show up out of nowhere. Papa George introduced them as old friends from the mines. Then they'd disappear into the cellar for hours at a time, coming up just to bring down more food and drink."

"Talking about old times?"

"I guess so, but why hide down there?"

Libby rested her head on Buddy's shoulder. "This place is special to you," she said. "And you wanted me to know this, and that's why we're sitting here."

"Yes, it is a special place. I'm glad you're here."

"All those men," Libby said, "the ones who worked in the mines with Papa George. Did they stay in the area and raise families?"

"You remember that kid I called 'Cousin Alex'? He and his dad used to visit every couple of years?"

"Skinny, dark wavy hair. From Chicago?"

"That's him, except we aren't actually related. He was the grandson of one of the miners Papa George worked with. Before Dad died he showed me a shoebox where Papa George kept letters. Alex's grandfather was a Greek guy named Dino. It's hard to read his English, but the revolutionary zeal was unmistakable. Anyway, it was this Dino guy that Papa George was closest to. When Papa George decided to build the bomb shelter, Dino came into town with a bunch of other guys, probably other miners, the summer before Dad started college. He said the property resembled a full-scale mining operation. Can you imagine a bunch of men in their mid-fifties and early sixties digging the place up, hauling everything out manually?"

Libby shook her head. "That's hard to imagine."

"About a year after Papa George died, Dino's son Spiros tracked down Dad. For some reason Spiros didn't know much about his father's coal mining days in Boulder County. Anyway, they struck up a friendship and kept in touch. That's how I met Alex, Spiros's son."

"Your 'honorary cousin.'"

Buddy laughed. "It's funny because I never took the 'cousin' part literally. I thought it was just a term of affection, and I went along with it."

They stared awhile at the foothills.

"I got a call from the water commissioner," Buddy said. "He wanted to remind me what *beneficial use* was."

"Okay. What is it?"

"Put it this way, irrigating my crop with federal water isn't Uncle Sam's idea of beneficial use. If I'm not careful, some good, patriotic boys might come a-knocking. Maybe break down the door."

"The water commissioner threatened you?"

"He thinks he's doing me a favor. You see, he knows a certain water lawyer who represents a certain ski-resort corporation that gives lots of money to lots of politicians. So the commissioner thought he'd give me a heads-up, to give me a chance to sell my water before someone takes it."

Libby closed her eyes. "I'm ready to file for divorce."

"Get a good lawyer."

"Damn it, Buddy! That's all you have to say? Are we going to be together or not?"

"I'm sorry. I want us to be together. But I'm not sure what the immediate future holds for me, and I don't want to make things worse for you."

Neither spoke for a while. "Let's stay in the past a bit longer," Libby said. "Tell me something, Buddy. Why did you love me so much?"

The question was as straightforward as it was confounding. He repeated the query to himself several times before the truth arrived. "I couldn't help it. The same reason I still love you."

"Then why did you push me away? You couldn't help that either? And don't blame the youth stupidity thing."

"We've had this conversation before."

"We haven't had it in a couple of decades."

"We wanted different things."

"We could've wanted different things and still have stayed together."

"You said the same thing back then. I knew you wanted a different experience, and I knew I wasn't going anywhere. I wasn't going to hold you back. No way."

Libby sat up. "This is what I never understood. Hold me back from what?"

"From success, an exciting life. I don't know. You were popular, motivated, a straight-A student with a scholarship. I was lazy, an average student with his head in the clouds. And your parents never liked me."

"You're nuts, you know that? I was perfectly happy to

go to CU and be your girlfriend. And my parents did not dislike you."

"Bullshit. I was a pot-smoker's son. I'm sure they were thrilled to get you away from me."

Libby cursed under her breath, something she rarely did. "I was wrong. You were young and stupid."

"C'mon, Lib, I was your first boyfriend. Don't you think you would've wondered what it was like to be with someone else?"

"Is that what it was about? Lots of people stayed together even though they went to different schools or did other things for a while. But you're so—so all or nothing about everything. You were afraid. Afraid of life, that's all. Just admit it."

Buddy sighed, returned to sitting with his back against the tree. "I knew my life wasn't going to be about making money and chauffeuring kids to soccer practice and making sure they went to the best schools and all that. My head was elsewhere. That kind of life would've killed me—"

"You don't know that! We were just kids ourselves. You have no idea how it would've turned out if you'd given things a chance. Somewhere along the line you just got scared and quit."

"Wow, you got it all figured out, huh? I knew who I was and who I wasn't. You were better off—"

"Did you ever consider how selfish you've been all these years? Just hiding in your own private world that nobody could be a part of because everyone else had it all figured out but you? I get it now. It's much easier to hide—"

"Easy? You think it was easy cutting out my own heart?"

Libby turned away. "What do you mean I was 'better off'?"

"You've got a nice life with a great kid."

She shook her head, laughed. "Got it all figured out, huh? I'm here with you right now. What does that say about my life?"

"I didn't say perfect."

"Tell me, Buddy. What do you like about Marty?"

"He's a nice kid."

"That's it? That's all you see? C'mon, Mister Deep Thinker, you can do better than that. What's so nice about him? *What* about him do you like?"

"He's a thoughtful, sensitive, curious, kid. What's *not* to like?"

Libby's face was calm now, eyes focused on Buddy. "And where do you think that comes from? Let me put it another way. Who does Marty *remind* you of?"

Buddy couldn't deny the whisper lurking in his consciousness, a conception too absurd, too irreconcilable to his self-image. Under the cottonwood tree, cloaked in Libby's gaze, Buddy watched his paradigm crumble.

"Say something," Libby said.

"Why didn't you tell me?"

"Really? It *never* occurred to you? You never—*maybe*—considered the timing of my last visit from LA, when we were together for what was supposed to be the last time? You didn't *ever* wonder why I went out of my way to make sure Marty could spend all that time with you growing pot?"

"You said you had a good job and a boyfriend in LA."

"And you just assumed—"

"That you were telling the truth? Why shouldn't I've assumed that?"

Libby said nothing, stared across the open space. "I gave

in," she said, "just accepted you weren't ready to be a father. And I wasn't going to trap you. So I made up the story about some guy running out on me. I'd go it alone if I had to."

"Your brother knew?"

Libby nodded. "Jake was adamant you should know the truth. We had horrible arguments over it. I made him promise that if I moved back, he would go along with my story. If you were going to find out, it had to come from me, and I would decide when that would be."

"So Jake talked you into coming back?"

"He thinks he did. But by the time Marty was a year old, I had already decided."

"Why did you return?"

Libby wrapped her arms around her knees, pulled them to her chest, then let her head fall forward. A tear disappeared into her jeans. "What do you think? Idiot."

Buddy put his arms around her shoulders, rested the side of his face against the back of her neck. "I'm sorry," he said. "You're probably right. I was afraid."

They stayed that way for several minutes before Libby straightened up, put a hand on each side of Buddy's face. "Give them what they want and end this."

Buddy took her hands in his. "I don't expect you to understand," he said, "but it's too late. I'm sorry."

Libby stood. "You're sorry," she said. "That's all you ever say about anything. Well, I'm sorry too."

Watching her follow the path back to her car and driving away, Buddy knew she was right. He was scared, and probably selfish.

25

H E DIDN'T REMEMBER driving home, only that he found himself in the cellar holding a joint. After several long drags, it occurred to him that symbolism also played a role in controlling the lives of the Fisher men, and that Papa George had symbolically hidden in the "magic of his newborn's eyes," just as his father, Abe, had built a symbolic wall to backstop a past he didn't want to think about, just like his father before him.

*

During breakfast in the summer of 1963, Papa George put down Rachel Carson's *Silent Spring* and said to his son, "I fear change is again happening." Abe nodded, assumed his father—in the midst of building a not-so-symbolic bomb shelter prompted by the Cuban Missile Crisis the previous October—was referring to Cold War rhetoric.

In September, Abe enrolled at the University of Colorado. His father's comment about change echoed in November.

"What you said before about things changing," Abe said. "Did you mean something like Kennedy getting killed?"

"No, no," Papa George said. "Only that things are changing."

Abe chose chemistry as his major, graduating summa cum laude during the period when the mechanism of DNA replication and the translation of genetic code had been discovered. It was also a time when the specter of the Vietnam War loomed ominously over the heads of draft-age men, a subject Abe and his father did not discuss, as if in implicit agreement. Papa George cried upon Abe's acceptance to the graduate biochemistry program, not only for his academic achievement, but for the draft deferment.

As Abe forged a path into the new world of biotechnology, Papa George continued his meditation on soil, particularly how mixtures of clay, sand, and humus affected its health and well-being. But just as the consequences of world events took years to fully manifest, so could an aging immigrant's past yield residual trauma.

Increasingly, Papa George's thoughts settled upon memories of a family that seemed more dream-like than real; the truth of his flesh and blood experiencing the horrors of the Second World War on the same soil from which he was born and raised weighed heavier and heavier. How could nature be so beautiful and so horrible at the same time? As Abe progressed through college, Papa George's thoughts also encompassed his graduate school pal Markus Lanzmann, who had died during the war, and the tragedy of his friend's unrealized passion. How better to honor Lanzmann's memory than to continue his research?

*

Nobody knew for sure where Papa George first acquired

cannabis seeds, but Abe remembered talk of his father's trips to Denver involving beet workers negotiating tea in parcels of "aces and deuces" on Larimer Street. He also remembered the bulletin board in the kitchen peppered with pre-war articles from *Popular Mechanics* and *Mechanical Engineering*, extolling the virtues of hemp. One article predicted hemp would become America's first billion-dollar cash crop. Another article from the USDA Bulletin cited hemp paper as superior to wood-derived paper, echoing Lanzmann's words: "Can you imagine a world in which no more trees have to be cut down?"

The change in Papa George was not lost on Abe. The sadness in his father's eyes, the stoicism in his voice, more and more time in the cellar, staring beyond the glow of a single candle. Abe could only observe with guarded concern. Then, toward the end of his first graduate semester, he detected an improvement in his father's mood. He also noticed woody cannabis plants appearing conspicuously in two different areas among the neat rows of hardy vegetables. By the end of the growing season, one area was bushy, full of flowering buds, while the other was covered with tall, thin stalks. In the kitchen, harvested stems soaked for days in pots of water before Papa George would start removing the fiber by hand.

Abe watched with detached amusement, indifferent as his father marveled over the cannabis fiber's tensile strength. Abe cared only that his father was showing an interest in life again. But alarm replaced contentment when Abe ventured down to the cellar and discovered paper bags covering the ends of male branches, a procedure suggesting those same bags would later be secured over the female plant's resin-filled flowers.

"Jesus, Dad, are you *crossbreeding* cannabis?"

"And why this should surprise you?"

He had a point. His father was a trained scientist after all. "Studying stalk fiber for textiles I can understand. But I hope you're not thinking of *smoking* that stuff—are you?"

"Everything about the plant is my interest. Why not also smoke? You should know that much about your father by now."

"And you should know it's against the law."

"You are going to call the police?"

Abe should've laughed but didn't. "Just be careful."

"Have you ever smoked marijuana, Abe? It is rather common nowadays among young people, no?"

Abe knew of marijuana's penetration into youth culture, primarily in the undergraduate world. "I've never tried it."

"So shocked you would be that I once smoked marijuana?"

He was indeed shocked, although hearing the story of his father's 1937 introduction by way of jazz musicians softened the impact, even piqued his curiosity. But for now, he thought it better to drop the matter. Research assistantships, qualifying exams, and writing a dissertation would leave little energy for his father's whims.

*

Just as Libby took the initiative to ask Buddy out on their first date, so did Evie Calhoun take the first step into Abe's life when she "suggested" they have lunch together. Evie would later claim it was Abe who cast the first spell, however, by making her fall in love with Papa George. "Raising a son while forbidding personal tragedy to cloud his vision of nature's beauty? How could I resist?"

In a short time they became that special type of couple, the kind seen now and then on buses, in cafes, or in other public places, a couple so in tune with each other, so obliviously happy, they seemed to exist only in public for the public, as a kind of example, perhaps. Evie's matured sense of silliness rubbed off on Abe, taught him to indulge in the absurd. From their playful banter evolved "Enigma Games," the art of applying scientific method to the unmeasurable, a game that could only be won by proving "legitimacy particles." Had the expression *soul mate* entered the lexicon back then, Abe undoubtedly would've used it. But many years would pass before his son, Buddy, would use the term when describing his parents' relationship. Meanwhile, Abe settled for a *knowingness* that Evie Calhoun had stamped an indelible image on his heart. For the first time in his life, Abe knew he wasn't alone.

Papa George delighted in his son's choice, and Evie returned his affections. The old man's enlightened spirit, his enthusiasm for her academic ambitions, proved irresistible to Evie's burgeoning feminist sensibilities. "He saw more in me than just a broodmare," she joked. Their relationship progressed in accordance with the changing cultural mores. Abe still lived at home but began spending evenings at Evie's apartment. Worried his father would feel abandoned, a nightly phone call became a priority. Papa George revealed only the joy a father felt knowing his son was with the woman he loved. Indeed, Papa George refused to get off the phone until he spoke with Evie and she told him everything that was new and wonderful in her life. After hanging up, Evie often wiped tears from her eyes.

Toward the end of their second year of graduate school,

Abe's thoughts turned to marriage. Faculty advisers had always been quick to discourage relationships between graduate students—no less marriage—stressing the unlikelihood of both finding employment at the same school. Abe's concern lay elsewhere.

"What's on your mind?" Evie said. They were reading in bed. "You seem preoccupied."

"Do you see marriage as a patriarchal system of slavery?" Abe said, then jumped out of his skin when Evie shrieked with laughter.

Evie said, "Is that your way of proposing?"

Abe joined in the laughter, saw how funny the question must've sounded when uttered with a straight face. "I'm not sure. There's a part of me that wonders if our relationship should be given a more legitimate appearance."

"Legitimate to whom?"

He thought about it. All potential answers had a connection to *society* per se, which sounded distasteful. "I don't know."

"Think about it. When you come up with something, let's talk again."

Abe knew he wouldn't come up with anything valid and said so. They agreed to keep things simple: cherish their time together and focus on comprehensive exams six months away. And that's what they did, rewriting notes, figuring out proficiency gaps, racking their brains over possible questions about fungi, bacteria, and plant metabolism. Time had a habit of speeding up when such milestones loomed on the horizon. Before long, spring's heavy wet snow was filling Boulder County's streams. The summer drained away quickly into August.

*

Abe noticed the subtle change just before the semester began. He gave her three days, then asked, "Worried about comps?"

Evie closed her book, set it on the nightstand. "I'm pregnant."

Dread dominated before giving way to more neutral, unidentifiable sentiments. Evie put her hand lightly against the side of his face. "Sweetheart, I said I'm pregnant. I didn't say I had cancer."

"Don't ever say that word again."

"Pregnant or cancer?"

"Not funny."

"Sorry. Talk to me."

"I had imagined this day. But not yet."

"Now we have a good reason to make our relationship *appear legitimate*."

The tenderness of her voice blunted the sarcasm. "You're not giving up your career."

"I agree. I'll just put things on hold awhile."

Abe smiled. "How long have you known—"

"Long enough to see the most obvious path we should take."

"It's not that obvious…Tell me."

"We move in with your dad—"

"Are you kidding?"

"Hear me out. He's already lost an entire family *and* his wife. Why not live in a beautiful place where your dad can watch his grandchild grow up? Don't you think he deserves to be surrounded by family? Is there a greater gift you could give someone?"

Evie had both logic and heartfelt sentimentality on her side. Abe almost felt ashamed for not immediately recognizing this *most obvious path*.

"I know how fond you are of my father, but he lives in his own little world. It may seem peculiar."

"I don't have a problem with peculiar."

"Baking soda and white vinegar. That's what he uses to clean with. *Everything*."

"That's the best you can do peculiar-wise?"

Life magazine had recently put marijuana on its cover, asserting twelve million Americans had tried it. Up to this point, Evie and Abe's attitude toward marijuana could best be described as *detached*. That is, both tacitly acknowledged pot's growing popularity but neither felt drawn to it. Papa George breeding and smoking cannabis had created a broader context for Abe to consider the so-called drug.

"Okay, how about this," Abe said. "The last couple of years my father has been crossing cannabis strains in the cellar. As far as I know, he's probably smoked more marijuana than all of our friends and acquaintances combined."

"How very progressive."

"Really? It's against the law. That doesn't bother you?"

It did bother her. "Well, it's the first you've mentioned of it, so I don't think it bothers you too much. And think of all the people we know who smoke it. And your dad's alone in the woods—I mean it's not like he's selling it. I doubt anyone gives a darn what he does out there. What's his next peculiarity?"

"Dad doesn't talk about his feelings, although he can get very emotional."

"You mean he's a *human being*?"

Silence. "I don't want you to think of yourself as the housekeeper looking after some older—"

"Maybe you can let *me* decide how I think of myself? I don't plan on upending the man's life for God's sake. It's possible I might organize some of the clutter, but would that be such a bad thing?"

Another round of silence. "All right then, let's move at the end of the semester." Evie didn't respond. Her expression said she had other plans. "Evie, you're a month away from comps—"

"I'm going to have a baby. You're going to be a father. Comps can wait."

"What'll you do all day? You'll go out of your mind—"

"There's plenty to do around the house. And I'll always have my research on cell membrane function to keep me company."

"You'll lose your funding."

"So what? We'll still have your stipend, and you know your dad isn't going to charge us rent."

There was nothing more to be said. When Abe asked his father how he felt about having a couple of roommates, Papa George could not contain his happiness. When Abe asked how he felt about becoming a grandfather, Papa George stepped away, buried his face into a handkerchief.

26

SHERIFF THOMPSON WALKED into Maria's house at 10:00 a.m. to find her sitting upright on the couch sound asleep with a paper cup balanced in her lap. On the coffee table, an empty bottle of ginger brandy lay beside several sheets of paper. Another bottle lay on the floor by her feet. Sheriff Thompson bent down, put a bag with two sausage McMuffins on top of the papers. Pain shot through his lower back.

"Wyatt?" Maria said.

"I got you some breakfast."

She looked at him squint-eyed. "I heard you leave the house so early. What on earth for?"

"Couldn't sleep. I thought I'd watch the sunrise."

Maria sat up. Sheriff Thompson watched her lift the cup to her mouth, tip it all the way back, then lick her lips. "We were supposed to talk this morning. Now sit down please."

Sheriff Thompson lowered himself to the opposite end of the couch, struggled to get comfortable. "What do you want to talk about?"

Maria sighed. "I expected you to be home this morning.

I was all prepared. Oh God, why weren't you here?" She rocked herself forward just enough to push the sausage McMuffin bag off the pile of papers, grab the top sheet, and fall back. "Look at this," she said, handing the paper to Sheriff Thompson. "This is how it works…"

Her voice meandered up and down, somewhat in relation to the way her eyes slowly opened and closed. The paper was covered with rows of short horizontal lines laid out in a triangular shape. Every line had a dollar amount that increased tenfold with each row. Deprived of context or reference, Sheriff Thompson could only stare at the paper. For some reason his mind digressed to a childhood practice of assigning personalities to numbers. The nine was happy; the six was frightened; the seven laughed. He noticed Maria's icy stare only when he looked up while pondering the disposition of a four.

"I don't understand," Sheriff Thompson said.

"It's what we're trying to accomplish here! You want me to help you, don't you?"

Maria straightened up, accidentally kicking an empty bottle across the room.

"Help me with what?"

"Shush!" Maria said. Sheriff Thompson did his best to listen as she described life-changing MP3s or, if he preferred, DVDs. "If you sign up three people…" But he had already wandered back to Hardscrabble Lane, dragging the demon backward by the armpits, straining his back as he loaded it into the truck. Maria grabbed another sheet of paper, leaned into Sheriff Thompson, pointed to a line that had his name typed underneath it. "*You* sign up under me, and then make that money back by signing up three others under *you*…"

Maria's bony finger made him think of how the nine-millimeter's grip felt in his palm. He didn't remember the first trigger-pull, just the thrill of the next nine. Ultimately, he knew the demon was but a minor figure in the fight against evil. As Carson said, the serpent's head needed to be cut off.

"You're not listening!" Maria screamed then reached for an empty flask under the table. Upon realizing the bottle would yield no more ginger brandy, she dropped to her knees and began sobbing.

Sheriff Thompson glanced at the sheet of paper then looked back at Maria. For a moment, he felt a pang of guilt, as if Maria's condition was his fault. If he had understood what she was talking about, Maria wouldn't now be lying in the fetal position under the coffee table. Grimacing through pain, he raised himself from the couch then bent his knees just enough to allow the sheet of paper to float safely to the floor in front of Maria's face, then hobbled back to his bedroom.

27

"**C**'MON IN, RAY. I hope you don't mind taking off your shoes. We have guest slippers if you want."

Castellanos did mind, but he sat on the mahogany entryway bench anyway, removed his boots, then followed Donald through the living room to an eight-hundred-square-foot natural stone patio with deck railings of patina copper panels. He had been to Donald's home a few times before with Suzanne, as guests for holiday parties or some tax-deductible function showing off Donald's reach into the chamber of commerce or upper echelons of law enforcement.

Donald sat in one of several chaise lounges, gazed out over the city. Castellanos took the lounge next to him.

"Some view, huh, Ray?"

"That's some view, Donny."

Silence. "You pissed off about something?"

"What am I doing here?"

Donny raised the angle of the chaise. "You know what's coming, right?"

It was the kind of intentionally vague question a

pretentious prick like Donald Campbell would ask. "I'm at your service, Godfather."

Donald turned to him. "You've always hated me, haven't you?"

"Bullshit."

"Sure seems that way."

"You're wrong. Growing up I only *disliked* you. As an adult I've always hated you."

"That's supposed to make me feel better?"

"Feel? Since when do you feel anything?"

Donald turned back to his view. "Admit it, you hate rich people."

Castellanos laughed. "*Ray Castellanos hates rich people.* Give me a fucking break."

"Okay why?"

Castellanos sat up, swung his feet off the side of the lounge. "The first thing you say after I walk in, 'Some view huh, Ray?' You said it as if you *owned* the fucking view and you're doing me a favor by letting me have a peek. *That's* why I hate you."

"What the hell are you talking about? It's my property. What do you want, a sign telling the public they can come anytime they want and sit on my patio?"

Castellanos lay back down, covered his face with his hands. "Why am I here, Donny? What do you want?"

"Hang on. You don't think people who've worked hard deserve to have a house like mine with this view?"

"Okay, let me rephrase. I don't like you because you're a *cunt.* Now why did you invite me here?"

"Jesus Christ. I just don't get you. I mean, I really just don't—"

"Donny, I'll give you ten seconds to start telling me why I'm here, or I'm gone. One, two—"

"It's all coming together. The Wichita guys, the Topeka guys, they're making a plan. Buddy doesn't have a chance."

"What kind of plan?"

"I don't know exactly, but—"

"You *do* know exactly—"

"Goddamn it, Ray, I'm trying to avoid needless—conflict! I don't want to see Buddy shackled and marched off to federal prison. It doesn't have to be this way."

Castellanos failed to keep a straight face.

"Tell me, Ray, what's the condition of your war chest these days?"

"Say what?"

"Your war chest, Ray. You got an election to start thinking about, don't you?"

Castellanos smiled. "You really wonder why I don't like you, Donny?"

"Here's the thing. I may be a cunt, but as far as you're concerned, I'm one *indispensable* cunt. Don't you think?"

"That's right. Without your patronage, Godfather, I'm nothing. And there wouldn't be a sheriff's deputy parked in the eleven hundred block of Timber Lane every night to ensure your well-being. Of course the deputies followed procedure, always informed dispatch of their whereabouts—which is all recorded."

Donald feigned howling laughter. "You really are out of touch, aren't you? That *patronage* came from a nonprofit—anonymously—and is one hundred percent legal. You think you can get elected from a bunch of old folks raiding their bingo money and sending you five- and ten-dollar checks?"

Castellanos matched Donald's phony laugh with one of his own. "Nonprofit, huh? And what was the purpose of this nonprofit?"

"To educate people on the issues."

Donald's tone had a sobering effect. Castellanos knew when he'd been beaten. "Okay, guys like you will control the message, I get it. Now what is it you really want from all this—conflict? What do you have against Buddy?"

"I'm trying to help Buddy. That's what you're doing here. I'm telling you he doesn't have a prayer, and I don't want to see him go to prison. If the feds take him down, he stands to lose everything—including his water rights."

Castellanos's face lit up. "Aha! You want me to get him to sell you his water!"

"It's about more than that. But if he sells me the water, he's got the money in the bank. Then if you can convince him to just cooperate, he stays put on his beloved land, and his future is up to him. He can still irrigate his garden. Nobody gives a shit about a few thousand gallons. But if he doesn't give Wichita what they want, then he'll be off the land and the feds will take all his assets—of which water is the most valuable."

"Why don't you just tell him what you just told me."

"Because he trusts you."

Castellanos knew it wasn't that simple, but there was no point trying to explain. "So how's Libby doing?"

"She's fine. I thought she'd be home." Donald sat up, stared at Castellanos. "Why're you suddenly asking about Libby?"

The sheriff laughed for real this time. "You bought the love of Buddy's life. Now you want to buy his water? What's next? He should bleed out for you?"

"Oh fuck you, Ray. Libby and I were old friends. She could've done anything she wanted. She didn't need me and you know it."

Donald spoke the truth for a change, although Castellanos never understood how Libby could've settled for Donald. "Fine, fine, point taken. But Jesus Christ, Donny, why do you have to be involved in this whole thing? Is there enough money in the world to make guys like you happy?"

"Guys like me? You think you're so much different than me?"

"God, I hope so."

Silence, then Donald said, "Are you going to help me or not?"

"You're crazy if you think Buddy's going to listen to me about selling his water."

"You can try, can't you? Is that asking too much?"

"What about the plan you're not exactly sure about? You gonna tell me some details you're not exactly sure about too? You gonna keep me informed on when you're not exactly sure it's going to happen?"

"Yes, of course! I want you involved."

Castellanos stood, took a few steps toward the house. "I'll see what I can do. But you should know by now that Buddy's gonna do whatever the hell Buddy wants to do."

Donald swung his legs off the chaise.

"Relax, I know my way out."

Castellanos walked to his car, drove down the mountain with no intention of engaging Buddy in a discussion of water rights. The thought of acting on Donald's behalf nauseated him. As the city's western boundary came into view, the radio crackled. Somewhere up Sunshine Canyon, a rural-route newspaper driver spotted an upside down pickup truck. The dispatcher broadcasted the license plate and vehicle description, then spelled the name of the registered owner.

*

Castellanos weighed nothing, felt nothing. He hovered above the cliff's edge watching first responders sever the battery cable, hammer wedges, and position airbags. A roadblock encompassed the approximate area where the vehicle went over.

"You want me to start the next-of-kin search?"

Castellanos turned to the young deputy. "Do you see the coroner anywhere? Because I sure as fuck don't. Go back to your car and make sure this area stays secure."

Castellanos waited until the deputy walked away then dropped to his knees. Several minutes later, the coroner's car pulled up. Castellanos stood, wiped his eyes.

"Hi, Ray," Emma said. He was always surprised at how young and pretty she was.

"Morning. EMTs call it in?"

Emma nodded, studied his face. He wasn't fooling anyone. "Non-viable," she said then took a cursory look around. "Straightaway. No skid marks."

"Yep."

Shouting from below as the airbags started inflating. "I'll call you on the radio," Emma said then began walking toward the belayer manning the rope anchor.

"You're going down there?" Castellanos said.

"Never pass up an opportunity to practice steep-angle rope skills."

He watched her get outfitted then rappel down. By the time she unhooked from the rope line, Alfie's body had been freed. Emma walked over, knelt beside the body. Castellanos could tell something was up.

"Looks like several gunshot wounds to the chest," Emma said over the radio.

The weightlessness reappeared, then anger. "Goddamn him," Castellanos said. "Goddamn him, goddamn him, goddamn him…"

"Ray? Did you copy?"

*

Castellanos stared at enormous sandstone slabs leaning against the foothills outside District Attorney Arnold Jaeger's window. Despite having gazed upon these "flatirons" his whole life, Castellanos had never pondered the geologic violence responsible for uplifting Boulder County's iconic symbol from the earth. And having just gazed upon the violent evidence of Alfie's battered, lifeless body, he had never felt so helpless.

"What do we know for sure?" Jaeger said.

News of a body found below Hardscrabble Lane had spread quickly thanks to the number of residents scanning police radio frequencies. Murders in Boulder County occurred infrequently, and suspects were usually announced or apprehended within twenty-four hours. The longer it took to release a statement, the faster the fire would spread.

"Alfie Beaubien was murdered," Emma said.

Jaeger had lived in the area long enough to know the name would echo loudly throughout the county. He rapped his knuckles on the desk a few times. "What else?"

"The cause of death was gunshot wounds to the chest. Any trauma from the vehicle's plunge over the cliff happened *postmortem*. I'll need to get him on the table to get an exact bullet count."

Jaeger looked at Castellanos. "Beaubien meets killer on the road. Killer shoots him, stuffs his body into vehicle, pushes vehicle over the cliff."

Castellanos brought his attention back indoors, glimpsed the desktop picture frame of Jaeger holding a cutthroat trout with both hands, then refocused on the man behind the desk. "That's what it looks like," Castellanos said. "Alfie lived about a mile up the road, and so far there's nothing at his house to suggest anything happened there. The vehicle's path down the embankment is pretty obvious. I've got men scouring up top for clues."

"Next of kin?"

"He was an only child," Castellanos said. "Both parents deceased. We're looking for aunts or uncles or cousins."

"Emma," Jaeger said, "I don't want to keep you from getting started on the autopsy. Ray, stay around awhile if you don't mind."

Emma stood. "I'll be in touch."

Jaeger waited for Emma to leave. "The word's out," Jaeger said. "Citizens and news agencies are all calling in. We have to make some kind of announcement. Something that doesn't suggest there's a crazed killer running loose."

"It wasn't a random killing."

"How do you know?"

"I'm sure of it."

Jaeger waited for more. "Jesus, Ray, tell me what you know already."

"It has to do with weed wars."

"What weed wars?"

"C'mon, Arnie, you know what I mean. That whole culture up there."

Jaeger grimaced, leaned his chair back. "In reference to a cold-blooded murder, you say, 'weed wars,' and I'm supposed to know what the hell you're talking about?"

"Sorry. Poor choice of words."

Again, Jaeger waited. "What's with this closed-mouthed crap?"

"There's just stuff going on I need to look into first."

Jaeger leaned over his desk. "How about telling me what you're looking into?"

"Well there's an interest group from Kansas in town, and they're not happy with Colorado's legal weed legislation and—"

"Interest group? Representing whom?"

"Agricultural interests."

"Kansas government?"

"Some government. Some not-so-government."

"What the hell does that mean? Organized crime?"

"Some would probably think of it that way."

Jaeger paused. "Are you trying to be *funny*, Ray?"

"Fuck you, Arnie. You have any idea how close I was to Alfie and his parents?"

"Then stop this vague bullshit, and tell me what's going on."

"Ask Will Brandt. He knows more than I do."

Jaeger groaned. "Brandt. God help us. He's losing his mind."

"Who isn't these days?"

Jaeger walked out from behind his desk, stood over Castellanos. "Look, I'm sorry for your loss. It's horrible what happened. But we've always worked well together. And suddenly, you're acting like you're hiding something. I've got to make an announcement—"

"Just do me a favor and call Will Brandt. There's more shit going on than I could possibly explain."

Jaeger stared at Castellanos. "Why is the chief law enforcement officer afraid to tell the chief prosecutor what he's thinking?"

"Fuck! Can you just call Will Brandt, tell him what happened, then get back to me with his reaction?"

Jaeger threw up his hands. "Sure, I'll do that. And in the meantime, we'll announce the murder was drug-related."

"Alfie wasn't a drug—"

Jaeger slapped his hand hard on the desk. "I'm not going to have a killer running loose in the foothills! Not on my watch."

"Relax, Arnie, I get it. We're both drinking from the same trough."

"What the hell's that supposed to mean?"

"It means I'm up for re-election too."

"Unless you give me something else—right now—the murder is drug-related."

"Just drag Alfie's corpse through the mud then spit on him, huh?"

Jaeger walked back behind his desk, sat. "The investigation is ongoing, but preliminary indications suggest the murder was drug-related. Take it or leave it."

28

BUDDY AWOKE THE next morning to see Ralston's pickup truck parked in the driveway with Ralston lying across the front seat wrapped in a sleeping bag. Buddy knocked on the window, led him inside, sat beside him on the living room couch. Neither spoke until Buddy said, "Whenever you're ready."

"They killed Alfie."

Ralston's words bore through Buddy's torso, starting fires along the way. He struggled to fill his lungs, forced an exhale before inhaling deeply. He repeated the process several times all the while seeing Alfie sitting on that same couch telling Stanley Carson to fuck off. "Who told you this?"

"Sheriff Castellanos came over last night. Said they found Alfie down the side of a cliff in his truck, about a mile from his house. They shot him."

"*They* shot him? Who shot him?"

"Castellanos didn't say. They're investigating." Ralston fell on his side, laid his arm across his eyes.

"Rally, you better not be blaming yourself for this."

"It's my fault."

"Bullshit! Why would you say that?"

Ralston sat back up. "That guy who got shot in the parking lot. Zeb thought I did it. I kept telling him it wasn't me. Then he came home the other night all shit-faced drunk and starts beatin' on me, telling me I fucked everything up and that he would be blamed and they'd be coming after him. I kicked him in the stomach, started shouting what a piece of shit he was and that Alfie shot the Kansas guy because Alfie had more guts in his little finger than Zeb ever had in his whole worthless, piece-of-shit body."

"You think Zeb killed Alfie?"

"No. But I'm sure he told Carson and those other assholes it was Alfie who shot the Kansas guy. If I had kept my mouth shut, Alfie would be alive."

Ralston's story fit together a bit too easily.

"I don't know, Rally. It's possible Alfie had been targeted all along, or maybe it was completely unplanned. It's one thing to destroy a man's property, but you're talking about pre-meditated murder here. Was Zeb there when Castellanos told you Alfie was murdered?"

"Yeah, he was there, on the couch passed out. I jumped on him, started pounding him. Castellanos pulled me off, dragged me outside, told me to go to your house when I settled down. I drove around most of the night. Got here a few hours ago."

Buddy thought the district attorney had probably called a press conference. He imagined the weed community would now blame him for Alfie's death, saying he should've just handed over the seventy kilos.

"I think it would be a good idea for you to stay here for

the time being," Buddy said. "Who the hell knows where your brother's head's at."

"I can stay at Alfie's. I've seen his will. He left me everything."

"Maybe it's better you're not alone for a few days— but it's up to you. You're a lucky guy to have had Alfie for a friend."

"I know."

*

"The death was ruled a homicide," Carson said, paraphrasing from an article in the *Daily Camera*. He was sitting on the couch of his hotel suite. "Of the ten direct hits, all were front to back, fired at close range." Carson skimmed down a few paragraphs, said, "DA thinks drug-related," then folded the paper, dropped it on the coffee table next to an open box of pastries.

Dahlgren stared at him from a leather club chair.

"Don't look at me like that, Dale. Maybe one of these two monkeys here can tell you what happened because I sure as hell can't."

"That kind of talk isn't helpful, Stan," Dahlgren said.

Gonzales and Lacerta stared at Carson. "We don't know anything about this event," Gonzales said.

"The governor wants to know this didn't have anything to do with our business here," Dahlgren said.

"Well you just heard these boys say they don't know anything about it, so go ahead and tell the governor there's absolutely no connection between this murder and our business here. Tell him somebody was settling an old score the way mountain folk do sometimes when they take matters into their own hands."

"What about that sheriff of yours?" Lacerta said.

Carson gave him a funny look. "Who? Wyatt? Sheriff Thompson? You can't be serious. He's a God-fearing man. He wouldn't just go out and kill somebody."

"Where is he now?" Gonzales said.

Carson jumped up. "Now just relax about Sheriff Thompson. In fact, you've had a bug up your ass about Wyatt from day one. What about all your renegade mercenaries—I mean *assets*? Or that Blues Brother freak with the lipstick?"

"Settle down, Stan," Dahlgren said. "You told me yourself Wyatt had an unstable side. Remember when you told me about his behavior at that meeting in the woods?"

Carson walked to Dahlgren's chair, stared down at him. "I told you—in confidence I might add—that Wyatt was an *emotional* man, *passionate* in his beliefs. You should also know that Wyatt loves the governor as a brother in Christ and wouldn't do anything to hurt the governor or put him in a bad light. If you don't believe me, ask the governor yourself."

Carson retook his seat on the couch.

"Maybe I'll have a talk with Sheriff Castellanos," Dahlgren said. "See how his investigation is going."

"Bullets have unique markings from the barrel," Gonzales said, looking directly at Carson. "At close range, powder residue can be found on the victim."

"Yes, I know," Carson said. "Forensic science is quite remarkable nowadays. But I'm telling you you're all jumping to conclusions. *It's just bad timing.* That's all. Shit happens, right? Nothing's really changed. You all got a plan, right? I mean our goal is in sight."

"The plan is forthcoming," Gonzales said. "But before it can be executed, we have to make sure all unknowables become knowable."

"I wish you'd stop talking in your goddamn secret-agent bullshit. *Unknowables.* I know you're talking about Wyatt. 'One hundred percent control of an asset is imperative'— you've been saying that since day one." Carson looked at Dahlgren. "But there comes a time you just gotta trust the people you're working with."

"I hear you," Dahlgren said, "and chances are you're probably right about this whole thing, but I'm sure you can understand how this kind of circumstance makes people nervous. But I get it. Until some kind of evidence comes to light, we'll keep things status quo. And I'll trust you've got things under control."

"I appreciate your support, Dale. You think Batman and Boy Wonder here can simmer down long enough to let us do our job?"

Dahlgren cringed. "These gentlemen are here to help us. And whether you know it or not, they've got our backs. As for the plan, we'll get together again tonight and go over things. Sound good?" Dahlgren looked at Lacerta and Gonzales. Neither objected.

Carson said, "Sorry, boys, didn't mean to be disrespectful. I'm just upset over the needless death of an innocent person. That's all. And I know the Cook brothers are just as upset as the governor and his people. How about we all relax and have a sweet roll?"

29

LIBBY WAS JUST about to take a seat in the waiting area when Castellanos stepped out of his office. "Hey there, Lib, c'mon back."

The phone call had surprised her. Their relationship the past twenty years had consisted of waves at the grocery store, friendly car honks, or maybe thirty seconds of stilted small talk at dinner parties. But that was to be expected considering Castellanos and Buddy had been close friends the entire history of Libby's relationship with Buddy—including countless double dates with the future Suzanne Castellanos. The toughest part about breaking up had been that longing to recapture how good it felt to be a Boulder County kid in those days, seeing the Samples or Big Head Todd at Tulagi's, going back to Buddy's house and staying up all night sipping beer, smoking pot, pigging-out the next morning on eight-egg omelets and heaps of hash browns at the Aristocrat Diner. She learned the hard way that the good old days only existed once they were long gone, and all you could do was look back in heartache. She took the chair in front of his desk.

"Thanks for coming in," Castellanos said. "How've you been?"

She knew Castellanos's words sounded just as empty to him as they did to her, but it didn't matter. Their shared history and kinship transcended time.

"Oh, you know," Libby said. "How are you and Suzanne doing?"

"We're good, we're good, thanks." Castellanos coughed. "Look, I don't know what you know or don't know—"

"As of this morning I know Alfie Beaubien's dead. I already knew that Roy Mitchell's being run off his land and that Colter McKenna and Billy Kittredge have been terrorized. And I know this has everything to do with Buddy and a stockpile of weed he's hidden somewhere."

Castellanos needed a few moments. "So you and Buddy are in touch?"

"I would've thought you'd know the answer to that."

Castellanos shook his head. "He stopped talking about you a long time ago, and I stopped asking."

"Well, I'm sure you know a lot more than I do. Buddy's only going to tell me so much about his business."

"I'm not going to bullshit you, Libby—"

"Thank you."

"I'm more interested in what Donny knows."

Libby straightened up. "Knows about what?"

"What's in store for Buddy."

"What's *in store* for Buddy? What am I supposed to make of that?"

"They're going to bust him, somehow, some way."

"And they're not going to keep you, the sheriff of Boulder County, informed of their plans?"

"When there's private interests involved, I don't take anything for granted."

"And you think Donny's got some inside info?"

"I was at your house yesterday. He told me the Kansas guys are making a plan and Buddy doesn't have a chance. He wouldn't elaborate—yet."

"Which means what?"

"Exactly. Is he really going to keep me in the loop? Or is he bullshitting me because—"

"Because he wants Buddy's water rights."

"Oh, you know about that." Libby didn't respond. Castellanos said, "I'm ashamed to ask you to spy on your husband—"

"Maybe I'm hearing things, but I could've sworn you just said something about not bullshitting me. I know you never liked him, Ray." It was Castellanos's turn not to respond. Libby said, "Go ahead, say it."

"Let's just forget it. I'm sorry to have bothered you."

"No way, Ray. *You* called *me*, remember? So here I am. You might as well go ahead and say what's always been on your mind."

Castellanos leaned his chair back. "Fine," he said, took a breath. "You could've stayed in LA and had a great life there. Instead, you came home with a kid, tail between your legs, and took up with Donny because it was *easy*—not because you had any real feelings for that prick. I mean—of all people! Did you have to go out of your way like that to hurt Buddy?"

Libby searched for a response, fought back tears, tried to keep her lip from quivering. She knew Castellanos wouldn't understand anything unless he knew who Martin's real father was. But now that secret belonged to Buddy.

Libby wiped her eyes, took a breath. "You're right, Ray. I never loved Donny—"

"Actually, stop. I was out of line. It's none of my business, and I have no right to judge you. All I know is that you're the only woman Buddy ever cared about, and that he was never the same when you two broke up."

"Geez, for a sheriff you're really a softy. I get a little emotional and just like that you let me off the hook?"

Castellanos smiled. "I'm the cowardly sheriff."

Libby laughed. "Speaking of cowards, did you know Buddy never asked me out for our first date?"

"Shut up."

"It's true! I had to ask him out. We went to see *Risky Business* at the Fox. Even at fourteen I could see what a coward he was. Although back then I saw it as shyness, which for some reason I kind of liked."

Castellanos leaned his chair back. "Yeah, well, he was kind of between worlds, wasn't he? Not sure where he belonged. At least that's how it seems looking back. You know his grandfather lost his wife early on, raised Buddy's dad all by himself. You never got to know Buddy's mom, but she was the nicest, friendliest lady you ever met. She treated anyone who came over like they were her own kid. His dad was the same way, which you know."

Libby smiled. "What did you mean by 'private interests'?"

"In retrospect," Castellanos said, "Buddy's dad and granddad were altogether different. Way ahead of their time, at least in our little world. I guess today we would say they had *vision*. Out here we got all these commerce department labs working with contractors, aerospace-whatever with the university. Huge money. I don't know why or how, but Buddy's dad and the old man saw the potential value in cannabis way back then. They predicted cannabis would eventually make its way back into the mainstream and that some multinational—like Cook Industries—would jump in and try to take over the whole market when nobody was looking."

"And that's what it's all about?"

"There's always more, but that's the bottom line."

"Get Buddy to go along, Ray. Don't let him throw his life away."

"I've tried, Libby. He's not going to listen to me. And if he doesn't listen to you, then I don't know what to do. But if I can find out what the feds have in mind, maybe I can help somehow."

"How do these things usually play out?"

"No-knock raid, agents swarming the property with assault rifles. They know he's a loner, so they're probably not too worried about people getting hurt. Not that someone getting hurt would stop them. But they want to find something. Their only worry is busting the place up and *not* finding a shit-load of something illegal."

"Why have they waited this long? I mean, why don't they just get it over with?"

"That's how these guys operate. First they nibble around the corners, harassing friends and comrades, hoping the real target—Buddy—will take the path of least resistance and just give 'em what they want. It costs money to organize and deploy officers and deal with any public relations fallout, etcetera."

"Will you be there when it happens?"

"That's the whole point, Lib. I want to make sure I'm there."

Libby stood, walked to the window looking over Canyon Boulevard. "And if they do find something? What'll they do to Buddy?"

"Prison probably. One way or another they'll take his freedom, ruin his life."

"And what will that accomplish?" Her voice broke. "What does it prove to ruin someone's life?"

Castellanos walked over to her. "It's a warning to others. It's their way of saying, 'Fighting back is useless. You're going to lose. We can and will destroy you.'"

Libby turned to face Castellanos. "They win. Buddy loses. Game over. And that's what scares me most, Ray, Buddy acting like a man who's got nothing to lose."

*

An unsettled feeling overcame Libby upon seeing Donald's car in the driveway. She had anticipated a few hours in an empty house, alone with her thoughts and a glass of wine, contemplating how to broach a discussion about Buddy. Pausing at the doorway to Donald's office, she watched his head rotate between laptop and books of revised statutes, then walked to the kitchen where she began opening cabinets. After transferring cans, condiments, and cereal boxes to the countertop, she sponged off the shelves, swept the floor, returned the items to the cabinets, then started on the sink full of dishes.

Donald had been part of their gang as kids, although not conspicuously so like Ray and Fernando. Buddy knew they would never really like Donald, but he never stopped hoping they would learn to tolerate him. She knew Buddy and Donald's gradual estrangement began during their college days.

She would run into Donald when she and Buddy would get together during breaks to "catch up," although passions invariably got the best of them. At the time, Buddy's versions of Donald's growing conservatism did not resonate with Libby as particularly significant. Her energies had been focused on enduring the emotional roller-coaster when coming home and seeing the man she loved. Not until Libby moved back from LA did she think of Donald as nice looking in that "pretty" sort of way that large eyes, straight nose, and rounded jaw line attracted some women. In LA, Libby had known many men like Donald, that is, excessively confident, completely focused on careers. She struggled to take the new Donald seriously—which added to her curiosity.

"What're you doing?" Donald said, startling Libby.

"What does it look like I'm doing?" Libby said, still facing the sink. He put his hand on her bare shoulder. She regretted having worn an off-the-shoulder top.

"Let Maria clean this up. That's why we pay her."

Libby had no choice but to turn around. His hand would fall away, but they'd be face-to-face, her back against the sink, and then he'd probably close the distance. She prayed he wouldn't start kissing her neck.

She turned around. "I clean when I'm upset."

He leaned in but didn't go for her neck. "What are you upset about?"

"Seriously? Alfie Beaubien murdered not five miles from where we're standing?"

Donald retreated. "Oh," he said then opened the fridge, took out a bottle of imported brown ale, then poured it into his favorite "imperial pint" glass.

"This doesn't upset you?"

"Of course it does. But what do you want me to do about it?"

Libby followed Donald back to his office. From the doorway she watched him set his beer on the monogramed fleur-de-lis sandstone coaster before sitting behind his desk. "What can you do? How about stop working for five minutes and talk about it?"

"What's there to talk about? They said it was drug-related. That's the way it goes with those guys."

"*Those guys?* You've known that family your whole life. Alfie wasn't a drug—"

"What do we know about Alfie? He grew up in a house smoking pot and worshiping crystals and sniffing weird incense and God knows what, and then the other halluci-nogenic drugs they were probably taking. And his best friend was Ralston Macky, another fringy foothills delinquent."

Libby could only stare. "You think Alfie got what he deserved, don't you?"

Donald took a long swig of beer, leaned back in his chair. "Did you even know the guy?"

"If this happened to Buddy, would you be so callous?"

Donald stared at his wife. "Oh, I get it. It's *Buddy* you're worried about. Why is that, Lib?"

"You know why."

Donald took a sip of beer. Before replacing the glass, he slid the coaster a few inches closer, then stood. "I do? Why would I? I mean, you two haven't spoken in, like, twenty years, right?"

"I know about the stash of weed he's supposedly hiding. And I know people are out to destroy him if he doesn't give it up."

Donald nodded. "Interesting. And how do you know this?"

"How do you think I know this?"

Husband and wife stared at each other until Donald said, "No. You tell me. I want to hear it from your mouth."

Libby laughed while lowering herself to the floor, bracing her back against the door frame. "Breaking news! I don't sit at home all day waiting for my man to come home. We tried that. It doesn't work. You care more about making money and becoming the king of Boulder County than you ever did about our relationship. We both know it's true, so let's stop the Kabuki-theater crap."

Donald returned to his desk chair. Libby remained on the floor viewing Donald from the neck up. Donald said, "You're leaving me. Say it."

"C'mon, Donny, this can't be a surprise. We've been living separate lives for a long time. But that's not what we're talking about—"

"Buddy's not some kid selling drugs," Donald said. "His situation is totally different."

"And when Buddy shows up dead and the district attorney says it's drug-related, you gonna just go along with it?"

"Dead? You're overreacting."

"That's good to know. So tell me what's going to happen to Buddy? What are these people going to do to him?"

"Why would I know anything about what's going to happen—whatever that means?"

"You told Ray—"

"Ray? So you're in touch with Ray too?"

Libby closed her eyes, sighed. "Jesus, Donny. Boulder County's not that big of a place."

"It'll be a DEA operation," Donald said. "The Controlled Substances Act classifies marijuana as a Schedule I drug, and Buddy's been illegally growing marijuana using water from a federal diversion project. Plus, there's strong evidence that the THC levels in his pot are far beyond the legal levels Colorado allows."

"When?" she said.

"I don't know. Could be anytime."

"How did you become so plugged into everything going on around Buddy?"

"Because Commissioner Brandt knows Buddy and I are old friends, and it just so happens I know water law. I'm Buddy's best asset, an inside man. I'm trying to help him stay out of prison."

"Oh my god," Libby said then rocked herself forward, momentarily balancing on her knees before standing. "Of course! Your true motivation for warning Buddy has to do with being an old friend. The county wouldn't be paying you a nice consulting fee for your water-law expertise, would they? Or maybe there's some other business-related motivation you're not telling me about?"

Donald stood. "Buddy knows *exactly* what's going to happen. And he knows exactly how to avoid anything bad from happening and even come out smelling like a rose. Ray knows too. He didn't tell you?"

"As long as Buddy hands over the stash of pot and stops growing it, they'll leave him alone? It's as simple as that, Donny? Look me in the eye and tell me it's as simple as that."

Donald sat back down. "That's true—as far as I can tell. But if he doesn't hand it over, the feds will take his water.

And I don't mean they're gonna buy it; they're going to *take* it. That's a lot of money he could use to start over."

Libby laughed. "And you've so generously volunteered to buy his water before the government can take it."

"You think I'm the bad guy?" Donald shouted. "I'm sticking my neck out for him so he can walk away with some money in the bank before it's too late."

Libby paused. "When will it be too late?"

"I told you, I don't know for sure."

"When will you know—for sure?"

"Why does it matter anymore? He's got no chance, Libby. All his weed's in the bomb shelter under the garden."

"I know about the bomb shelter. Everyone does."

"You're damn right everyone knows, and that includes the *real* bad guys of this whole drama, the ones who have ground-penetrating radar. They know what's on every inch of Buddy's land, and that includes an escape tunnel leading into the forest."

"He's never mentioned that."

"Why would he? I don't know if Buddy even knew about it way back when. My theory is that Papa George built it when they first dug out the bomb shelter but kept it sealed. Maybe his dad told him about it. I've seen the images. The tunnel leads right to the bomb shelter. A year ago it was still sealed. Not anymore."

"A year ago? You've known for a year this was all going to happen?"

"No—*they* knew. They've been watching for a long time. But can't you see how deluded he is? If you really want to help Buddy, make him understand there's no escaping this, Libby. I don't care how many tunnels he digs."

"I'll just say, 'Give it up, Buddy. It's no use. Your old friend Donny says you can't dig your way out.'"

Silence, then Donald said, "It doesn't have to be this way. Buddy knows this better than anyone."

It doesn't have to be this way, Libby thought. *How true.* Nothing had to be any way. Everything was just a choice, after all.

30

THAT EVENING, BUDDY parked in Alfie's driveway where crystal energy glowed through the living room window amid a multicolored display spinning over the outside of the house. Alfie's mom had always saved the "magic lantern" show for the winter solstice week—her way of celebrating light and the sun's rebirth. Alfie continued the tradition for those driving around the foothills searching for elaborate Christmas displays, but changed the orbiting images to pentacles, moons, fairy stars, spiral goddesses, and other pagan symbols—Alfie's "fuck you" to the hypocritical world, Ralston said.

Ralston was glad to see Buddy, welcomed him in as if that morning's tragic news was but a shared memory from long ago. The house smelled fruity. Buddy sat on the couch, spent the next two hours listening to Ralston ramble on about all the fun he and Alfie had over the years. Several times Ralston was overcome with laughter, needed a couple of minutes to collect himself. Buddy had never seen him like this, guessed he'd been smoking Pineapple Kush or one of the other "giggly" strains.

As the night wore on, Ralston gradually unwound, became more and more contemplative, until he stretched out on the couch and closed his eyes.

Buddy looked around the room, saw an afghan draped over the back of a rocking chair. Not until he covered Ralston with the blanket did he notice the crocheted pattern of an angel on a crescent moon, wishing upon a star. Driving home, he reflected on how suddenly Ralston's life had changed then began ruminating on whether Alfie's death had been inevitably connected to his own *inability* to change. Tomorrow he would give Castellanos a call, suggest they take turns keeping an eye on Ralston, to help him get through this dark time.

Sitting in the quiet depths of the cellar, Buddy applied a small flame to the tip of a joint, carefully rotated it between thumb and forefinger. *Dark times, changing times.* He recalled how Papa George feared change as if it were a bad omen, wondered if his grandfather had recognized Abe and Evie's wedding day as marking *joyful* change on a lovely September afternoon beside an aspen grove quaking in a soft breeze. Or had Papa George recognized his *own* celebration of change when he filled the couple's bedroom with phlox, freesia, thistles, and hyacinth, while anxiously awaiting his grandson's homecoming from the hospital? Or did he share in the simple delight of whimsical change when Roy Mitchell inadvertently renamed "Bennet" Fisher after the newborn's tiny hand closed around Roy's finger, thus provoking the typically reticent man to exclaim, "Well, aren't you my little buddy-boy!"

And what of the changing seasons? Did Papa George not feel joy when encouraging toddler Buddy to fill his lungs with autumn's dry, sweet fragrances of butterscotch and vanilla? Or when his grandson discovered a splash of red, pink, and purple among brown and yellow grasses, did Papa George not feel joy explaining how one could plant wildflowers to bloom in fall as well as spring?

Ultimately, Evie's sudden illness would usher in change too dark to overcome. Even when a virus was still thought to be causing Evie's nausea, Papa George behaved with a pre-ternatural sense of doom, shuffling between the garden and cellar in a daze. When pancreatic cancer was officially named, thirteen-year-old Buddy watched his grandfather decamp to his bedroom like an animal acknowledging its mortality.

With the shock of Alfie's murder not yet fully assimi-lated, Buddy wasn't surprised that thoughts of his mother's death should also arise, both tragedies having shared an untimely, if not random, quality. He couldn't help but wonder if his unwillingness to change was pushing him toward the same fate.

31

CARSON WALKED INTO the presidential suite at the Hotel Boulderado surprised to see Major Davis sitting comfortably in a high-backed leather armchair. On the couch sat Lacerta, Gonzales, and Dahlgren.

"Good to see you again, Major Davis," Carson said, shook Davis's hand. "Nice place you got here, Dale. Quite an upgrade from the Motel 6. I guess the governor's budget problems aren't as bad as reported."

"The state of Kansas is not paying—"

"I'm teasing! I know who's paying for this. Who do you think made the call? And you damn well deserve this room if anyone does."

Carson sat in the middle of the love seat, extending both arms along the top of the backrest.

"Dinner's on the way," Dahlgren said.

Carson glanced into the attached dining room with its Neo-Renaissance dining table. In the corner, an easel displayed an aerial photograph with a red X outside a boundary of black dashes.

"I bet that's Buddy Fisher's property," Carson said,

smiling at Lacerta and Gonzales. "How long till jump-off?" Neither man responded. He looked at Dahlgren.

"Uh, thirty-six to forty-eight hours was the last estimate," Dahlgren said.

"How's Sheriff Thompson doing?" Major Davis said. "I'd imagine he's ready to get back to his wife and kids."

The four men stared at Carson.

"Wyatt's doing just fine, Major. I'll let him know you asked about him."

"You keeping track of his whereabouts?" Dahlgren said.

Carson sat up, gave everyone a queer look. "'Course I know his whereabouts. What is this, a grand jury investigation?"

"Dale and I met with Sheriff Castellanos," Major Davis said then unsnapped the breast pocket of his shirt, took out three folded pieces of paper, and handed one to Carson. "You know what this is?"

Carson took reading glasses from his breast pocket, said, "Looks like a St. Michael coin."

Major Davis handed Carson another piece of paper. "Take a look at the other side of the coin."

Carson examined the bas-relief emblem of the Marine Corps, then laid both sheets on the cushion beside him. "So what about it?"

Major Davis handed over the third piece of paper. "This is a casting of a tire track found on the firebreak road. The coin was found on the slope between the firebreak and Hardscrabble Lane—where Alfie Beaubien was murdered."

Carson peeked at the photo, dropped it on top of the others, took off his reading glasses.

"Any idea what kind of gun Sheriff Thompson carries?" Major Davis said.

Carson slid to the end of the love seat, leaned on the arm. "Don't know, never asked. I think you're all overreacting if you want to know the truth. I bet there're lots of vets living in those foothills. Tire tracks as evidence of something? I'd like to see the science behind that."

"The science is pretty good, actually," Major Davis said. "And they're checking for DNA on the coin. That science is pretty good too."

Loud knocking. "Hang on," Dahlgren said. The hotel staff set up the table with fried calamari, prime rib, mashed potatoes. Dahlgren said, "Gentlemen, shall we?"

Carson was the last to join in, even considered acquitting himself of the meeting, but realized how such an action might be interpreted. The others wasted no time digging in. Under different circumstances, being a Kansas boy with a proud ranching pedigree, Carson would've commented on how his companions ate with a single-mindedness only an expertly marbled Angus or Hereford could've inspired. When everyone had put down their cutlery, Dahlgren looked at Gonzales, who then stood up from the table, pulled the easel out from the corner.

"This satellite image was taken recently," Gonzales said, and began pointing out the logistical advantages the property offered. "…The south and west boundaries terminate at national forest with a forward slope…"

Carson thought the military jargon comical, Gonzales throwing out terms like *delaying action, envelopment, line of departure,* as if preparing to assault an enemy with superior firepower and pre-sighted artillery, instead of strolling across some pot farmer's backyard. Anyone with half a brain could see the agents would assemble on Quartz Way, descend the slope, surround the property, pay special attention to the bamboo enclosure. Other agents would approach up the driveway, probably bash their way through the kitchen door—or something like that.

"…Fanatical partisan combatants occupying the bunker could present difficulties. We should treat the bunker as if assaulting a fixed, fortified position. Boobytraps cannot be ruled out…"

Self-centered fool, Carson thought, then saw visions of fire.

"Excuse me, Special Agent," Carson said. "You think Buddy's going to blow up his precious kilos, kill and maim government agents, and destroy his sacred home? Let's not let paranoia distract us from the goal. This is not a suicidal religious cult we're dealing with. It's one man with no history of violence—"

"History is not a predictor of future activity," Gonzales said. "Metrics suggest a resentful, alienated personality with an overburdened sense of justice who sees a special obligation to address an outrage. All possible contingencies will be taken into account."

"I understand the safety of your men is important," Carson said, "but getting those seventy kilos out, intact, is the goal. Your boys go all seek-and-destroy on us—well, uh, that's just not going to work."

"Stan," Dahlgren said, "we all know Buddy Fisher isn't a dangerous person, per se. But the governor agreed that Special Agent Gonzales will be in charge of the operation with the support of Mr. Lacerta's SLS—"

"I get that, Dale, but maybe the governor needs to call

Wichita so he can rehash with Cook Industries the priorities that account for us being here."

Dahlgren stood, took a few steps toward Carson. "The governor is well aware of the priorities."

"You sure about that? Because the way Agent Gonzales is talking here, they're gearing up for a big Waco, Texas–style weed barbecue, and that's gonna piss off a lot of people who give a lot of money to support the governor's agenda—if you know what I mean."

Carson had always admired Dahlgren's even-tempered nature, which was why the agriculture secretary's throbbing jaw muscle appeared significant.

"Incendiaries are not part of the procedure," Lacerta said, his first words of the night. "But maybe it's time for Mr. Carson to disengage."

"How's that?" Carson said.

"The operation is in the final stages of planning," Lacerta said. "Your role is perimetric at best."

"Peri-what?"

Dahlgren said, "At our previous meeting we agreed that at some point we both have to trust each other. You've done your job, Stan. Now let Special Agent Gonzales and Mr. Lacerta do theirs."

Carson stood. "Let's get something crystal clear. I will be present to supervise the removal of that weed—"

"These operations often take on a life of their own," Gonzales said.

"Yeah, I know. That's why—"

"We can't guarantee your safety," Lacerta said.

"Afterward maybe," Dahlgren said. "When they've secured the property."

Carson took turns staring at the men in the room. "I'm gonna put in a call to Wichita. And then you, Dale, will get a call from Topeka. Then, perhaps, we'll all meet again with clearer heads."

Carson moved to leave. Major Davis said, "There's still the issue of Sheriff Thompson."

"Not for me. Unless you want to show me an arrest warrant."

"For his own good," Major Davis said, "you might want to suggest he turn himself in, to assist Sheriff Castellanos in clearing his name."

Carson walked to the door. "I'll do that, Jay. And I'm sure Wyatt'll be more than happy to cooperate. Thanks for dinner."

*

Carson parked the Navigator in front of Maria's house, called Sheriff Thompson. This time he left a message. "Now I'm in front of your goddamn house, Wyatt. Where the hell are you? Call me ASAP." Using the Lord's name in vain was a mistake. He pushed redial, heard a sequence of beeps, then said, "Fuck it."

Carson banged the knocker three times; the door creaked open. Maria snored on the couch in her bathrobe. Empty half-pint bottles lay across the coffee table. Confetti covered the floor. Carson walked to Sheriff Thompson's room, saw a closet and dresser bare of clothing, Jesus and lamb missing from the nightstand. He sat on the bed, thought of the two St. Michael coin photos, recalled Sheriff Thompson choking Zebulon, jamming his gun into his mouth. Then he remembered the drive to Chief Black Kettle's Inn—after Buddy turned down a hundred grand—when Sheriff Thompson said the Lord gave him the choice of not blowing Buddy's head off. Just his luck the Lord offered Sheriff Thompson a different option up on Hardscrabble Lane. Carson wondered if he was partly to blame for Alfie's death, the way he agreed with Sheriff Thompson about the Lord speaking through him and that *His* choice could only be the right choice. But that's how you rolled with guys like Sheriff Thompson; those who trusted the Lord would, in turn, be trusted. Carson checked his watch. The dinner meeting had probably ended. Something told him Dahlgren would call, start ass-kissing to gauge his sincerity about calling Wichita. The phone did in fact ring a few minutes later, but with Sheriff Thompson's name appearing on the caller ID.

"Hello, Wyatt—"

"I don't appreciate you taking the Lord's name in vain the way you did."

"Oh yeah, I'm sorry about that, son. Just a moment of weakness because I was upset about these accusations against you. And frustrated over you not being around to defend yourself. It's not fair and I don't believe any of it. Not a word. Where are you?"

"My actions—"

"Whoa there, hang on, Wyatt. I don't know anything about your actions, and I don't want to know. Understand? Not a thing. All I know is what *other* people are saying. And that's how I want it to stay. Okay? Just tell me where you are."

"In the woods."

In the woods. Intentionally vague. That's a good thing. "Got it. And do you have a plan?"

"The Lord has a plan."

"Of course He does. How can I assist you in carrying out His plan?"

"I don't need no assistance."

"Yes, that's true. The Lord saw it proper the Marine Corps trained you in wilderness survival and all. But we're supposed to work together, remember? That mercenary raid of yours at Buddy's? Not SOP, no sir, but I let it go 'cause I knew your heart was in the right place—"

"I can stop the sorcerer from his evil ways."

"I know you can, Wyatt. And that's what we're gonna do. We're oh-so-close, my friend, but you gotta cool it until I tell you it's zero hour. We need to get ahold of that weed he's hiding. If those seeds get dispersed, well, I don't even want to think about the damage it'll cause. That's why we gotta stay on the same page, or the whole mission could end as one big Charlie Foxtrot."

"Can't wait forever."

"A day or two, that's all. Remember, we *might* know where he's hiding the pot, but if we're wrong, we may have to talk to him a little bit, convince him to cooperate. But this all needs to happen under the guidelines set by Topeka, so it's done by the rule of law—"

"The Lord's law is the highest law."

Carson stood, dropped the phone on the bed, kicked the dresser, then picked the phone back up. "Can you just take thirty seconds and look at the situation as an ordinary grunt soldier—I mean marine? If your platoon's assaulting an enemy position, you'd wanna know where all your fellow marines are, right? Otherwise you might get friendly fire casualties, right?"

"Ain't gonna be but one casualty. Cut off the serpent's head, just like you said."

Just like you said. Sheriff Thompson's words clanged loud enough for Carson to realize he'd been ignoring his own advice, that he'd been self-flagellating with a bag of lemons instead of making lemonade. "As God is my witness, Wyatt, I will personally deliver the son-of-a-bitch to you. Just promise to wait until the weed is secured before taking any action."

Silence lifted Carson's spirits. "Okay."

"That's the way! *Semper fi!* Oh, uh, wilderness survival these days includes portable phone chargers, right?"

32

DAYBREAK FOUND BUDDY clearing away thorny shrubs and rotting branches six paces along a forty-five-degree angle from a Gambel oak. He dropped to his knees and dug through the debris until he caught the edge of a five-by-five piece of sheet metal he then stood on end and let fall over. One by one he dropped garbage bags into the hole, fourteen in all, each holding fifty waterproof containers of medical-grade plastic.

Buddy pushed the empty wheelbarrow past the pine trees below Quartz Way, saw the SUV in the driveway. Libby stepped out, leaned against the door, watched Buddy push the wheelbarrow to the shed. They hadn't spoken since their conversation at Porphyry Open Space. Buddy's messages had gone unanswered.

"Does this mean you're talking to me again?" Buddy said.

"Shut up."

"Awesome."

Libby followed him into the kitchen, pulled a chair from the table, sat staring into her lap. Buddy sat across from her, waited. "I would've had breakfast ready if I'd known you were coming over."

Libby looked up. "Tomorrow night," she said.

Buddy had never expected a formal warning, only signs: a drifting helicopter, a strange car idling in the driveway, "birdwatching" hikers along the property line.

"How do you know?"

"Ray told me last night."

"Ray? Since when—"

"Does it really matter?"

"He told you to tell me?"

"You don't think Ray *assumed* I would tell you?"

Buddy nodded. "Of course he would. Who told Ray?"

Her hesitation was scarcely perceptible. "Donny," she said. Buddy could only smile. "You think this is funny?"

"Sometimes people smile for reasons not funny."

"Jesus, Buddy. Donny's giving you one last chance to avoid losing everything. Hate him all you want, but at least you'll have a life. I knew coming here was a waste—"

"You could've—"

"And don't give me your 'you don't understand' crap! Oh, the tragic hero, Buddy Fisher, destined to carry on the family tradition of heartbreak and pain. A symbol of suffering for all the world to see. And for what? You think people will look back on your sacrifice and be inspired to change the world? And what about Marty? Don't you want to be around to see what kind of man your son becomes? All you'll accomplish is hurting those who care about you. That's what you'll be remembered for—" Her voice broke.

Buddy left the room, returned with a box of Kleenex and a cell phone. Libby's purse buzzed. She blew her nose, took out her phone, read aloud, "I'll give them what they want on one condition." She looked at Buddy. "I don't know anymore when you're serious."

"I just texted you from a smartphone."

"Congratulations."

"If I go to prison, they'll take the phone away before I've even figured out how to use the damn thing. I'll call Ray and Donny tomorrow morning and tell them I'll give them what they want. But they have to hear it from me first. You can't say a word."

Libby stared at him. "Out of nowhere you decide to go along with the program? Suddenly you see the light because I show up and start crying?"

"Maybe if you'd called me back you would've known I'd been reconsidering."

"You couldn't have said so in your messages?"

"I don't like talking to answering machines."

"All you had to do was say, 'I'm reconsidering. Call me.' But that's too much effort, isn't it? And the way you sounded at Porphyry, it was like you'd already resigned yourself to martyrdom, looked forward to it even—despite being told Marty's your own flesh and blood. Now I'm supposed to believe you've been sitting on the fence until this morning?"

"Yeah, why not believe that? Maybe what I needed was for you to show up like you did and tell me Donny and Ray had been talking. I mean—are you kidding? Ray's *always* hated Donny's guts, yet they're working together to help me? If I cooperate, Donny and his beloved Cimarron won't get my water. That's a lot of money he's giving up. Maybe he's not as pathologically greedy as I thought. He also knew Ray would tell you and that you would warn me. I know

Donny could've told you himself, but maybe he thought it would've had more meaning if you heard it from the sheriff of Boulder County. So yeah, I think you should believe I was on the fence until this morning."

Libby returned to staring into her lap, then said, "So tomorrow all the drama ends."

"I thought you'd be a little happier."

"I'd be happier if I believed it."

Buddy held up the smartphone. "I got one of these, didn't I? Isn't seeing believing?"

*

Roy Mitchell first noticed the low monotonous rumbling that evening, while sitting on his deck admiring the unusually red, pink, and orange twilight, the result of wildfire smoke west of the divide. The noise sounded like earth-moving equipment. Excavating this late in the day seemed odd.

Lorraine joined him on the deck holding a cordless phone. "Blood-red moon tonight, they said." She handed the phone to Roy. "It's Buddy."

"Hi, Buddy. Got some work going on at your place?"

"No, just an uninvited guest problem. Can you do me a favor and call Sheriff Castellanos? Tell him there's a lot of commotion coming from my land? I can give you his direct number."

"Hey, now it's glowing real bright your way. You okay, Buddy? Where are you?" Roy walked into the house.

"Safe and sound. Ready for the number?"

"Hang on." Roy opened a drawer, found a pencil, looked around. Lorraine put a piece of paper in front of him. "Go ahead." Roy wrote down the number.

"Don't tell Castellanos you talked to me. Just say all hell's breaking loose at my house or something like that. I'll explain later."

"You sure you're okay, Buddy? You got me kind of worried."

"I'm fine, Roy. I swear. Can you call Castellanos and say that? I'm sorry to put you on the spot. I'll explain everything later. I promise. But I gotta know you're going to make the call."

"I'll call him right now. But let us know what's going on, will ya? Call me back, I don't care how late."

33

CASTELLANOS HELD THE phone to his ear chanting, "…
You mother*fucker*! You mother*fucker*! You mother-
fucker!…" Occasionally, he substituted "I'll fucking
kill you…" Donald's voicemail picked up after two rings;
Castellanos almost swerved off the road searching for the
redial button. The second and third calls both rang eight
times. The next call saw his mantra change full-time to "I'll
fucking kill you…" When voicemail picked up the fourth
time, he tossed the phone to the floor.

*

The Road Ends sign hung from a chain traversing Feldspar
Lane. Beyond lay a quarter-mile remnant of narrow-gauge
rail line that once transported miners to gold fields near Por-
cupine. After the mines played out, the tracks were torn up,
leaving a rocky, jagged path marginally suited to four-wheel-
drive vehicles. Eventually, this unauthorized "jeep trail" had
to be closed off due to the number of cars ending up at the
bottom of Grizzly Gulch. Castellanos adjusted his backpack
and miner's headlamp, set off on the trail. It should take

about fifteen minutes to get past the ravine. On the other side, a huge granite slab marked the path he and Buddy had hacked out of scrub growth down to Quartz Way. He called the slab "Donny's Doubleback," because that's where the piece of shit always turned around, saying he was tired.

Castellanos had felt more hopeful since reconnecting with Libby, even daydreamed about Buddy, Libby, Suzanne, and himself growing old together right there in Boulder County. Roy Mitchell's phone call blew it all up. Walking settled Castellanos, helped him see consequences over pounding Donny to a bloody pulp. There were better ways to hurt a rich man: give him something to worry about so he suffers slowly, from the inside out. Donny's friendship with Carson was well known, Castellanos reminded himself, as was Carson being Sheriff Thompson's keeper. Judge Irvine had granted an arrest warrant that morning. Maybe Donny should be linked to an accessory-after-the-fact rumor. How much fun would that be, watching the anxiety seed sprout, chew at his stomach lining?

Castellanos descended quickly, catching a boot toe now and then but never falling. The glow from Buddy's property helped him maintain proximity to Quartz Way. He dug in his heels about twenty yards above the cutout, crab-walked close enough to look down at three personnel carriers. A man walked out of the forest at the dead end. He stared at the ground, hands in pockets. Dress slacks and tweed blazer gave him away. Castellanos watched Carson walk to the SUV at the other end of the road. Then he lowered himself over the edge of the cutout, hung for a moment before dropping to the ground and sprinting across Quartz Way. He'd only

254 | MARC KRULEWITCH

gone a few yards down the slope when a flashlight beam hit his eyes. "Freeze."

Castellanos raised his arms, badge and ID in hand.

"Drop to your knees."

"I'm Sheriff—"

"Do it now!"

Castellanos got to his knees. The agent approached slowly, gun over flashlight. Two other agents flanked him. None of them had insignia on their jackets. "I'm the sheriff of this fucking county. Put the gun down."

The light bounced around Castellanos's uniform. "Toss me the ID. Keep the other arm raised."

Castellanos did as told. The agent stepped back, put the ID under the light, then spoke into his shoulder-mounted mic. Castellanos assumed they were wearing wireless ear buds.

"Copy," the agent said then holstered his weapon, handed the ID back to Castellanos. The flanking agents moved back to their original positions. "I'm sorry, Sheriff, you're not authorized to be here."

"Copy that," Castellanos said. He got back to his feet, dusted off his legs, continued down the slope expecting to be grabbed or tackled. Instead, the agent just shouted, "Sheriff, we can't guarantee your safety!"

At the bottom of the slope, Castellanos took out binoculars. Inside the house, agents drifted past windows. Some loitered in plain view. In the meadow, agents wandered in twos and threes, rifles slung over shoulders. A radio beeped. Castellanos looked back, saw the agent he had just encountered waving his flashlight in broad, sweeping motions. Next to him another agent stood in a hole, handing up objects wrapped in plastic bags. Castellanos turned back to the driveway. A man in camouflage pants and black turtleneck stood beside a guy in a bomber jacket talking on the radio. They both looked pleased.

He knelt down, leaned against a tree. Something seemed off. He hadn't expected to get past Quartz Way, yet there he sat in the front row, watching agents acting with all the urgency of groomsmen at a wedding rehearsal. And what about those guys posted near a hole in the ground full of bags? And where the hell was Buddy? He looked at the driveway again. Bomber Jacket was talking on a cell phone. Camouflage was yakking it up with agents who had taken off their helmets. Castellanos thought it was time he joined in on the fun, but by the time he stood up, everyone's attention had shifted to the woods bordering the opposite side of the driveway.

He trained the binoculars on the forest, watched as Buddy came into focus, his right hand resting on the stock of a shotgun balanced over his shoulder.

Castellanos dissolved as he had done while overlooking the wreckage of Alfie's life. He no longer held binoculars, having become the prism itself, magnifying rifles at the ready, pistols pointing from extended arms, and his old friend's disbelieving grin. Buddy stepped on the driveway. Primeval screams returned Castellanos to the material world. He saw agents in the meadow reorganizing into a skirmish line, advancing halfway to the scene. *What the hell for?* Castellanos thought. Their path of fire had already been compromised by the guys on the driveway about to blow Buddy away.

Then it was just Bomber Jacket's voice shouting orders. Castellanos also wanted to shout, tell Buddy to drop the goddamn shotgun and quit fucking around. Hell, it was practically pointing at the ground already. Just lift your hand and let it slide down your back. Every time Bomber Jacket repeated the order, Castellanos saw Buddy's lips move, probably making some smart-ass comment through that grin. Son-of-a-bitch was asking to get shot to pieces, didn't give a damn his friend would have to carry around that image forever.

Resignation seeped in, then a sense of loss. Years from now, Buddy's death would be an afterthought, the logical result of a fool's resistance. It was while Castellanos imagined Libby's reaction—watching her collapse to the floor—that Buddy began raising his left hand before doing the same with his right, letting the shotgun fall to the ground behind him.

Castellanos sank to his knees, rubbed his forehead. The agents broke formation; some laughed. He couldn't see much from the ground, but he didn't have to. He knew they'd have Buddy flat on his stomach, hands zip-tied behind his back. Now that the seventy kilos had been found, he dared hope everyone would settle down, realize Buddy was harmless, and not make him do too much prison time. Either way, he would be there for his old pal when he got out, make sure Buddy had a place to stay, some kind of job. Thoughts of Donny throwing money at Buddy, buying forgiveness, spawned more refrains of "You mother*fucker*!…" If not for the light gradient covering the property, Castellanos may have been too absorbed in his mantra to notice movement in his periphery. As it was, he lifted his binoculars to see a figure double-timing it across the meadow in camouflage fatigues, black ski mask, gun in hand. Castellanos took off running. He had the angle to make up for the gunman's head start, assuming those agents in the meadow didn't interfere. He shouted, "Sheriff-Boulder-County!" losing a step to the wasted oxygen. Most seemed not to notice the running sheriff, a few smiled, waved, watched him cover the remaining forty yards as another man closed in from the west. Castellanos reached the driveway, bent over gasping, managed to unsnap his holster the same moment he straightened up and saw the gunman's arrival.

34

CARSON SAT IN the driver's seat talking about the moon. "...Harvest moon, hunter's moon, I can never remember..." Donald wished he'd shut up about the moon already. The spotlights were going to drown it out anyway, blood-red or not.

Donald's phone vibrated: *Sheriff.* He declined the call. The phone vibrated again; he changed the ringtone to "silence."

"Wife?" Carson said. "Supper gettin' cold?"

Donald looked through the windshield. "How many agents fit in those trucks?"

"Eight or ten I would guess."

"Three trucks here. Probably another in the driveway. All for one guy with no history of violence."

"Oh, that's just bureaucracy for you. They gotta follow some protocol in case an agent scrapes a knee and sues for disability, then blames government negligence because there wasn't someone to catch him when he fell, or something like that."

"What're they doing?"

Carson glanced at his watch, although time had no relevance to the question. "Well, all the lights coming on tell me they've already sneaky-walked down the hill, surrounded the house, knocked on the door, and asked him to pretty please c'mon out."

Donald kept his gaze through the windshield. Carson puffed out his cheeks, exhaled, slid his palms along his thighs. He stepped out of the Navigator, began walking along the edge of the road, stopping halfway to peer down the slope. Two agents were on their knees digging with hand trowels. A third agent held a flashlight while a fourth stood watch, rifle ready. Carson remembered the red X on the landsat photo. He continued along Quartz Way, past the idling personnel carriers, until he reached the dead end. Once there, he walked several yards into the woods, looked around, returned to the car.

"Man, I'd love to get me a pair of those newer-generation night vision goggles," Carson said. "Maybe Gonzales can throw one my way."

Still looking through the windshield, Donald said, "He's gonna call you when it's over?"

"Dale's gonna call. Gonzales doesn't like me much."

"Gonzales deputize Sheriff Thompson? I thought he'd be sitting here with us."

"Wyatt? Oh no, he was never intended to play such an active role like that. He's more of a note-taker, to help the sheriffs of western Kansas understand what's going on."

"I thought for sure he'd want to be around to see it through."

"I know what you mean, Don, but he's got a wife and two boys waiting back home, and he was real anxious to see them. At least that's what he told me a few days ago, before he dropped off the radar. I told him he might as well go on back to his family. I could always send him a message when it was over."

"He'd leave without telling you?"

Carson laughed. "Yep, he's a strange one, all right. Guys like him answer to only one authority." Carson pointed up even though Donald still looked straight ahead. "You could say his marching orders come divinely inspired."

"You never did tell me how Sheriff Thompson got Zeb to go along."

"Uh—you didn't talk to Zeb or those other boys that were there?"

"Not my crowd, Stan. I just arranged the meeting."

"Sure, I get it. Wyatt said they talked real serious. Things got a little heated for a while, but Zeb came around. They're both country boys, so they probably realized how much they had in common."

"You weren't there?"

"I stayed in the car. Thought it would look better if it was just Wyatt showing up on their turf."

Donald angled his seat back. "Castellanos said they had a suspect in Alfie's murder."

"He say who it was? Drugs?"

"Nope."

Carson waited. "Then what'd he tell you for?"

"Power games. Jealousy. I-know-something-you-don't-know."

"How do you mean jealous?"

"He doesn't like people who have money. Me being successful pisses him off."

"You guys go way back, huh?"

"With Buddy I go way back. Ray never liked me. But Buddy wanted everyone to be friends. He wouldn't exclude me just because of Ray. If you wanted to hang with Buddy, you had to be cool with whoever else he was hanging with."

Carson grunted his approval. "Loyalty's admirable."

The comment hit a nerve. "I did everything I could to get him to cooperate, Stan."

"Easy, Don. Just saying I value loyalty in friends."

Neither spoke for a while, then Donald said, "Let's hope those guys don't have itchy trigger fingers."

"We haven't heard any shooting. That's a good sign."

"Everyone knows the weed's in the bomb shelter or that escape tunnel. They should just take it and leave."

"And that's what they're going to do, I have no doubt. Don't let Lacerta and Gonzales's worst-case-scenario approach bother you. This whole show of force—like I said, that's just their training. It's them telling the world how serious they are about getting their way. The truth is, if they were *really* serious, they would've been watching Buddy twenty-four-seven like they would a Pablo Escobar. But they didn't do that. You wanna know why? Because the folks that really matter in this operation don't give a good goddamn about Buddy Fisher."

"You don't think Buddy'll do time?"

"Nah, not hard time. They'll stick him in the county lock-up while they put a deal together. Buddy gets his freedom, but the feds kick him off his land—or force the county to do it—something like that."

A short silence then Donald said, "He wasn't expecting this. Not tonight, I mean."

"Yeah? Well there you go. The lack of fireworks probably means he's cooperating." Carson rotated in his seat to face Donald. "They're not going to hurt him, Don. If he resists, they may rough him up a bit, but just whatever it takes to get a guy on the ground and cuff him. Now if he does something stupid like show a weapon? That changes everything. But I don't see something like that happening. Do you?"

Carson stared at Donald waiting for an answer, noticed how weirdly overexposed Donald's profile looked in the reflected light. Carson's own face must've looked blacked out to Donald, which explained why he preferred looking straight ahead.

"What was that?" Donald said.

"What was what?"

"Someone shouted."

Carson opened the door, listened, turned back to Donald. "I don't know—"

Another shout. This time Donald turned to Carson. "Sheriff? Did he say, 'Sheriff'?"

"Not sure."

"Sounded like they were just down the road. Everything's blocked off. Can't be Ray. They wouldn't let him in. What about Sheriff Thompson?"

"Wyatt? I don't see how that's possible, Don. I really don't. He went back to Kansas. I'm sure of it. That's the only thing that makes sense to me."

Donald settled back in his seat. Carson closed the door.

"What I meant about *making sense*, Don—is like what I said before. Guys like Wyatt get *divinely* inspired. If a voice told him to go back home, well then that's what he's going to do. And to be perfectly honest, I'm glad he's gone. He had this unpredictable aspect about him that troubled me. I was starting to think that maybe—and I haven't said this to anyone else—that maybe he's a little nuts. Don't get me wrong. I don't mind religious folks as long as they don't take it too far, you know? As long as they don't get all blinded by fanaticism and use their beliefs to justify absolutely anything they feel like doing. You know what I'm saying?"

Carson was pretty sure Donald knew what he was saying, although he wished Donald would admit it—say *anything*, actually. Jesus, the guy was hard to read.

Carson's phone rang. "It's Dale," Carson said. "Talk to me, Dale…They did? That's what I wanted to hear! Great news. Uh-huh. Really? Uh-huh…Well, okay then. Alrighty. Will do." Carson hung up. "They found the stash. Everything went smoothly."

"What about Buddy?"

"No sign of him."

Carson was supposed to call Sheriff Thompson, tell him they found the pot. He didn't give a damn what happened next but hadn't figured Buddy's absence into the equation. For the moment, he could only wonder why the hell Donald wasn't celebrating. They found the pot, and his old pal wasn't hurt. Maybe not getting Buddy's water on the cheap bummed him out?

"The feds are going to charge you a lot more for that water, huh?"

Donald straightened his backrest, rotated to face Carson. "Aren't you going to call Sheriff Thompson? Tell him the good news?"

Carson caught a whiff of attitude, said, "That's one hell of a good idea, Don." Then shots rang out.

35

VOLUNTEER FIREFIGHTERS CARRIED an American flag draped over ladders extending across Main Street. A horse-drawn buckboard followed, carrying a coffin of unfinished pine holding Sheriff Thompson's body. At the gravesite, a marine honor guard sounded "Taps" before folding the flag and presenting it to the grieving widow. Pastor Bynum called attention to the twenty-four notes comprising the bugle call, referred to Christ's thirty-three miracles—twenty-four of which were cures. Having welcomed Christ into his heart, Sheriff Wyatt Thompson had been cured of death. Pastor Bynum removed two lilies from the standing wreath, handed one to each of Sheriff Thompson's young sons. Lilies symbolized their father's resurrection into a peaceful state, he said, then did the same with two chrysanthemums, comparing them to the sacrificial honor of serving God and the Marine Corps.

Carson stood several feet behind the mourners. *Sacrifice,* he thought. A more profitless offering there never was. A man should have more to show for giving his life than seventy kilos of catnip buds and sesame seeds, although Wyatt's family would get a fiber-glass swimming pool. And what about the sacrifice to ensure the whole debacle never happened? That is, the *resources* required to keep mouths shut? Nobody ever talked about that. Never mind the hundred grand he'd never see. Carson felt he was owed the truth about Wyatt's death, shouldn't be shoved aside, left to dope out fact from fiction on his own. "Need-to-know" my ass. But he also knew fiction was a bureaucracy's stock-in-trade, the ever-evolving, cover-your-ass gift nurtured by the passage of time. The people of Ellsworth County didn't give a damn about the particulars of Sheriff Thompson's last moments on earth. They knew only that their son died a hero, cut down in a crossfire between good and evil. Everything else was just commentary.

*

"What Does Ellsworth County, Kansas, Know That Boulder County Doesn't Know?" shouted the *Boulder Weekly*'s blood-splattered cover three days after the funeral.

District Attorney Arnold Jaeger paid no more mind to the provocative cover than he normally gave the alternative press. Six days earlier, he had defused public angst by holding a press conference declaring Alfie Beaubien's murder "drug-related." On the same day, he phoned Commissioner Brandt and learned of powerful Kansas interests threatening a federal lawsuit apocalypse. "*Marijuana is heroin* as far as the feds are concerned," Brandt reminded Jaeger. "And don't think that ignorant cracker for an attorney general won't use his influence on a judge or two, send a message by bankrupting Colorado…"

Jaeger had heard the paranoid babble before, gave

Brandt's corporate-Bible-Belt-crazies rant the same attention he did the *Weekly*'s cover. His assistant paraphrased
the article in a memo, highlighted the Ellsworth County
multitude affirming Sheriff Thompson's journey to Boulder
County before returning in a shipping container packed with
dry ice. "All hearsay," Jaeger replied. "Small-town gossip.
How do we know that guy was even here? Castellanos doesn't
know anything. The body miraculously shows up in front
of the medical examiner's office? I don't have time for tab-
loid conspiracies."

Later that afternoon, the *Weekly* published an online
addendum featuring Sheriff Thompson's landlady, Maria,
holding a cancelled check, prompting phone calls to the
DA's office from the *Daily Camera*, *Denver Post*, and all local
TV stations. Jaeger downplayed his staff's concern, ignored
advice to issue a statement, said the appearance of hiding
behind written words could hurt re-election prospects.
Instead, he held a press conference reassuring the public a
random killer was not at large. When pushed for details,
Jaeger's self-conscious manner, his obvious avoidance of
provocative language—an over-reliance on the noun "incident"—worked only to invite scrutiny. Smelling blood, the
Weekly came out with a special edition dubbed "Incident at
Fisher's Forest," a catchphrase inspired not only by the district attorney, but from unnamed sources claiming to have
heard gunshots somewhere north of Grizzly Gulch.

The Incident evolved as Carson envisioned, Jaeger's
inertia helping transform the narrative with each passing
hour. Frustration and fatigue likely played roles in Jaeger's
next lapse of judgment, when he implied Sheriff Thompson's
death was *somehow* connected to Alfie Beaubien's murder.

Pastor Bynum led the condemnation from Ellsworth County, declaring in an open letter to Colorado's governor—published by the *Weekly*—that drug-related characterizations of their son's death were a blasphemy not to be tolerated. Jaeger was forced to apologize. In a written statement—published by the *Weekly*—he categorically denied any evidence suggesting Sheriff Thompson's death was drug-related.

"Before the FBI or state's attorney takes over," Jaeger said to Castellanos, "tell me how a sheriff could be murdered in Boulder County and taken back to Kansas, and all we have is an anonymous report of gunshots—which happens every goddamn night around here."

Castellanos heard the district attorney's despair, thought of telling him not to be so hard on himself, that the Incident owed its life to the *Weekly* stumbling upon a Kansas county's public mourning. Instead, he told Jaeger not to worry about the FBI or a state prosecutor, then described a quasi-governmental entity serving at the pleasure of unelected corporate elites. "An Incident that didn't happen won't ever be investigated."

"The Ellsworth County medical examiner's report says Sheriff Thompson was shot nine times. You're telling me that didn't happen?"

"No. I'm telling you we don't live in Ellsworth County."

36

"SHERIFF THOMPSON WAS carrying a gun either on his hip or in his hand," Libby said. She was sitting in the garden with Buddy under a fleece blanket. "But that's where the consensus ends. Some said the sheriff's face was painted camouflage. Some said he glowed with the holy spirit. You pointed a shotgun at the sheriff when his gun was still holstered or after it was already drawn—depending on the version." Libby paused. "Okay, what about the door?"

"The door?"

"Your front door. Was it really unlocked?"

"Hang on. Who shot Sheriff Thompson?"

"One of the agents, all of the agents, none of the agents, he shot himself, nobody shot him, he's still alive but knows too much about something he wasn't supposed to know so he's hiding. Or he's been raptured. Now what about the door? Did you really leave it unlocked?"

"Why would I lock it? Since when do those guys try the doorknob before bashing it down?"

"And the cookies?"

"Yes, I made chocolate chip cookies. Yes, I left a note

saying, 'Help yourselves.' No, the cookies were not laced with anything psychoactive. The garden was full of vegetables, and the bomb shelter was full of junk. That's it. How come you haven't asked if they found seventy kilos?"

"Did they find seventy kilos?"

"They did find seventy kilos—just not *the* seventy kilos."

"What do you mean?"

"I mean they found seventy kilos of the finest catnip buds and sesame seeds this side of the Mississippi."

Libby started laughing then abruptly stopped. "Wait a minute. Are you saying all this chaos was for nothing?"

Before Buddy could answer, a text message clanked on his smart phone. "Ray and Suzanne just left. I'll explain the *other* seventy kilos when they get here."

Oddly, Buddy's words echoed between his ears with an unusual resonance, as if someone else had spoken. He felt as he did in the cellar, smoking a joint in the candlelit darkness, but this time with an overwhelming sense of peace. He saw Papa George, a sound engineer, mixing, routing, processing the garden's timbre, channeling vibrations through his grandson. Then he saw Ray and Suzanne merging onto Highway 36, knew they would greet their old friends in front of the house, exchange hugs, walk to the living room, try to recall the last time they all sat together around a fire. A lull in the conversation would give Castellanos a chance to talk about the previous ten days as one who had just recovered from a brutal strain of flu, that is, sweating, shivering, unable to distinguish reality from fever dreams. An emotional discussion would follow, in which Castellanos, Suzanne, and Libby would implore Buddy to stop torturing himself with guilt over a deranged sheriff's decision to murder Alfie in cold blood. Then Buddy would talk about coal tunnels under Porphyry Open Space, how Libby noticed the ground below the winding gear tower had appeared freshly dug up. It wasn't supposed to look that way, but Cousin Alex had been in a hurry to load the seventy kilos of weed and seed before driving back east.

In the meantime, Libby pulled her knees up under the blanket, leaned into Buddy. "Marty's going to like it here."

"How's he going to feel about finding out who his real father is?"

"He'll be thrilled—and you know it."

"We'll get a paternity test so I can prove he's my son. He needs to know he can live here forever. It's his birthright, as it will be for his children."

"I'm scared he's going to be angry at me for not letting him know sooner. I don't know how I'm going to explain all—"

"Let's not worry about that now—and I'll share the blame. It won't be just on you. I promise. And besides, Marty's wise beyond his years. He may see everything that unfolds as completely logical. He may say, 'Don't worry, Mom. I knew you thought you were doing what was best for my future. I'll always love you no matter what.'"

Libby thought about it. "He'd have to be quite an old soul to have that reaction. But who knows?"

Buddy laughed, then described his mother's angry response when Abe and Papa George once referred to his seven-year-old self as an old soul. "She worried that I spent too much time with adults doing adult things in the garden. 'There's nothing old about Buddy! Stop trying to make him older than he should be! Let him be a child for chrissake!'"

Libby stayed strangely quiet.

He leaned forward, saw the fear in her eyes. "What's the matter?"

"But what if Marty *doesn't* take it so nicely? It could take *years* for him to get over his anger. He may never get over it. What if he asks the county to kick me out?"

Buddy wanted to laugh. "Time out. Now you're being ridiculous. Just calm your nerves. We'll get married as soon as your divorce is final. Then it'll be a married couple with their biological son all under the same roof. One happy family protected by birthright—and the conservation easement."

Buddy waited, hoped the logic of his words would calm her fears. To his relief, she said, "Sounds great." A long pause followed, then, "Where should we honeymoon?"

"Oh, I don't know. Anywhere is fine with me. I've heard Kansas is nice."

For his sixth novel, author Marc Krulewitch changes the venue to Boulder County, Colorado, where he's lived since 1992. His previous books, *Something to Call Your Own, Maxwell Street Blues, Windy City Blues, Gold Coast Blues,* and *Doubt in the 2nd Degree*, all take place in Chicago, where he was born and where his family has lived for generations.